To

Considering Us

Jenn Bouchard

Thank you
for your support!

Jenn
Bou[...]

Black Rose Writing | Texas

ISBN: 978-1-68513-552-2
LIBRARY OF CONGRESS CONTROL NUMBER: 2024945056
PUBLISHED BY BLACK ROSE WRITING
www.blackrosewriting.com

Printed in the United States of America
Suggested Retail Price (SRP) $21.95

Considering Us is printed in Georgia Pro

*As a planet-friendly publisher, Black Rose Writing does its best to eliminate unnecessary waste to reduce paper usage and energy costs, while never compromising the reading experience. As a result, the final word count vs. page count may not meet common expectations.

Praise for
Considering Us

"Set in small town New England, *Considering Us* is for readers who know sometimes the right person comes along at the wrong time, but that fate has a way of bringing us second chances. Bouchard weaves a story full of romance and found family that will keep readers rooting for Devon to figure out exactly where she needs to be, and who she needs to be with, to find her happily ever after."
–Sharon M. Peterson, author of *The Do-Over, The Fake Out,* and *The Fast Lane*

"Bouchard dishes up the sweetest second chance romance that will warm your heart to the end."
–Caitlin Moss, author of *You First* and *Goodbye Again*

"Nobody writes a New England story like Jenn Bouchard, especially with mouth-watering food you can taste while you read. I need those cookies! I loved this second chance love rom-com bursting with ordinary Jane vs highfalutin boarding school vibes that made me want to rewatch all the old movies mentioned and make a mixed CD. *Considering Us* is a feel-good, humorous yet realistic book that I'll hold in my heart as a new classic."
–C. D'Angelo, award-winning author of *The Difference* and *The Visitor*

For Grant and Avery, who have cheered me on for all of it.

Considering Us

1

"This is pasta salad with chicken. It's already dressed with a red wine vinaigrette, but here's extra if they want it. The gazpacho will taste better tomorrow because the flavors will be more developed, so maybe someone can have that for lunch." I dug out one more container from my cooler bag. "And this is the broth Mrs. Preston requested. Oh, I don't think I caught your name. I'm Devon."

The housekeeper nodded, almost shaking from what was likely an overwhelming first week on the job. Staff never lasted long in the Prestons' house. "She told me she asked you for vegetable instead of chicken," the young woman said with a nervous quiver in her voice, smoothing her unwrinkled apron. "I'm supposed to make sure it's vegetable." Despite her novice status in the Preston household, she had already learned that she didn't want to piss off Julianna Preston. "I'm Angie," she squeaked out.

I groaned to myself. I had been through this sort of thing with multiple housekeepers at this address. "It's vegetable, I promise. You won't get in any kind of trouble." I zipped up the cooler. "Thanks, Angie. I'll be back on Monday. I can show myself out."

I walked out into the hallway from the kitchen slowly, peering through open doors to see if anyone else was home. I knew my way around the Prestons' stately four-floor Commonwealth Avenue townhome much more intimately than the rookie housekeeper likely realized. And I was in the mood to see one particular resident of the house.

Bentley Preston stepped out into the hallway from the den at the sound of my footsteps. Clad in khaki shorts and a Tommy Bahama polo shirt, he had likely been working from home while also watching a golf tournament on TV based on the noise I could hear in the background. A smile curved onto his lips as he looked me over. I couldn't help but feel a bit giddy at his focus on me and the possibility of what might happen next.

"Delicious Devon," he murmured, as cheesy as he could be. I relished the attention.

We both looked around, and seeing no one else, he grabbed my hand and drew me into a large hallway closet. I shut the door behind us and breathed in, smelling a mix of the musty sporting equipment surrounding us and Bentley's spicy aftershave.

"The closet?" I whispered just before I felt his lips reach mine. Being with him was always a thrilling mix of excitement and fear of getting caught.

"Not the first time we've done it in a closet," he said, accidentally knocking over a lacrosse stick. He was correct; we had been having a clandestine affair for the past ten months and had found ourselves in all kinds of odd places. I enjoyed the way he looked at me and appreciated me—*all* of me—but part of me had no idea why I was involved with him. Was it boredom? Convenience? He was fifty years old—fifteen years my senior— and married to a woman most people either despised or were terrified of. Who, as far as I could ascertain, left my delicious food to her husband and teenage daughter while she survived on overnight oats with chia seeds from a nearby coffee shop and the broth I made for her. Life was too short for that kind of self-inflicted torture and deprivation.

Bentley seemed to agree with my feelings about food and joy, often sneaking out to meet me for ice cream. He grabbed onto my well-fed thigh and gave it an appreciative squeeze. "What did you bring for me today?" he murmured. "Any Chicken Milanese?" He kissed my neck and slipped his hand down my shorts. Two months earlier, I would have found the whole scenario exciting, but I found myself trying to enjoy the moment despite the hangers I kept bumping into.

I tried to answer his question despite where this was going. "There's some pasta salad and—" I was interrupted by a teenage girl's voice yelling outside the closet door about her tennis racket. Bentley and I locked eyes in the dim light, and our bodies froze, realizing what was likely to happen soon. Sure enough, the door swung open, and sixteen-year-old Adrienne Preston stood before us with a horrified expression.

"Mom! Mom!" she shrieked, and that moment marked the end of my employment in the Preston household.

•   •   •

I had taken the T three stops from Park Street to Copley on my way to the Prestons' just an hour earlier, but the thought of jamming into a Green Line subway car with a sweaty crowd that had just come from a Red Sox game on a hot August Thursday evening was not appealing. I stumbled down Comm Ave until I hit the Public Garden and stood at the edge, staring at the tourists, families, green grass, and trees. People were laughing and happy, while I was in a daze as if I had a migraine without the actual headache. What the hell had I done? And why? Another roll in the hay with Bentley Preston certainly wasn't worth this.

Julianna Preston's words burned in my brain as I watched the world go on in front of me in the late August haze. *"You're through, Devon Paige. Your days in Boston are over."* And I knew she meant it. I heard a hysterical Adrienne Preston screaming every nasty word imaginable at both of her parents, blaming them for ruining her life. And as if I was watching a movie of the whole damn thing, I saw myself tripping over the tennis racket in question, grabbing my purse and cooler, and making a beeline for the front door.

I forced myself to move forward, deciding to meander through the park's paths instead of taking the sidewalk around, past the swan boats, until I got to the Common. An ice cream stand was set up, selling various bars, popsicles, and Italian ices. It wasn't J.P. Licks—that was in the opposite direction, way down on Newbury Street—but this would do for now. As cliché as the whole thing was, ice cream was always my go-to. In a cloud of chaos, it was the only thing that made any sense.

I cut in front of a line of kids who were hemming and hawing over what to get and threw a ten-dollar bill on the little window ledge. "You have anything with toffee? Heath bar something?" The confused worker handed me a Blue Bunny Heath ice cream bar and started to get me change, but I walked away and headed across Tremont to Avery Street. The ice cream tasted cool and creamy through the chocolate and candy crunch, but the heat coming from the still-prominent sun above and the sidewalk vents below me caused it to melt way too quickly. By the time I walked into the front doors of the Ritz-Carlton, I was sweating and dripping ice cream all over myself.

"Ma'am, may I help you?" the doorman asked as I walked past him toward the Avery Bar just off the lobby. One of my favorite drinking spots in Boston, I sat on a leather stool and grabbed a few cocktail napkins to wipe off what I could. There was something about a hotel bar when you wanted to be anonymous. I ordered a drink and finally took out my phone to call Tam.

"I've been waiting to hear from you," she said as she answered the call. My best friend and the closest thing to a sister I had, Tamara Sparks was an anchor and reporter for the NBC affiliate in Boston. If there was any buzz east of I-495, she likely knew about it. And she had definitely heard what had just happened less than an hour earlier. "How are you, Dev?"

"So, it's already out there," I grumbled, taking a swig of my beverage. This was what happened when you were stupid enough to have an affair with the husband of one of the most well-connected women in Boston. "She moves quickly, that one. Are you doing the eleven o'clock?"

"No, and I'm not letting you watch it, either. Where are you?"

"I'm at the Ritz. Avery Bar. Huge whiskey sour with Angel's Envy."

Tam sighed. "I should have known. You and the hotel bars. Let's get you out of there and have something delivered to your place. We can order ice cream and whatever else you want. We can get more bourbon. I don't think you should be in such a public venue right now. You don't want to get recognized and have people—"

"Talk shit about me to my face?" I laughed wryly. Tam didn't swear much, but I certainly did. "It's all tourists in here. There's a dude in a huge cowboy hat. Trust me, these people have no idea who I am or who you are, for that matter."

"Okay, okay. I'm on my way over there. Just, well, don't get into it with anyone. Do a crossword or something."

I couldn't focus on a crossword, but it didn't matter because my phone soon blew up with messages. One by one, my clients fired me. Some made excuses, such as upcoming vacations, which I knew was bullshit since almost all my clients had children who were starting school in the next two weeks. Others said things along the lines of due to "recent events," they felt as if it was time to end our working relationship. Each message felt like a punch to a different part of my body, and I knew I would have to go home soon and crawl into bed. Tam had probably been right about needing to leave. By the time she arrived twenty minutes after we had hung up, I was gutted.

She hugged me and sat on the stool adjacent to mine. "This is bad, huh?" she posed, knowing that it was awful. "Is there anyone left?"

"David Anders," I said quietly with my head in my hands. He was the one client that some people in the bar might be familiar with. "I haven't heard from his mom yet."

"She might not know," said Tam, tapping on the counter. "What are you going to do?"

"I'll call her later," I said. "She's a smart woman. She might be in Atlanta, but she works at a big hospital. I'm sure she's told some of the doctors that I cook for her son. I owe it to her to let her know."

"Good idea," she said. "I feel like I'm to blame for some of this."

"Why?" I asked, chewing on an ice cube from my empty glass. "Because Julianna met me at that networking event three years ago? You didn't bring me there; you just interviewed me at it. The organizers invited me. The only reason you and I are friends is because of that event. And I got most of my clients because of it, so I am grateful for it. I just had to screw everything else up by banging her husband in a closet."

"You were mid-bang?" Tam asked, wide-eyed. I couldn't imagine Tam ever getting herself into this situation. *Nope, never.*

"No, no, no. We were just fooling around at that moment. But the optics were terrible." I grabbed my phone back. "Seriously, how did the media—how did you—find out already? I get it that she texted all her friends and told them to fire me, but how did everyone else find out?" I typed my name into the search bar on Twitter. "Oh my God."

"You're trending, my friend," Tam said softly. "We got a brief press release from her publicist."

"She has a *publicist*? She doesn't even have a job," I gasped, scrolling through all the tweets that included my name. "*Former Minx chef de cuisine-turned-private chef Devon Paige caught having affairs with married clients she met through Back Bay Women's Network in apparent homewrecking plot*," I read aloud. "Homewrecking plot? I wasn't trying to wreck anyone's home. I just thought she was a horrible person. And Bentley loved my food and paid attention to me. A lot of attention." I threw my head in my hands and pulled on the back of my hair. "What did I get myself into?" I wailed.

"Everyone loves your food, Dev," Tam said, putting her arm around me. "Look, I'm not going to judge anyone here. I'm sorry about what's happening to you. I want to help you figure out what to do next because you definitely need a plan." Tam's phone buzzed, and she looked at the screen. "Ugh, it's that Boston public service announcement TikTok lady again," she said, clicking on a message. "She posts something every day, and I think she's onto you." I lifted my head to see what had caught Tam's attention.

A woman with big blonde hair, heavy black eyeliner, and a very strong Boston accent was on the screen. "Ladies of Boston, this is your public service announcement of the day. Watch out. There's a chef in town named Debbie who tricks women into cooking for them and then has sex with their husbands. So don't let nobody named Debbie cook for you. This woman is gonna be lookin' for new customers, so you are warned, Boston." She lifted a Dunkin' coffee cup and signed off.

"Only one! I had sex with one husband! And I'm not Debbie!" I moaned, and people started to turn to look at us. The bartender began walking toward us. It was time to go.

"And that's enough for today," Tam said, pulling out two twenties from her wallet and dropping them on the bar counter. "Let's go order that ice cream."

2

"They didn't have Heath or toffee vanilla. Best I could do was chocolate chip," Tam said, handing me the pint that she had ordered through DoorDash. I traded her a whiskey sour for the ice cream and grabbed a spoon.

"You sure you don't want any? This is my second ice cream of the day," I said, in between spoonfuls of Edy's and sips of my cocktail.

"I'm good," she assured me. Tam did not share my ice cream obsession—her attitude was one of indifference, which baffled me. "I'm supposed to meet this new guy at nine tonight at Woods Hill, but I'm not sure I want to go all the way to the Seaport," she said with a yawn.

"You live in Southie. You're literally around the corner."

"Maybe not for much longer," she responded. "My lease is up next month. And you know me, I can't stay in an apartment or with a man for long. I get so bored." It was true; other than her job or her friendship with me, Tam always seemed to be looking for something else. No guy or landlord hoping for longevity stood a chance.

"Is that why I got involved with Bentley?" I mused, poking the bottom of the pint with my spoon. I was making quick work of it. "Was I just bored? I don't know."

"I did wonder," Tam said, scrolling through her phone. "Oh geez. My Yale classmate Andrea Lark. Did I ever tell you about her?"

My cell phone rang, and I put up a finger to signal that I'd be a minute. "Dr. Anders! Elaine!" I never knew what to call her. "Thank you so much for calling me back."

"Of course, dear," she said. "David said the enchiladas last night were better than ever."

"Oh good, I'm so glad. Look, Dr. Anders, I'm in a bit of a situation. I don't know if you saw—"

"Yes, it's all over the Boston media feeds—which I follow closely, of course. I never know when David will be mentioned."

"So, okay, yeah. I'll be honest with you. It's true. Not the intentional homewrecking stuff—and it was only with one person—but yes, I did have a relationship of sorts with Bentley Preston. And I totally understand if you don't want me—"

"Now stop right there, Devon," she ordered in a voice she must use with noncompliant patients. "My son loves your chicken enchiladas. And everything else you make for him. Those cookies. Mmm. I dream of those cookies after I visit him. Why would I care who you're involved with?"

"Oh, thank you so much, Elaine. Seriously, I'm so grateful."

"You know I can't always be there for him, but you can."

"Yes, yes, one hundred percent. I'll bring him food tomorrow. Oh wait, he'll be in Toronto for that scrimmage. You must be there right now. Sunday, then!"

"Yes, I'm in Toronto through tomorrow night. Sunday will be wonderful. He'll look forward to it. Thank you, Devon."

"No, thank you!" I said and ended the call. I took a deep breath and looked at Tam. "Okay, I have one client. One client."

"And how much of your expenses will that cover?" she asked, picking up my checkbook from the coffee table and tossing it at me.

"Probably my car insurance," I scowled, setting the checkbook aside. "Maybe my electric bill, too." I was in so much trouble.

"So, hear me out," she began. "My classmate Andrea Lark has very suddenly become the Head of School at Rockwood. It's a boarding school in New Hampshire on George's Island, just next to Portsmouth. You can walk into town; it's that close."

"What does that have to do with me?"

"She needs a Dining Services Director. Like immediately. Housing is included."

"Me? A boarding school? I've never done anything like that. Come on, Tam. I would have no idea what I was doing."

"Think of your experiences," she said. "Didn't you say you shadowed staff at events during your semester in DC during college? The White House and State Department, right? Nothing shabby about that. And ten years in multiple high-end Boston restaurants, followed by private chef services for some of the wealthiest families in Boston?"

"And David Anders."

"How could I forget your reclusive Celtic? What I'm saying, Dev, is you are flexible, innovative, and can work with anyone. Your name is mud here in Boston, at least for now. But people have short memories. You'll be able to come back. You just need to do something else for a little while."

I swirled the ice in my glass and decided to change the subject, not wanting to fully entertain this idea. "Who is this guy you're seeing tonight?"

"He's a professor at BU. That feels old and serious, doesn't it? Is that the life stage I'm in? Dates with professors? I still feel like I'm twenty." She stretched out her hands and examined her manicure. "Maybe I won't go."

I sat up suddenly, my mind cycling back to fifteen years earlier. "What if he's the one you're meant to be with? And you don't go, and someone else snags him? But he's actually meant for you."

Tam laughed. "Do you really believe in that? That these missed opportunities really mean we're denying ourselves our destinies? Come on, Dev, I've never heard you talk like that. I'm the one who clings to rom-com movies, and even I don't think it's true."

For whatever reason, I couldn't shake the image of a twenty-year-old boy with dirty blond hair and a hand that felt so perfect in mine. When I had bad days, my brain often went back to 2007 for no apparent reason. It had been amazing until it was so disappointing, so why think about it? Maybe I just liked to wallow in more misery when things took a downward turn. "Did I ever tell you about Kyle?"

"Who's Kyle?"

"I guess not then." I curled up tighter into the elbow of my small sectional couch. "The night before I left for my DC semester—this was January 2007—all the Norwell College students who were leaving on school-affiliated programs had a dinner. We had come back from our semester breaks before everyone else, had brief orientations with our groups, and stayed in temporary dorm rooms for a night before departing. People were going all over the world. This, of course, was when I thought I wanted to be a lawyer and was going to DC to immerse myself in the rat race of government and politics."

"Which you hated," inserted Tam, who had known that much about me. She actually knew almost everything. I had just never told her about Kyle.

"Yes, which I hated. The rest of my group loved it, but it wasn't for me. Anyway, I knew Kyle the way you knew people at small liberal arts colleges who you didn't really know. We had been students in the same Intro to Sociology class our freshman year, but it had been a big lecture hall. He was the goalie of the soccer team, so I knew of him, but that was really it. We were sometimes at the same parties, but he lived in the soccer house for his sophomore year and the first semester of his junior year, and I had stuck with the same group of friends from my freshman dorm. Our lives hadn't intersected in any sort of meaningful way until that moment. But there we were, grabbing for the same last slice of watermelon in the food line with our own pairs of plastic tongs."

"How romantic," mused Tam. "I mean it. Now, this sounds like a nineties rom-com movie that I can get on board with." Tam loved rom-coms, and by extension, I had grown to enjoy them, too. But she was the expert and could relate most of life's circumstances and scenarios to specific movies. It was impressive.

"I guess it *was* romantic, at least at first," I replied, knowing where the story was going, which was where the magic died a humiliating death. "He offered to split the watermelon slice with me, so naturally, we ended up sitting together. He suggested we sit in the smaller room that was adjacent to the main room, so I sat across from him, and we talked for the next two hours. It was one of those conversations without any spaces or awkward pauses. It just kept going and going. Like one of those really good 'Dinner with Cupid' matchmaking columns in the *Globe*."

"I love those," Tam quipped. "I need more dates like that. It rarely happens."

"Agreed," I said, continuing with the story. "And it was unusually warm for January—like fifty degrees at eight at night, which you know is crazy for New Hampshire in winter. So, we took a walk around the Loch. You've never been to Norwell, but there's this lake in the middle of campus. It's small and technically called Lake MacGavin after some Scottish donor, so Norwell students call it the Loch."

"I'm learning so much." Tam laughed. "It's eight-thirty. I need to make a decision. Do I stay or do I go?"

"Give me five more minutes, and then you can decide," I said. "I'll give you the express version of the rest of the story. We walked around the Loch like five times. After the second time, we were holding hands. After the fifth, we kissed for the first time."

"Oh, was it good?"

"Like the best kiss of my life. I still go back to it in my head. Nothing has come close to matching it." I felt my body temporarily relax and flush warm. Despite what eventually happened with Kyle, that was one of the greatest moments in my highlight reel.

"Aww, I love that. Okay, keep going. Three more minutes."

"We went back to the dorm where we were temporarily staying, we listened to Oasis on his iPod, and we drank Coors Light that he bought from a guy staying in the next room over."

"And I'm guessing...."

"Yes, eventually, but not until like three in the morning. There was a lot of talking. He talks a lot, but it didn't annoy me. He was fun to talk to. I liked everything about him. And then we went to breakfast and ate a bunch of bacon. Other things, too, I'm sure, but I remember the bacon. For some reason, it tasted like the best bacon ever."

"And then you had to leave each other? This is excruciating."

"It was pretty awful. We had shared this magical night, and suddenly, I couldn't care less about going to DC. He left for the London School of Economics, and I went to American University. And I never talked to him again."

"Oh my God, Dev! Did you try to reach him?"

The happy, warm feeling drained from me, and I found myself grabbing for a throw blanket even though it was ninety-five degrees outside. "I tried to get in touch about thirty times. I sent him emails. I sent postal mail, but I have no idea if it ever reached him. Once, when I was drunk, I spent twenty dollars calling various switchboards at his school, trying to find him. Even if I had connected with him, I would have sounded like a wacko stalker at that point. I finally gave up."

"And you haven't Googled him or anything? You could still try now. Who knows? Maybe he's single and has been thinking about you for years, too."

"I don't let myself," I conceded. It still made me sad. "That rejection was so intentional, so purposeful, I just can't put myself through it again. He made a choice." I sat up and tapped my watch, snapping out of my emotions. "You have about ten minutes to somehow get from Beacon Hill to the Seaport. What's it going to be?"

Tam stood up and readjusted her outfit, even though she always looked newswoman-amazing. "I think I need to go. On the off chance that he's my Kyle." She grabbed her bag and walked over to hug me. "Are you going to be okay?"

"Eventually," I said. "Thanks for being here for me tonight. Have a good time with Professor Plum."

"With the candlestick." She laughed.

"In the study. If he's a total dork, come back here, and we'll watch *Clue* again." It was one of our go-to movies, even though it wasn't technically a rom-com.

"Deal. And Dev? Seriously, think about the boarding school and talking to Andrea. It's worth an email."

3

The drive to St. George's Island was easy. I almost wanted it to be annoying or difficult or riddled with traffic, so I would find an excuse not to pursue the job (and do what else—I had no clue). But on a sunny Monday morning in late August, I was going against any Boston commuter traffic and made it to the Portsmouth exit on I-95 in under an hour. Soon, I was crossing a tiny bridge onto St. George's, a small island adjacent to its sister island of New Castle. Once on St. George's, I passed a cute farmstand selling tomatoes and corn, a combination convenience store/tackle shop/post office/Dunkin' Donuts, and an ice cream stand. *Bingo*. If I was going to even entertain this possibility, iced coffee and frozen dairy were necessities.

The wrought-iron gates to the Rockwood School were open, with a large green area and stately oak trees welcoming me. It felt a little like a smaller version of my alma mater, Norwell College, which was only half an hour west, except the students at Rockwood were as young as fourteen. *I would have loved a place like this*, I thought, shuddering at memories of my high school years with a mother who never really "got" me and a father too weak—both physically and emotionally—to say much of anything. Boarding school might have been fantastic.

Andrea had responded within thirty seconds of receiving my text two days earlier with even more enthusiasm than Bentley Preston had expressed for my Chicken Milanese, which was saying a lot. We made plans to meet in her office at Rockwood at 11 AM on that Monday, and I followed her directions to the administrative building. I was expecting something in red brick and ivy, but instead, I found myself staring up at an old Victorian house with three floors and a gorgeous turret with the most charming violet-framed windows. If someone could fall in love at first sight with a building, it was me in that moment.

"Hello, Devon!" proclaimed a tall, lanky woman with curly brown hair and large, purple-framed glasses in a floral dress. She waved from the porch as I walked to greet her. "At least, I hope it's you! Now, wouldn't that be embarrassing?"

"It's me," I said, sticking out my hand to shake. "Thanks so much for meeting with me today, Andrea."

"Any friend of Sparky's is a friend of mine. Let's head up to my office."

"Sparky? I hadn't heard that one." By up, she meant up several staircases to the third floor. Andrea bounded up the stairs, skipping random steps with her long legs while I may have been panting. Without Bentley Preston around anymore, I was going to have to find other ways to exercise.

"Ask her about the time she blew the circuit breaker with her million-watt hair dryer when twenty girls were getting ready for a formal. Tamara Sparks became Sparky forever that night."

I sat opposite Andrea in her cluttered office, moving a stack of books off a chair to the floor to do so.

"Excuse the mess," she said, gesturing to the stacks of papers and files all around her. "I assumed this role, shall we say, rather suddenly."

"So Tam said."

"Did she give you details?" Andrea asked, drumming her fingers together as if she couldn't wait to spill the beans.

"No," I said. I wasn't sure if Tam knew what had happened to even tell me anything. All she had said was Andrea needed someone immediately.

"I was the Director of Admissions for the past five years. Before that, I worked in development at Exeter. It was my first job out of Yale. Anyway, I felt good in the Admissions Office. I knew what I was doing, and I had a great little staff. Everything was going fine until this." She handed me a flyer with the header *The Underground Stallion*. There was a large black-and-white picture of a naked man and woman, with key body parts blocked out and stunned looks on their faces. The article underneath the image called for the resignation and/or removal of the Head of School and the Dining Services Director, with concern about the reputation of the school and worries that the scandal could affect students' future college acceptances. Given everything I had just gone through, it felt hauntingly familiar.

"I'm guessing this was more than just a passing dalliance," I said, handing the paper back to her.

"Yes, a full-fledged affair between two people married to other spouses, who were also employees here. One worked for me in Admissions."

"And someone caught them and took this picture." I felt a shiver up my spine. At least Adrienne Preston didn't take any photographic evidence. Tweets, texts, and press statements were one thing. Images with nudity were another. "A student, I presume."

"Indeed, at least we think so," Andrea said, sitting up a bit straighter. "I'm not sure who writes for *The Underground Stallion*, but I have my suspicions. Anyway, the Board of Trustees launched into full panic mode and didn't want to go through the media attention that a firing and national search would entail. So, they asked both of them to resign, and I was pressured into assuming this position." She sighed and looked around, almost as if she didn't know where she was. "I'll be honest; I really didn't want this. But given everything that was happening, I didn't feel like I could say no. Now, I am trying to figure it all out, plus hire for the vacant roles."

"Look," I began, knowing that I needed to be transparent, particularly after everything Andrea had been through. Plus, it wasn't in my nature to be demure or evasive. Sometimes, it was better to lay all your cards on the table. "You should be aware that I was just involved in a similar situation and—"

"Trust me," she interrupted, shaking her head. "I know what happened. I have an unfortunate addiction to internet gossip. I watch that Boston PSA on TikTok every day." She must have noticed my worried expression because she put up her hand as if to stop me from stressing. "Things happen. I'm not judging anyone in your situation or in this situation, for that matter," she said, gesturing at the flyer. "What happens between adults is their business. I am just stuck in a job I feel ill-prepared for now, trying to find a Dining Services Director while the students eat subpar meals."

Eww. If there was anything I had little tolerance for, it was bad food. Life was too short for that, and I had grown up eating some terrible things. My mother's awful casseroles came to mind. "What's going on there? Don't you have mostly the same dining staff you had before she left the role? Or did they all leave with her?"

"Yes, they're all still here, but they are really struggling without her. Donna planned all the meals, ordered all the ingredients, and led all the staff meetings with that department. She wiped out all her computer files when she left. We have old archives of menus, but that's about it. We don't even know which recipes she used. Plus, Marnie, the interim director, if you want to call her that, is obsessed with boxed meals. It's just the fall athletes here so far, but she's got everything set up in cardboard boxes as grab-and-go. Everyone's groaning about it and leaving the boxes everywhere. Tons of waste, plus there are pizza deliveries coming to campus every single night. Two of the cars hit each other in the parking lot yesterday."

"You need a leader," I murmured, mulling this over. "I have absolutely no experience in this kind of environment," I added, almost as if I was trying to convince her that I was the wrong person for this job. I couldn't tell if I wanted to take this on or not. *Maybe I'll move to another city and start my business over.* I didn't really have the money to do that, and my thoughts kept darting back to David Anders. *I would have to leave him.* For whatever reason, I was attached to that quirky six-foot-five guy who never left his condo building unless he had a game or practice. Even his trainer met with him in the small gym of his luxury Seaport high-rise at odd hours so as not to interact with many onlookers. Despite his oddities, he lit up whenever I came over and actually talked to me—David Anders hardly talked to anyone—probably because I brought enchiladas and cookies.

"Devon, I know you were chef de cuisine at Minx before it burned to the ground," she retorted. "That is no small feat, managing that kind of kitchen. I ate there once, back when I worked at Exeter. We had a dinner meeting with some prominent Boston alumni there. It was excellent. Everything was well-executed. And since then, you've run a successful business dealing with people who I'm sure are not easy to please. These teenagers and our staff might be your easiest customers yet."

What do I have to lose? I couldn't be humiliated much more than I already had been, and my bills and expenses would stack up quickly after I got my last checks and Venmo transfers from the clients who had fired me. Boston was a ridiculously expensive place to live. Maybe I could do this for a year and regroup and figure out what the hell I actually wanted. "Are you offering me the job?" I asked.

Andrea stood up to fiddle with the air conditioning unit. "I'm sorry this thing is so loud. I don't think these window units are meant for days like this. Makes you long for those cool fall days, huh?"

"Love the fall," I replied. "But I dread what comes after. I'm not a big fan of winter, which I know makes no sense since ours goes on for about eight months." It never stopped me from drinking my iced coffee and eating my ice cream, though.

"Right?! I do think there's something cozy about living up here on this campus during the winter, though, plus there's no commute." She made a good point. I wouldn't be hauling cooler bags and groceries all over the city in snow, ice, and wind. Walking to work–from wherever I'd be living–would likely be a hell of a lot easier. "I want you to take this job," she continued. "Um, I should probably ask you some kind of interview question to make this more formal. You know, in case the Board wants some details of your hiring process."

"Sure. Go for it. Ask away."

"Well, like I told you, we are not making our constituents very happy right now when it comes to food. It's just the fall athletes for the next couple of days, but later this week, everyone else shows up. Staff will start eating in the dining hall more regularly then, too. What will you do early in your time here to connect with students and staff to make meals a more pleasant experience for them?" She shuffled through some papers on her desk, looking for something but apparently not finding it. "Was that a good question? I'm so new to this."

"Great question. I think listening to people is the first step. I had to do this with my private chef clients. I sat down with them and found out what their food needs were, but more importantly, I discovered what foods made them happy. What meals had positive nostalgia associated with them. I would imagine—especially for students who are away from home for the first time—that if I can make them some things that are familiar to them, this transition can be much easier and more positive. So, I think I'll run some small focus groups. That'll help me get to know everyone better, too." I felt a bead of sweat run down my temple. I was thinking on my feet, and it was starting to show. And that clunky air conditioner wasn't keeping up with the scorching day outside. "How's that for an answer?"

Andrea clapped her hands together. "Perfect. Are you in?"

I took a deep breath. "One more caveat. I have one client left in Boston. He's really important to me. I need to make him food, which I can do in my own kitchen if you're giving me a space with one. But I'll need to go down there once a week to deliver some things to him. Would that be okay?"

Andrea gave me a smirk. "Is it, you know, the *guy*?"

"No, no, not him. They fired me. At least, his wife and all her friends did. It's a professional athlete, and he's twenty-two, and his mother employs me to feed him. It's sort of a unique situation."

"Of course you can still work with him," Andrea said. "Let me show you around campus."

We spent the next half hour or so meandering through buildings, both old and new, stately brick structures and charming wood-frame houses. I saw the expansive dining room and met a few staff members, who seemed excited that I was coming aboard. The kitchen was modern and well-equipped. I witnessed a few students picking up boxed lunches, inspecting the contents, and throwing them out in a big barrel outside of the building. I had my work cut out for me, but anything I could come up with was probably going to be an improvement.

Andrea led me to a dorm and up four flights of stairs. I had to practically haul myself up the last few. "And here it is," she said, flinging open the door. "Your apartment."

I didn't know what to expect, but given how out of breath and shaky I felt, I hoped I wasn't seeing a mirage. It took up the entire fourth floor of the building—a large Victorian house similar to the administrative building but without a turret—and had huge windows on all four sides. The back window had a fire escape so tall I felt dizzy looking down it. Air conditioning window units buzzed from the side windows. There was a large living space, a bedroom big enough to fit a king-sized bed, a walk-in closet, and a bathroom with a claw-footed tub as well as a stand-up shower. A full-sized washer and dryer were stacked in another closet. The eat-in kitchen was obviously recently renovated, with granite counters and gleaming stainless-steel appliances. It would have rented for at least six thousand dollars a month in certain areas of Boston, probably much more.

"This would be, um, mine?" I choked out. My Beacon Hill place was lovely but a small studio. My dining table doubled as a second kitchen counter. This was a whole different world.

"Yes, included in your benefits package," she replied, smiling. "We just ask that you're available for any student issues as they arise in the dorm when you're here. There are staff living on each floor of the house, but I promise you this is, by far, the best apartment on campus. I might like it better than my house!"

She sold me. Tam had expressed interest in leasing my condo, so with living at Rockwood—even at a salary less than I was accustomed to—I would be saving money. And in a year's time, I could decide my next move. Despite the hellscape that the past few days had been, things were turning around. "This is great. Thank you. I look forward to moving in."

We walked down all the stairs and worked out the logistics and plans for me to get started on the job. As we headed down the path back to the administrative office where my car was parked, I noticed the boys' soccer team heading in the opposite direction. A tall, thin man with sandy blond hair and a bit of scruffy facial hair, dressed in athletic clothing and carrying a clipboard, was at the back of the pack, chatting with one of the players. His voice was so familiar, causing me to stare at him in a way that he must have felt. He looked up at me and stopped talking, and our eyes briefly locked. As I walked past, I kept looking, turning slightly to continue trying to determine if he was who I thought he was. He did the same until we were too far apart to keep doing that.

"Everything okay?" Andrea asked once we got back to the front of the building where our tour had begun.

"Who was that? The soccer coach?" I asked, but I already knew. It had to be him.

"Kyle Holling," she said. "Coaches soccer, obviously, but he's also a history and government teacher. He's been here for years. Just went through a nasty divorce. His wife used to teach here. Ex-wife, I should say. She and their daughter moved to Boston. I probably shouldn't have told you any of that. Another part of the job I need to get used to. No more gossip," she said, somewhat wistfully. "Why do you ask?"

"I know him," I replied. *How is this happening?* "We went to college together." The words came out of my mouth as if they were in slow motion. I felt lightheaded and wobbly on my feet.

Andrea winked. "I'm guessing there's more to the story than that. Kyle's a doll. Never shuts up, but he's a sweetheart." She followed me to my car. "I should probably advise you to stay away from each other to prevent any more controversies around here, but that would be silly. You're both adults. Just don't do it in front of the students, okay?" She laughed and waved, heading back up to the path toward her office. "See you soon, Devon!"

Speechless, I started my car and headed back to Boston. When I turned on the radio, Oasis was playing.

4

"How did I somehow end up packing your bathroom for you? And all your clothes, for that matter? By the way, I think it's time for a wardrobe refresh. Some of these tops need to go. I almost put them in the donation pile." Tam picked up a dingy, frayed, olive-green waffle knit L.L. Bean shirt that had clearly seen better days. I may have had it since college.

"You wanted to move in this week," I replied, taking the glass baking dish of bubbly chicken enchiladas out of the oven. "And I love that shirt. It's perfectly worn in. But I am eternally grateful for your help. I now have enough food for David Anders to last a week until I can get back here." I wasn't sure how I was going to handle the three enormous cooler bags I was bringing him that afternoon. Tam had to go to work, and I couldn't afford to pay anyone to help me like I used to do with big jobs like this. Until I got my first Rockwood check, I was puttering along on fumes.

"And it'll be October before you know it, and you'll have some breaks from him when the season gets underway. This is always a tough stretch for you," she said. I swore Tam knew me and my life better than I knew myself sometimes. "How are you feeling about everything?"

"Sweaty and gross after making a huge batch of cookies and all these enchiladas in late August. Oh, you mean about Rockwood? Totally fucking perplexed. I was all set to take the plunge. I mean, it's a weird job for me, completely different from anything I've ever done, you name it. Still, I looked at it as a one-year opportunity to make some money, have very few expenses, and figure out the next stage of my life. But, *Kyle Holling* on campus? And recently divorced? A huge monkey wrench in the whole damn thing."

"And Oasis on the car radio as soon as you turned it on. You said you listened to it with him on that fateful night. It's got to be some kind of sign. I'm channeling a major *Sleepless in Seattle* vibe here." Tam could truly tie a movie into almost any scenario.

"But a sign of what? The guy ghosted me. I tried to get in touch with him every which way, and nothing. And obviously, he wasn't pining away for me. The dude got married. He has a kid, for God's sake. And I've been here, living some sort of arrested development."

"You have not," she insisted. "You're only thirty-five. *We're* only thirty-five. If you are, then I am, too." She looked around the studio condo. "I'm excited to move in here. I'm covering so many stories at the State House these days, and I'll be practically next door."

"And closer to Professor Plum." Tam's date had gone well, and they were going out again that night.

"Yes, that's true. Cambridge is just across the river. But you know me, I'm sure I'll get bored soon." She examined a pair of wind pants that were riddled with holes and tossed them in the recycling pile without even consulting me. "What about Bentley? Have you heard from him?"

"Nothing," I muttered. "I mean, I don't know if I should expect to. It was a bad scene. And Julianna's Instagram is just pictures of her doing volunteer work all over town. Feeding people at homeless shelters, wrapping gifts for children, that sort of thing."

"Saint Julianna," said Tam with a nod.

"I guess she's trying to put an angelic image out there. In contrast to me." I sighed, scooping up the donation pile into a trash bag. "Where was any of that going, anyway? Decent romps and secret ice cream dates? Fun for a while, but I'm starting to need more, I think." *I need more.* It was a significant revelation for me.

"You do deserve more, Dev," agreed Tam. "Now, I get a cookie before you leave, right?"

•   •   •

"'Sup, Dev?" said David Anders as I opened the door to his Seaport condo. I was one of only four people, including his mother, housekeeper, and trainer, who had a key. One of the doormen had graciously offered to help me as I unloaded the huge cooler bags from my Jeep at the valet stand. David's building was the epitome of luxury in a city where people like me thought they had made it big time when they were able to buy a seven-hundred-square-foot condo in a good neighborhood with a dishwasher and street parking. Even three years into our arrangement, I still was in a bit of awe every time I came over.

"How's my favorite Celtic?" I asked while dropping the bags onto the enormous marble kitchen island and going back into the living room, where David was intensely gaming on his PlayStation.

"Stressed, Dev. My shooting sucks, and I keep getting these groin muscle strains. Sorry for the TMI, but you know how it goes." I did. He told me almost everything.

"Okay, so here's the deal, kiddo," I said, sitting down next to him on the big leather sofa. "I need to talk to you. Can you pause this, whatever it is?"

"PGA Tour 2K21. See, I'm playing on a course in Scottsdale here."

"You don't play golf."

"A man can dream, right?" he drawled. David always worried me. He hardly ever left his condo unless he had a game or practice. I couldn't imagine him spending four hours on a golf course, especially with other people. "So, what's the deal? Don't worry about the whole 'Dev in the news thing.' They just don't have much to talk about until we start our new season and dominate the news cycle with our brilliance." He put down the controller and gave me a high five. I knew he didn't act this relaxed with anyone else. David Anders, on the bench and on the court, was quiet, focused, and extremely shy. I liked being a person he was comfortable with, but it felt heavy sometimes.

"You know it. Can't wait to watch you guys. No, I'm putting the whole mess behind me." I took a breath. "Which is why I've taken a job running the dining services at a boarding school near Portsmouth. It's a nice place. Pretty campus. I'm just looking at doing this for a year. You know, so I can get my shit together again."

He nodded slowly, digesting the information. "What about me?" he asked with a shakiness in his voice.

I patted him on the knee. "You are part of the deal. I'll still come down once a week with a bunch of food for you. My new boss knows. I made sure I could still do this before I said yes. I'm going to call your mom and let her know after I leave, but I wanted to talk to you first."

He stood up and walked to the kitchen. "Good," he called back at me. "Because no one makes a cookie like this," he said, opening the bags until he found what he was looking for. And with that, I had David Anders' blessing.

•   •   •

Despite the two air conditioning units whirling from both sides of the fourth floor of Wentworth House, the ice in my extra-large iced coffee had melted, and the drink was growing lukewarm too quickly for my liking. I turned on the icemaker in my new freezer, but I knew it would be a while until it yielded anything. Somehow, I doubted I could get an iced coffee delivery to campus. I wasn't in Boston anymore. And even if I could, it would most certainly be melted by the time it reached me. And I'd have to climb all those stairs yet again. Those were going to take some getting used to.

It had felt so strange to load up the Jeep and the rented U-Haul trailer and just drive away from Boston with Tam waving goodbye from outside my condo building. I had lived in Boston for the thirteen years since I graduated from Norwell. My whole adult life. *Was I making the right decision?* I didn't feel like I had a better option. Word had spread about the scandal to the point where reporters were following me down the street, asking me questions that I tried to ignore. I finally told someone who claimed to be from *The Raucous Bostonian*, an online paper I had never heard of before, to shut the fuck up. For someone who represented a supposedly unhinged news source, he didn't take it well at all *and* included my outburst in his story. It was probably a good idea for me to leave town for a while.

The Rockwood maintenance staff hauled things up to the fourth floor with me, just as Andrea had promised. Still, the whole thing was overwhelming. I really had no idea how to start the job. Considering I had seen big stacks of cardboard meal boxes and takeout bags strewn outside the trash barrels when I pulled up to campus, the sooner I got going with everything, the better.

"Yoo-hoo! You're here! I'm so glad!" proclaimed Andrea in her brimming-with-positivity way. I wanted to bottle some of that and inject it into my veins. I wondered if she was on some sort of drug. It really was something.

"Hey there," I said, slurping more of my tepid coffee. "Want a cookie?" I asked, pointing to the Rubbermaid bin on the counter.

"Absolutely!" She gobbled one down in about five seconds. Yes, some kind of mood-altering substance was possible. Andrea might have had the munchies. "Oh my! What are in these? They are amazing!"

"Semisweet chocolate chips, white chocolate chips, and dried cherries. I chill the dough before baking, too. And I use organic sugars, which seem to make a difference in the consistency. Glad you like them. They'll be around a lot."

"Well, I think you'll win everyone over quickly with these. Yum," she said. "Can I get you anything?"

I finally poured the rest of the coffee down the sink. I couldn't take it anymore. "What's the coffee situation on campus?"

"Oh, I can't believe I didn't tell you on our little tour. So unlike me! We have a student-run coffee shop next door in Hartley House. It'll open tomorrow for the school year. Hours aren't probably what you're used to in the city, but it's open before and after classes, plus after dinner during study hours for breaks and some special events. You'll see me there a lot."

"Big coffee drinker?" I asked.

"I average eight cups a day." So, there it was—caffeine-fueled energy and optimism, with a penchant for gossip.

"Excellent. I usually only have one, but it's a big one."

"Well, I won't keep you, but I do have a favor. I know I said I didn't need you to start work until Monday, but we have an apple-picking event tomorrow afternoon. Many of the students will be with their parents here on campus, moving in, etc., but for the students who come early or are alone because they live far away, we like to offer an activity. I'm short on chaperones. One of the teachers I was counting on has food poisoning. She's blaming it on the boxed lunches. I think it might be because she drank multiple margaritas at Las Noches in Portsmouth last night, but I don't have any proof. I guess I need to take her word for it."

"How do you know she was drinking margaritas?" I asked, opening my new oven to inspect it. It was at least one-and-a-half times bigger than my Beacon Hill one. I'd be able to get David's food made so much quicker here.

"A bunch of us were out last night," Andrea said, shaking her head. "I probably shouldn't go to these gatherings anymore. It's a tough transition from colleague to boss. I'm seeing things I shouldn't be seeing. Two of the new teachers started making out at the table," she declared with a mix of unease and fascination.

"Yikes. I bet that was awkward," I replied, stashing my coffee mugs in the cabinet. "So, you're asking me to chaperone, I take it. If the staff member who bailed is only hungover, won't she be okay by tomorrow? I mean, just hypothesizing, given my vast experiences with hangovers. I did work in restaurants for many years. They are vicious but often short-lived."

"I agree, but she's sticking to this food poisoning story, so I'm a bit stuck. Yes, I really could use your help. How about it?"

Early New England apples were some of my favorites. The Jonamacs were great for snacks, and the Ginger Golds were surprisingly good for baking. It would also give me a chance to talk "food" with some students informally. But I had a nagging feeling deep in my gut. *Would Kyle be there?*

"Will there be a lot of, um, people there?"

"Not too many. I planned on two minibuses. Don't worry; you don't have to drive. I have that covered. It'll be a great opportunity for you to ease into the community. Also, I really need some help. Pretty please? I'll buy you a doughnut!"

"Do they make apple cider doughnuts there?" I felt like she was breaking me down. It didn't take much. I was a sucker for cider doughnuts.

"The best ones I've ever had. How about it?"

There was really no way I could decline on my almost first day on the job. "As long as we can bring back apples for the dining hall. I have a favorite apple crostata I'd love to make if that's okay."

Andrea clapped her hands together and beamed with anticipation. I was going apple picking.

5

I spent Saturday evening in a literal and figurative sweat after Andrea left. I needed to unpack, but I had no food in the apartment beyond the random condiments I had brought in a cooler from Beacon Hill. Instead of heading right to a grocery store as I should have, I drove my Jeep through the crowds of people in Portsmouth, held my breath, and drove over the big green Piscataqua River Bridge into Kittery, Maine. My home state always made my heart jump around in my chest, and I was not totally sure why. My upbringing was weird, and I didn't have warm feelings of home, but my father was kind despite his weaknesses. My mother was confusing, and she did not understand me. And growing up without money in a place like Kennebunkport was hard. I left there to go to college on a ton of financial aid and never went back in any sort of permanent way.

I drove twenty-five miles up to the Kennebunkport exit and looped around the Maine Turnpike service plaza parking lot. After such a physically and emotionally depleting day, I was starving. *Was I really going to eat here? At Burger King? Or should I drive five more minutes to my parents' little house just outside of Dock Square?* It had been months.

I snapped out of it and got back on the highway, heading south this time. I was overtired, overheated, and not in the mood for the judgment of my recent career moves or for the God-awful food that would likely be served. My mother's idea of a Saturday night dinner was a tough broiled pork chop, and whatever canned vegetable was on sale at Hannaford that week. I hadn't learned my cooking skills—or much else—from her.

I went back to Kittery and grabbed a little outdoor bistro table at When Pigs Fly, a place I knew because of the delicious bread they sold in Boston-area markets. With my most recent paycheck from David Anders' mother, I treated myself to a feast, with bread and breakfast to bring home with me.

The campus was abuzz with activity when I pulled back in after dinner, with friends shrieking at seeing each other after summers away and parents dropping their kids off after meals and shopping in the surrounding towns. *My new home.* There was so much to get used to. I dragged my weary body up the four flights of stairs, hoping this was going to get easier with time. When I brought my baked goods into the kitchen, I saw a yellow piece of lined paper taped to the outside of the window atop the fire escape. As I walked closer, I saw that it read "Hi" and had an arrow pointing down. I opened the window and saw that sitting at the top of the fire escape, in a plastic sand pail filled with almost melted ice, were two Coors Lights.

•   •   •

I did not sleep. I finally drank both of the Coors Lights at two in the morning, along with the pastries I had bought for breakfast. I didn't know what to do with myself. Just knowing that Kyle was somewhere on the campus and had left me beer, *the very beer we had drank together over fifteen years earlier*, made me an absolute wreck. *What was I doing at Rockwood? Why had I put myself in this position? What was I going to say when I actually saw him again?* I finally opened my laptop and streamed *It's Complicated,* one of my go-to movies for when everything went to shit. Somehow, seeing Meryl Streep, Alec Baldwin, and Steve Martin fumble around through their messes made me feel a little better. It also made me crave chocolate croissants, but that was another problem that I didn't have an easy solution for.

Even dressing myself and getting ready for apple picking was a monumental task. I ended up on a Pinterest board for apple-picking attire. Soon, I found myself down a rabbit hole of articles, websites, and advice columns about what to wear when one goes apple picking. *Who the hell am I,* I thought, scouring image after image of happy twenty-somethings in lush apple orchards enjoying their hayrides and taking bites out of shiny pieces of fruit? I had no idea if Kyle was even going to be on the excursion. Feeling ridiculous, I finally pieced together some jeans cutoffs, a white tank top, and a thin flannel shirt with the sleeves rolled up. I flat ironed my hair, applied minimal makeup, and flossed my teeth twice. I hadn't slept in a very long time and felt the weird sensation of exhaustion combined with jitters from the extra-large iced coffee with two shots of espresso that I bought from the student-run coffee shop that had mercifully opened next to my dorm that morning, just like Andrea had promised it would.

We were supposed to meet by the admin building at one in the afternoon to board the minibuses to take us to the orchard. I didn't know if it would be better to be early or to show up a minute or two before one. I paced around the apartment, which I still hadn't really unpacked or done much of anything with. I ate a piece of dry toast because I hadn't bought butter or jam or any other real groceries. Finally, I looked at myself in the bathroom mirror. An overtired woman in her mid-thirties stared back at me. Despite the bags under my bloodshot eyes, I looked okay. Kyle had walked away from me fifteen years earlier, and I deserved better than that. The beers were obviously some sort of nostalgic peace offering, and given that I would have to coexist with him in this new living arrangement, I would talk to him and hear what he had to say. But he still did what he did, and I didn't need to pretend that never happened. I took a breath, dropped some Visine in my eyes, and walked out the door.

"Devon! Over here, Devon!" crowed Andrea from in front of two white minibuses with The Rockwood School emblazoned on the sides as I walked down the path. She hadn't said that she was coming along, but I realized then that I should always assume that Andrea was everywhere. A small group of students gathered, along with a slightly pudgy man with brown curly hair and a full beard streaked with white, wearing glasses. No Kyle. *Okay.* "Devon, I'd like for you to meet one of the esteemed members of the English department, Ryland Dennis. Ryland, this is Devon Paige, our new Director of Dining."

He shook my hand and said, "I think I speak on many people here's behalf when I say I am *so* glad you are here. My favorite dessert is key lime pie."

"Oh," I said, taken aback. I hadn't asked anyone what they liked to eat—I had only met Andrea so far, for God's sake—and this felt so forward.

He must have noticed my discomfort and started to laugh. "I'm just joking with you. But I do enjoy key lime pie, I must say. Not sure I could pull it off in my apartment here. My kitchen isn't anything at all like the top floor of Wentworth House."

I didn't know what to make of this guy at all. Was he jealous of my apartment? He seemed, well, odd. Andrea chuckled awkwardly at our interchange. "Don't take Ryland seriously. He wouldn't know what to do with that kitchen. He spends most evenings at the Library Bar in Portsmouth, isn't that right?"

"Among other places," he said with a smug smile.

"I'm here," yelled a breathless Kyle Holling, running down the path. His sandy blond hair was a floppy mess, he hadn't shaven, and his clothes looked like he had picked them off the floor. He was a far cry from the preppy, put-together, forward-thinking twenty-year-old I had known. If it wasn't for his familiar voice and the fact that I knew he worked at Rockwood, I wouldn't have put two and two together that it was him.

"Oh, good," exclaimed Andrea. "You, Kyle, know Devon. Devon, Kyle. A bit of a college reunion this is, for you two!" Ryland looked puzzled, and I tried to stay even and calm.

"Good to see you, Kyle," I said, nodding at him carefully and giving a tight, closed-lip smile. I tried not to think of things that had happened in our past, but it was hard not to. My memory flew backward to his hands, tracing my back, his lips on my neck, his voice in my ear. I attempted to clear my head by looking in the direction of a confused Ryland. Yep, nothing sexy at all there. He was my temporary antidote.

"Oh, yeah, hiya Devon," Kyle replied, his eyes big as he looked over my face. He saw me looking over at Ryland, and he rolled his eyes. *What is going on here?*

"Okay, time to get on the road!" announced Andrea. "Kyle and Ryland shouldn't ride together, so you each get in a bus. Devon, if you could pick a bus, that would be fantastic." She walked over to the students and divided them into two groups. Not wanting to have to deal with this weird Ryland character, I didn't have a choice. I followed Kyle into the bus. He was sitting in a front-row seat, and I sat in the opposite row across from him. Students started filing in and sat behind us.

"Why can't you be on the same bus as him?" I whispered just loudly enough for him to hear me.

"Oh, that's a story," he said with a harsh laugh. "Not one I can repeat on this bus in this present company, but I'll be sure to tell you later. Most of the kids know about it, but I'm really not supposed to say anything anymore," he said, slumping back in his seat. I looked behind me, and students were staring back at me. A few started whispering to each other, using their hands to cover their mouths. "Did you get the delivery I left you on your fire escape?" he asked, perking up a bit.

"Yes, um, thank you. Kinda risky, leaving beer out in the open among teenagers, huh?"

"They were mostly with their parents and moving in, so I took the chance," he said, shrugging his shoulders. "Figured it was a good welcome given our history," he murmured, giving me a wink. I reddened instantly. This was the Kyle I knew. And I had to try not to react to him like that.

Browning Farm was in Lee, New Hampshire, so close to where Kyle and I had gone to college that I knew exactly where we were. "I think I picked apples here once," I said as we pulled into the parking lot.

"Probably," he said. "We go here every year around now, and usually, there's a trip further into the fall for those later varieties."

"Great," I said, following him out of the bus. "I want to make some crostatas this week from these apples, and the ones later in the fall will be great for some other things I have in mind."

Everyone was given baskets from the staff and led out to the orchard to start picking. I tried to keep my distance from Kyle, wanting to use this opportunity to talk to some of the students. I then realized that I wasn't used to talking much to teenagers, and I didn't quite know how to approach them. Then I thought of David Anders. He was in his early twenties, but he wasn't exactly worldly, and maybe these students would be of similar maturity. It was worth a try.

"Hi," I said to a small group, attempting to appear self-assured. "I'm Devon Paige, the new Director of Dining. I'm starting work tomorrow. I'll organize some focus groups, but I want to get a sense of what kind of food you'd like to eat at Rockwood. Any ideas?" I plastered a smile on my face, sure that they could see right through me and would immediately label me as a fraud.

A girl in an off-the-shoulder crop top looked me over critically and gave a scowl in reply. "I'm on a raw food diet. Nothing cooked." The other girls in her little group giggled.

I couldn't tell if she was serious or not. "Okay, so run me through your day. What's for breakfast?"

She tossed her blonde waves over her shoulder. "A smoothie, of course. Or an acai bowl."

She was full of shit. "Would those include yogurt?"

"Yes, of course," she replied with a haughty laugh.

I gave her a big smile. "Yogurt is cooked, you know."

The other girls nervously laughed, and the ringleader rolled her eyes at me. "Nice outfit," she said, looking me over and then walking away, her followers scurrying after her.

"Good one," said Kyle, coming up behind me. I could feel his breath on the back of my neck, and I tried not to let it get to me. It wasn't easy.

"Who on earth was *that?*"

"The meanest of the mean girls, the most obnoxious and entitled student at Rockwood. Ashlyn Lark."

"Lark, Lark... Any relation to Andrea, or just a coincidence?"

"Her niece. Andrea has no control over her. Ashlyn does whatever she wants because she knows Andrea won't do shit."

"Sounds like a great person," I said, shaking my head as I went back to picking apples.

"You just have to feed her," he said, joining me but picking twice as quickly, not inspecting the apples like I was. "She's such a pain in the ass in class—always thinks she's right, clearly pawns off her work on others, you get the idea. Can't wait to have her in my Political Science class this year."

"You know that was my major," I said.

"I do," he said, picking another apple and placing it in my basket since his was already full. "And I majored in Econ and thought I was going to be some big corporate exec type. Now I teach your major, and you are a chef. Funny how life turns out."

"*Was* a chef. Not sure I call this that. This is likely to be more about keeping a ton of people reasonably happy or at least well-fed."

"You didn't cook when I knew you," he said, taking a bite out of an apple. I was still filling my basket, examining each apple thoroughly before I twisted it off its branch.

"We knew each other for about twelve hours," I said, realizing how that sounded. A lot had happened in those twelve hours.

"Still, it's cool, you know," he continued. "The food aspect of you."

"That's one way to phrase it," I replied, trying hard not to smile. He was trying to engage, and part of me really wanted to. And part of me was still angry about him ghosting me, but I knew I couldn't delve into that in the middle of the apple orchard with so many ears around.

"I've never eaten anything you've cooked," he said. "Want to go get a doughnut?"

"Yes, but one second," I insisted. I looked around and discovered we were alone in the orchard aisle. "You and I obviously need to talk about some things. I have no groceries. If you are willing to go buy some food, I'll cook it. But this is just to talk, okay? I don't want you to get the wrong idea."

A big smile curved across his face, and in that moment, I saw twenty-year-old Kyle. "I'd love that. What should I buy? I don't know where to begin."

I shook my head. "I honestly don't care. Think of something you really like, look up a recipe for it, and buy the ingredients. I worked in restaurants for years and then cooked for some of the most high-maintenance people you've ever met. I can figure out almost anything." I picked one last apple. "Okay, let's get that doughnut."

We walked up the hill to where there was an open-air doughnut stand. The batter was being fried in hot oil for all to see, and Ashlyn Lark was standing nearby, munching on a fresh doughnut. "Raw food, huh?" I asked Kyle, and we both had a laugh.

6

Kyle was standing in my doorway with three overstuffed grocery bags—one from Market Basket, one from Whole Foods, and one from Trader Joe's—and I could see the veins bulging in his tanned forearms. Part of me wished this was just a cute guy coming over to make dinner with me, but it wasn't. This was Kyle; there was a lot of baggage, and we were going to be living and working in close proximity to each other for at least the next nine months. It was complicated.

"Three different stores, huh?" I asked, opening the door the rest of the way for him to enter the apartment.

"So, I was watching Food Network when we got back from the orchard," he began, setting the bags down on the kitchen counter. "And they went to this food truck that specialized in croque monsieurs. They looked awesome, and you said anything, so I started looking up recipes; there were so many variations, so I bought it all. Yes, at three different stores. Plus, potato chips because they served those with the croque monsieurs from the food truck, but I didn't know which kind you liked, so I bought four different ones."

He really did talk a lot, as I remembered from years earlier, but he was also thorough. There were several kinds of bread, cheese, ham, mustard, milk, butter, and flour; indeed, all the things I needed. I plucked the prosciutto, gruyère, and parmesan from the spread. "This is great," I acknowledged. "I actually prefer my croques with prosciutto, which isn't traditional at all. But I think you'll like it. And these," I said, setting aside the crinkle-cut kettle chips. "Are perfect."

"And there's this," he said, pulling out a six-pack of Coors Light from the bottom of a bag.

I shook my head. "Although I did enjoy the trip down memory lane when I cracked them open when I couldn't sleep last night, I'll admit that I hadn't drunk one of these since 2007."

He set them on the counter. "That night, then."

"Yes, that night," I replied. Flashes of laughing, sipping from the silver cans, lying next to each other on the twin bed in the sparsely furnished temporary dorm room, his hands on my hips, his mouth... I had to stop letting myself think these thoughts. "Anyway, I prefer whiskey sours. The only groceries I did bring from Boston were lemons and sugar to make them. You want one?"

"Oh yeah, I remember you telling me your dad drank them every evening."

"And sometimes before the evening. Seriously, that one is obscure. I don't even remember telling you that."

He smiled. "Devon, I remember everything." He raised an eyebrow. "*Everything.*"

Don't think about it, I instructed myself, as I felt the blood rush through my body. I cleared my throat and started making simple syrup in the microwave. "Okay, we need to talk. We're living and working in close quarters and obviously have a past."

"We do," he agreed. "And the more I've been thinking about it, the cooler I think it is."

"Why is that?" I asked, reaming the citrus halves through my strainer to separate out the pulp and seeds. While my dad mixed his whiskey sours using a neon yellow mix that my mom picked up at the local package store, I saw mine as a subtle, nuanced work of art—not too sweet, with an amber hue from the high-quality bourbon I chose, plus lemon juice, simple syrup, and just one Luxardo cherry. *Perfection.*

"The way I look at it," continued Kyle. "Considering us for a moment—"

"Wait, wait," I insisted. "First of all, there is no 'us.' I haven't seen you or talked to you in well over fifteen years. I tried to get in touch with you multiple times. I never heard from you. That was humiliating for me." It was time to lay all my cards out on the table; I had nothing to lose. He needed to know where I was coming from. "The only reason we're talking right now is because I took a job at the school you happen to be teaching at."

"You didn't realize I was here?" Kyle asked, clearly surprised and maybe a little amused.

"No!" I replied, horrified at what Kyle might be assuming. "Not until the very end of my tour with Andrea, after I had already agreed to the job when I saw you walking with the soccer team. What kind of person do you think I am? That I followed you here? After fifteen years? Like some kind of stalker?" Even though I hadn't followed him to Rockwood, I felt so embarrassed. "Tamara is my best friend in Boston—Andrea's college classmate! That's how all this happened. This had *nothing* to do with you. Don't flatter yourself," I said, handing him a whiskey sour. I was incredulous but somehow continued to go through the motions of mixing drinks. Years of working under pressure in restaurants were excellent training for moments like this.

"You never even Googled me?" he asked, taking a sip. "This is really good, by the way."

"Nope. Ask Tam. I told her that." I immediately regretted this revelation.

He smiled. "So, you were talking about me."

"Yes, because I almost withdrew from the job after I saw you," I said, starting to heat the milk for the roux that would be the base for the cheese sauce. "But I need it for now, so I didn't. But I never Googled you. When you ghosted me, I decided I didn't want to know anything else about you." Maybe it was harsh, but it was the truth, and he needed to hear it.

Unfazed, he continued, "Well, I Googled you. I Googled the hell out of you. For years." *Why does it sound sexy when he talks like this?* "You had a feisty reputation as a chef. I never saw that in you."

"Once again, you knew me for twelve hours."

"Those were twelve good hours," he said with a sigh. "Okay, I get it. You're pissed. I should have gotten in touch with you to let you know what was going on. I was putting together something for you in London that I wanted to send you when things changed for me very quickly, and then I threw myself into a relationship that ended up being a complete and utter disaster. It just took almost two years for me to realize it."

I poured the hot milk into the butter and flour mixture and whisked vigorously. The whisking was therapeutic. I had no idea if he was telling me the truth about his intention to mail something to me, but I decided to hear him out. "Okay, continue. Tell me what happened."

He poured more straight bourbon into his glass. "This girl, Lila, knew my roommate Jack. She came bursting into our room to ask him if he had finished, in her words, 'the blasted international politics assignment.' British girl, obviously. Jack wasn't there, but I was—sitting around by myself, feeling a bit lonely. Thinking of you."

I rolled my eyes, trying to remember what I might have been doing at that same moment. Probably stuck in a seminar related to Washington, D.C. internships or scurrying around free receptions and happy hours throughout the city to find decent food to eat. "I'm guessing Lila is the almost-two-year relationship gone wrong," I said while adding gruyère and parmesan to the sauce.

"Yes, she was. And everything was going well, or so I thought. There were weird signs along the way, which I didn't initially see. I was all in, as I am with everything I do." *So I gathered.* "I transferred to LSE. Stopped playing soccer on organized teams. Abandoned so much of who I was to spend my time with her. I told her I wanted to spend the rest of my life with her. But then I started to realize that I had never met her family or any of her friends from home. There were tons of excuses. Then, finally, two weeks before graduation, I started asking a lot of questions. She broke down and told me that no one from her hometown, including her parents, knew about me. I gave her an ultimatum: that I needed to meet them, or we were over. She said she didn't want that, so she brought me to her house way out in the countryside." He took a long sip of his drink. "Once we were there, it was terrible. It was clear that her parents weren't happy, and within hours of our arrival, her next-door neighbor showed up. His name was Nigel, and he was super nerdy. When he realized that I was Lila's boyfriend, he started crying. And she's comforting him and telling him that she loves him and that we're not really serious, and *I'm standing right there.* I might as well have had a sign on me that said 'idiot' or something like that."

"Or at least 'pushover,'" I said, shaking my head while brushing toasted bread with mustard. It was a strange story, and even though I still wasn't over what Kyle did to me, I did feel bad for him. I had certainly been in my own tough situations. "What on earth did you do then?"

"I got my bag and called for a cab. It cost me a fortune, but I took it all the way back to London. Lila barely apologized or got up from the bench she was sitting on with Nigel. I think her arms were still wrapped around him, and he was still crying, even though I was leaving. They got married the next summer."

"That's ridiculous. How did you find that out?"

"The alumni magazine. I think their marriage was almost arranged by their parents in some way. The magazine said they grew up together," he answered. "You bake the sandwiches with that sauce on them? They didn't show that part on the show I watched."

"And then I broil them at the end. They probably showed you that part, but it was a food truck, so who knows."

"Yeah, I don't really remember. I was busy looking up recipes at that point," he said. "Anyway, I packed up my stuff, booked a one-way plane ticket, and flew to JFK. I emailed LSE and told them to mail my diploma to my parents. And then I sat in their basement in Connecticut for a month, feeling like the biggest loser and looking at job ads. I had something lined up in London, but there was no way I was staying after that debacle."

"Okay, let these cool for a second," I said, pulling the sandwiches out of the oven. "Was Rockwood your first job after that?"

"Yeah, they needed a dorm proctor, and my parents were driving me crazy, so I jumped at it. I actually lived in this dorm on the first floor. I love this building. It was horrible pay, but I got free room and board, and they hired me to help with the soccer team, so it was a good diversion for me. Gradually, I started taking on more responsibilities and eventually became a teacher and the varsity boys' team coach."

"And you got married," I said, cutting the sandwiches in half.

"Guessing Andrea told you. She talks almost as much as I do," he said, taking a huge bite. "Delicious! This is so amazing, Devon! Thank you so much. Really."

"It's just a sandwich," I said, secretly happy he liked it so much and that his first food-impression of me was a good one. "Yeah, she realized afterward that she probably shouldn't have told me, but it was already out there."

"Well, I am super into this sandwich. I could eat five of them," he said. "Yeah, Andrea talks. So, anyway, Cora was an English teacher here. Once again, I was all in. We got married, had a baby girl, and lived a pretty good life here for a while. At least, I thought so. And then she became best friends with Ryland Dennis last school year, and everything fell apart."

"The guy who I met at apple picking? Oh, that's why you couldn't sit on a bus with him. Did they have an affair? He's kinda gross."

"I have no actual proof," he said, grabbing a second sandwich. "Yeah, nasty, right? They both denied it, just said they were emotional soulmates, whatever the fuck that means. But she became convinced through their friendship that she and I were no longer compatible and that I wasn't supportive of Annie—that's our daughter—and her dream of performing on stage, so she filed for divorce and moved to Boston. And Ryland is still here. The former Head of School—before she left in disgrace—drew up this ridiculous contract with HR. I swear it's like something from *The Office*. Ryland and I aren't allowed to be within a certain proximity of each other, so that makes faculty meetings interesting. I also have a letter in my file with a big warning about contact with him. But I know they don't want to fire me unless I do something colossally stupid. Most of the kids and their parents love me, and we have a killer soccer team. So, I have that going for me."

I pulled out the container of cookies that Andrea had discovered the day before. I felt like he needed one. "I'm surprised you didn't kick his ass," I said, offering him a cookie. "You have an intensity about you, as you may have realized."

"I went about my revenge in other ways," he said, chomping on a cookie. "So, so good, Devon. Love these. Yeah, I sent a stripper to an English Department meeting for him. She was dressed as a librarian. It took a while for anyone to realize what was going on in the meeting, and Cora hadn't left for Boston yet and was there, and things got ugly fast. She threatened to take full custody of Annie after that, so I had to tone it down."

I felt my eyes widen at Kyle's story. "Wow, that's extreme. Very creative, though, I must say. Glad you like the cookies. I'll make them this week in the dining hall to try to win over some students."

"And the staff. This will help most definitely. Anyway, I've learned a lot about myself throughout these fifteen years, Devon. I want you to know that about me. I realize that anything I do, I'm one hundred percent in. Maybe it's more like one hundred ten percent. It was good for playing soccer when I was younger. Coaching now, too. Super focused, eyes on the prize, all in. Not sure how great it was not for driving a spouse crazy. Or parenting a kid who is into something I don't totally understand. I'm working on that, too."

I began mixing another batch of drinks. "At least you know this about yourself. That is, shall I say, more introspection than I've heard from most men."

"I went through a bunch of therapy when Cora left. Used every single visit available to me through the Employee Assistance Program. I've got all kinds of insight now."

"So, what's the verdict? How do you not drive a future romantic partner away with this, um, intensity?"

"My therapist said to lay it all out there early on. This is me, working every day to channel all this energy for good." He looked into my eyes for a solid five seconds. I felt all the feelings throughout my body. *All* of them. He pushed his disheveled hair off his forehead and smiled as if he knew the effect he was having on me. I was trying to keep it together the best I could, but I had no idea what my face looked like. "You know, just in case you're still considering us," he said with a wink.

I couldn't. Not yet. It was too much, too soon, and there was too much damage and complexity between us. "Look, I sometimes make terrible decisions," I explained, trying to snap back into a normal state of being. "You need to know that about me. You probably saw me on TV."

"I don't watch much TV, other than episodes of *The Office* and sports," he said. "I do spend way too much time, however, online. Hence, all the Googling. I know what happened, Devon. It's okay. Things happen."

"They do," I said. "And there is a lot going on right now for both of us, and I think we need some time. We obviously had a very strong connection years ago, and I've really enjoyed talking to you tonight. For now, I want to be friends with you. Get to know you for real this time. As an adult. I could use a friend here."

Kyle nodded. "I can't help but think the stars were aligned for us to reconnect here at this stage of life, and I'm not going to lie, I find you very attractive. You're smart and sexy, just like you were fifteen years ago. Like I said before, I'm laying things out there. But I respect you and want to be your friend, too." He took a sip of the fresh drink I put in front of him. "Is it because you find me annoying?" he asked somewhat sheepishly.

"No," I answered, shaking my head. "I mean, you talk a lot, but it's not annoying. Not yet, anyway. Maybe I'll change my mind about that." I couldn't help but laugh.

"Okay, cool. I think I really annoyed Cora after a while. Thinking you actually might be dodging a bullet here," he said with another wink. Then I saw a bright flash, and Kyle ran to the window by the fire escape. He flung open the window, and I rushed over to see what was going on. Kyle yelled, "I see you! You're going to fail my class this year!" He shut the window, and I backed away quickly so no one else could see me, even though I lived there.

"Who was that?" I asked, not expecting people to be sneaking up the fire escape to take my picture.

"Probably some kid from *The Underground Stallion* looking for dirt."

"Andrea showed me a copy of the scandal with the old head of school. Who are these kids?"

"They were all over my separation and divorce, too. No one knows for sure, but I have my suspicions."

"Ashlyn?"

"Likely, or at least some of her minions. I'd get some curtains for that window, Dev," he said. "I should probably leave before it gets too late and they pull the fire alarm to get us to walk out of the building together." I shuddered, realizing the possibilities of total embarrassment. "Thanks for dinner. Best night I've had in a long time," he said as he let himself out and headed down the Wentworth stairs.

I cleaned up our dishes and let everything from the evening sink in. *Kyle was back.* I felt a strong attraction to him in so many ways; he still looked great. I loved talking to him, and I knew that physically we had once clicked. It would be easy to jump into some kind of relationship with him, but it was also so complicated given the living and working situation we were in. *And I haven't even started working here yet,* I thought as I started the dishwasher. Plus, he had so much baggage, both past and recent, to work through. I did not want to be his rebound or easy fix. Time would tell, but friendship—for the time being, anyway—seemed like the right answer.

It was dark outside, and I could hear the soft chimes that I read about in my staff handbook that sounded each night at ten o'clock, signaling quiet hours. There was something nice about a ritual and a cadence to my days. The past few years had been hectic and at the whims of others, and life at Rockwood might be more structured and predictable. I could handle that for a year or so.

I was about to shut off the kitchen light and retire to the bedroom when I heard a knock on the window by the fire escape.

Kyle's face was peering at me, lit by the flashlight on his phone. I opened the window. "I thought I said we were going to try to be friends. No late-night booty calls," I teased.

"Shh," he said. "I promise you I'm trusting the process here. But I remembered something else you told me from fifteen years ago." He handed me a plastic bag and headed back down the fire escape. I looked inside the bag and saw it. It was a hand packed pint from Georgy Porgy's Ice Cream, the stand right outside Rockwood's gates. Vanilla Toffee, my absolute favorite.

7

The first few days on the job were hard. I tried to ease into the role, working with the staff to see what they had in stock and what they needed while figuring out what the hell to actually cook for the students. We kept running out of things and improvising, and when Andrea stopped by, I found myself buckling. "I have no idea what I am doing," I admitted. "If you want to fire me now and find someone else, you might be better off." I knew she would probably tell everyone else on staff at Rockwood what I had said, but I didn't care. I was sweaty, exhausted, and completely bummed out.

"That makes two of us," she said in her usual cheery, up-tempo voice, pulling up a stool from the corner of the kitchen and sitting down. "I feel like I'll never know what I'm doing in my job here. But you're serving food that's not in a cardboard box, so that's a great first step." She looked around and saw Marnie, the former interim Dining Director, glaring at her from across the kitchen. "Oops," she said, chuckling softly. "How are things with her?" she whispered. "Is she pissed you took over?"

"She seems okay," I said. In all honesty, I hadn't had time to consider other people's feelings that much. "Anyway, I think I need to set up some focus groups like I told you I would in my interview. Sooner rather than later, or else I worry I won't be able to connect with the students. How should I go about reaching them?"

"Just send out an all-student email with a sign-up form attached. Search for one that I've sent to get the address. And maybe try to get a variety of grade levels so you hear different perspectives. I think it's a good idea," she said. "Nice picture in *The Underground Stallion*," she added.

"What? I haven't seen it." *Ugh.* It must have been from my dinner with Kyle. I had pushed it so far out of my mind, and with everything else going on, I hadn't mentally revisited it. "How bad is it?"

"Considering you're both fully clothed and the only mildly questionable thing in view is a six-pack of beer, I think you're doing quite well," she said, standing up. "They usually keep stacks of the paper in that little birdhouse outside the library if you want to see one for yourself." She patted my shoulder. "You're doing fine, Devon. I'm looking forward to dinner tonight. I can't miss Taco Tuesday."

"Yeah, we'll have tacos," I mumbled. "We didn't even drink the beer, just so you know. If you don't mind, I'm going to go—" I really wanted to see this newspaper or flyer or whatever the hell it was. Apparently, I had fled one scandal-ridden situation for another one.

"Please, be my guest. But try not to put much stock in that rag. It's just a few kids stirring up trouble. You'll make yourself sick if you let it get to you."

I nodded and bolted out of the back of the kitchen, through the empty dining hall, and out into the grassy quad. Students were milling around, swinging in hammocks, throwing frisbees, and chatting in small groups. I ran across the lawn to the library and found the birdhouse Andrea had mentioned. Sure enough, there was a small stack of white papers sticking out of it, with the words *The Underground Stallion* emblazoned across the top.

There was a black-and-white picture of Kyle and me, standing across from each other at my kitchen island, laughing and smiling. Sure enough, the silver beer cans were shining, as were our faces mid-conversation. It was so strange to see us through the eyes of whatever little shit snuck up my fire escape and took the picture; we looked happy and well—*into* each other. My heart sank a bit. I was a little embarrassed and very confused.

"Nice picture there, Chef," yelled Ashlyn Lark in my direction from the middle of the quad, then went back to laughing with her friends.

"I'm not going to feed you," I muttered to myself, knowing that I couldn't withhold food from her. But boy, did I want to. *Why does she make me bristle so badly?*

Once I was back in my apartment and safe—hopefully—from intrusive eyes, ears, and cell phone cameras, I gave Tam a call. I never knew her work schedule, as it changed at a moment's notice, but she always told me to try calling if I needed her. This was one of those times.

"What's up, Chef?" she asked, and I could hear the lilt of the newsroom behind her. She probably wouldn't be able to talk for long.

"Ugh, that's what *she* just called me. Ashlyn Lark."

"Who the heck is Ashlyn Lark? Any relation to my Andrea?"

"Niece. And I don't know who Andrea's brother pretends to be because his dear daughter is clearly the spawn of something God-awful. Yeah, in other words, I don't like her at all. She's a mean girl. Reminds me of a few girls I went to high school with." There it was. I knew something about her was familiar and terrible.

"Oh, those are the worst," she said. "I only have a few minutes, but I'm so glad you called. Tell me something. How are things going otherwise?"

"Well, Sparky, I have already been featured in an underground newspaper if that gives you any kind of idea."

"I'll ignore my nickname, which I like to pretend never existed. Did they write about Bentley and the scandal? Eww, that's harsh. What'd they say?"

"No, nothing about that, at least not yet. I'm sure they're onto me, so I bet it'll be soon. But it was about Kyle and me. No article, just a picture and a caption. It says, 'Chef cooks up something spicy with Rockwood's newest bachelor.' And there's a picture. Hold on, I'll send it to you." I took a quick snap of the newspaper and texted it to Tam.

"Whoa, that's Kyle? Dev, he looks good. What are you doing drinking beer with him? Are you two already an item? I thought it would take at least a couple of months, given your trepidation."

"We did not drink those beers. We drank whiskey sours. And no, we are not an item. He's been through a lot. He has a ton of baggage. I heard the whole story about what happened when he went to London and the girl he met there, plus all about his recent divorce from a teacher who used to work here. He has a *kid*, Tam. Her name is Annie, she's ten, and she does theater in Boston. It's all too much. I told him I wanted to be friends for now. He's sort of on board."

"Because he really wishes he was cooking up something spicy with you," she replied with a laugh.

I sighed. "He brought me ice cream."

Tam cleared her throat. "What flavor?"

"Vanilla Toffee," I said weakly, and I heard Tam gasp. "I know, I know," I said. "But I'm trying to take this one step at a time."

"Gotcha," she said. "Well, I love your condo. I'm not there much right now due to Professor Plum, but I really like it. Great location."

"Ooh, I want to meet him. That is, if you're ready for that."

"Definitely. When are you coming down to feed D-Dawg?"

"D-Dawg?" I scrunched up my nose at the nickname. "Where did you hear that one?"

"The new sportscaster has been calling him that. Too cheesy, right?"

"I think so. Yeah, I'm making my schedule around his, so this week, I'm taking Friday and Saturday as my weekend. I'll be down on Friday afternoon with a ton of food for him. Are you free?"

"Shoot, I'm covering this huge book event on Nantucket this weekend. But soon. Just let me know when you'll be back." I heard some people talking near her. "Okay, Dev, I gotta run. Don't let this Ashlyn get to you. And Kyle's cute. Whatever you decide to do, I support you. But if you decide to play pots and pans with him, I'm good with that."

"What does that even mean, Tam? Pots and pans?"

"I have no idea. It just sounded like something some chef in a rom-com would say."

•   •   •

I only had four students reply that they would come to the focus group, but I messed up the online form, and somehow, it only captured the numbers of "yes" replies and not actual student names. Out of the three hundred students, only four agreed to help me. And who knew if they would even show up?

I set up a space in the corner of the faculty dining room that had some comfortable chairs and a low table for us to meet. I brought my favorite fresh sparkling lemonade and a tray of the cookies that Andrea and Kyle had liked. When I made them in the dining hall kitchen that morning, the staff couldn't get enough, and I had to set aside some for the focus group. I promised I would make more for dessert that night if I had time. As they enjoyed the cookies, it seemed like Marnie and the rest of the crew were softening a bit to my presence. Maybe it would work with this group of students, too. Or else I could just sit in the room by myself and eat cookies.

I grabbed a chair and scrolled through my phone, too fidgety to do anything else. "Someone told me the cookies were here," announced a familiar male voice. Kyle came into the room in shorts and an old Counting Crows t-shirt and plunked himself down on the chair across from me, helping himself to a cookie.

"Where've you been? Is this, like, a day off?" I asked, gesturing at his attire.

"Class. I just entertained a group of sixteen-year-olds with tales of presidential assassinations. My favorite, of course, is that of James Garfield. A sordid, unfortunate, gangrene-ridden story." He smacked his lips. *Oh, those lips...* "This is delicious. Hits the spot."

"You wear that to teach?" I pondered, thinking of my uptight, old-school teachers back in my Maine public school days.

"Yep," he said. "Another thing Ryland Dennis complained about last year to the former Head of School was my attire. But she's gone, and Andrea couldn't care less. You want me to tell you about James Garfield?"

"Seeing that I'm just sitting here waiting for students to show up to this focus group, sure. But we're not exactly helping our cause by hanging out here together."

"Old friends, Dev. We were college classmates. Anyone can look up our bios on the Rockwood staff page and figure that out."

"True," I acknowledged. I needed to ease up a bit. There was only so much I could control. "Okay, tell me about James Garfield."

"His vice-president was Chester Arthur. He was in an off-shoot political group called the Stalwarts. Charles Guiteau wanted a government job and kept getting turned down. He was also a Stalwart. So, being a presidential assassin-type, he got the weird idea that killing the president might help him achieve his goals. Not exactly of sound mind and body, right?"

I giggled. I imagined Kyle in front of a class of students, managing to get teenagers to pay some degree of attention, which was impressive in a world where they were used to being entertained with YouTube and TikTok. He continued, "Anyway, Guiteau shoots Garfield at Union Station in DC just before Garfield is taking a train trip. He's a terrible shot. All these people try to help him, so they lay him down on the floor of the nasty-ass train station."

"You said nasty-ass in class?" I couldn't imagine my million-year-old U.S. History teacher in a three-piece suit using such a description. I also had no recollection of ever learning this story in school.

"You bet," Kyle said, smiling. "It's an important part of the story. Anyway, they're digging around in his open wounds for bullets. Bare hands, and we're talking 1800s. No Purell on the scene in those days. No luck. They bring him to the White House, put him to bed, and continue to try to help him for months in a sweltering Washington summer."

"I'm guessing they weren't much help."

"Nope. They fed him huge meals, but he kept wasting away. They even brought in Alexander Graham Bell with a metal detector at one point, but the bullet had moved, and they only checked one side of his body. Stupid shit like that. He finally died of gangrene."

"And the guy who shot him? What happened to him? I'm guessing he didn't get his dream job."

"Arrested, tried, convicted, and hanged," said a boy as he walked in the room. He gave Kyle a high-five. "Best teacher on campus. Tells the good stories." Three other students followed him and sat down. One of the girls looked familiar, but I couldn't place where I might have seen her before. Possibly just at mealtimes so far; I had seen so many students that they all blurred together.

"There you go," said Kyle, grabbing another cookie. "Glad young Sam here remembers everything he learned forty-five minutes ago. All right, you four. Make sure you give Ms. Paige here some good ideas about what you want from your dining experiences. No smartass snarky crap. And definitely eat these cookies. You won't regret it," he said as he walked out, waving at me as he left.

I cleared my throat, thankful for the introduction and cookie endorsement, but also all too aware that I was following the great Mr. Holling. "Hi, everyone. Thanks for coming today. As you can see, I didn't get an awesome response to my email, so I'm very grateful to you four for signing up and coming to talk with me. Please help yourself to cookies." In true fake-it-'til-you-make-it fashion, I pretended to know what I was doing. "Maybe we can go around and introduce ourselves. Tell me your name, what grade you're in, and where you're from. I'll start," I began. "I'm Devon Paige. I'm the new Director of Dining, and up until a couple of weeks ago, I lived in Boston. I grew up in Kennebunkport, Maine."

The students went through the requested motions, and finally, the girl who looked familiar spoke for the first time. Looking directly at me, she said, "My name is Adrienne Preston. I'm a junior, and I just transferred here from a private day school in the Boston area this week."

• • •

The rest of the focus group meeting was a blur. I managed to keep it together—to engage in conversation with the other three students—while Adrienne sat in silence. I didn't even try to talk to her, having no clue what to say. I had never seen her in person, as she had typically been at school or playing sports or on some kind of extravagant getaway with her mother or with friends, but I had seen her picture in a million places throughout their house. And when she discovered Bentley and me that fateful afternoon, I had only seen her in the shadows and frantic chaos as I stumbled out the door. But I heard her voice as she asked about her tennis racket, followed by her screaming for her mom. And now she was sitting in front of me, as her schoolmates told me of the lasagnas and chocolate cakes they missed from home.

I thanked them all for joining me and promised to start including their input in our menus. I had distracted myself from Adrienne by taking pages of notes. She was the last to stand up, so I quietly asked, "Would you mind staying for a minute?" and she sat back down. Once the last student had left, I offered the plate of cookies to her again. She took one, and I poured her a glass of lemonade.

"I've had these before," she said, chewing slowly. "But I've never had the lemonade. I wish I could say it's awful, but I can't. So, you have that advantage over me."

"What are you doing here?" I asked. "I thought you were going to that school in Carlisle."

"I was," she said. "They kicked me out after three days."

This was a pattern with Adrienne, at least from what her father had told me. "What happened?"

"I borrowed the Dean of Student's daughter's horse for the afternoon. I rode it to Walden Pond. I figured it could use a swim. Hot day," she said with a shrug.

I tried to imagine this scenario playing out and suppressed my laughter the best I could. It was a ridiculous prank. "You took a horse that wasn't yours and rode it all the way to Walden Pond? Down actual roads?"

"I used my maps app and figured out some trails. But they had to close down the pond for a bit and kick paying guests out because I was in there with a horse, and it was a whole scene. So yes, I was asked to leave the school immediately."

"You could probably get your own horse if you asked your parents," I said with a sigh.

"I know," she replied. "But I would have to keep it out in the suburbs, and I wouldn't get to see it much. It wouldn't be very practical."

She was an odd child but likely correct when it came to being able to spend time with a horse. "I can see that. Okay, so you're here. Why Rockwood? I would think your mother wouldn't want you anywhere near me."

Adrienne fiddled with her shoelaces. "She doesn't even know you're here. I didn't know you were here until I showed up to lunch the other day. For whatever reason, my mother thinks this place is fantastic. They were willing to take me despite my impressive record, and she sent me up here with the driver. She didn't even drop me off."

I had to ask. "And your, um, father?"

She rolled her eyes. "She sent him off to Canyon Ranch in the Berkshires for a month to find inner peace or lose weight or something. She calls the shots anyway. You know the money is hers, right?"

I didn't. Bentley and I had never discussed the origins of their family's wealth, but I knew he worked as a hedge fund manager, so I had made assumptions. But if the real money was Julianna's, it made sense that she was the one making the big decisions. "There's obviously a lot I don't know," I said. "And you and I are going to have to coexist. So, let's start here. What's something from home you miss eating? I didn't ask you with the other students around, but I'd love to know now."

Adrienne looked to the side like she was trying to avoid something. "Your Chicken Milanese," she acquiesced. "I hate to admit it, but it was my favorite."

I was getting somewhere. "It *is* good, isn't it? I'm afraid to know what you three ate after I left."

She made a face. "It was really bad. She started getting food delivered from all these different restaurants, but everything was cold or soggy. Too much salt. Dad refused to eat more than a bite. He'd leave and go get ice cream. And then she decided he was eating too much of that and booked the Canyon Ranch visit."

I groaned. Strangely, I didn't miss Bentley at all, but we had bonded over our shared love of dairy. "Well," I said, clearing my throat. "You lucked out then, coming here. We're going to make Chicken Milanese tomorrow night." I hadn't planned for it, but now I knew we had to.

8

"'Sup, Dev," David Anders grunted from a weight bench in the middle of his living room where his coffee table used to be. His trainer, Johnny, was spotting him as he bench-pressed a ridiculous amount of weight. "One more set, Dev. Sorry 'bout this," he murmured in his Southern drawl. I walked past them and into the kitchen, where I silently started unloading the cooler bags on the counter.

"Okay," he said, sitting up and wiping the sweat from his forehead with a towel that Johnny handed him. "I'm good, man. I'll see you tomorrow." Johnny waved goodbye to me and left the condo, leaving us alone.

"What's going on?" I asked, sitting on the leather chair next to the weight bench. "Since when are you working out here instead of the gym downstairs?" David didn't like going anywhere he didn't have to, and it worried me that he might be leaving his condo even less now.

He shook his head, taking a gulp of Gatorade. "Since some punk-ass down there told me that my game sucks and the Celts should trade me. I don't need that shit. But the thing is, then I start thinking maybe he's right. And it's stuck in my head. I've been playing like crap, and I can't seem to snap out of it."

"You scored eight points last night," I said, handing him a cookie. "That's not horrible."

"That was the most I've scored so far this season. I need to break into double digits again."

"Dude," I said, shaking my head. "The preseason literally just started last week. I can't believe it's October already. But you have plenty of time. And you're home now for a few games. That'll be good."

"Oh yeah, my mom's going to call you. I've got a game in LA at the beginning of December that she can't go to—some medical conference. She wants you to go."

"Oh," I said with a nod, trying to keep a smile on my face. I had done this a few times during my tenure working for David and his mother, but I used to have more control over my schedule. I didn't want to give him anything else to stress about, considering his uncertain state of mind. "Sounds good. Just tell her to give me a call."

"Cool," he said, giving me a high-five. "So, how's it going? How's fall up there in the north woods?"

I laughed. "I wouldn't exactly call it that. If there's a Whole Foods nearby, I consider it a place that is at least suburban. But yeah, the leaves are changing, and there are a ton of confused tourists going through St. George's trying to find Wentworth by the Sea in New Castle. Wrong island! They get confused because there's a dorm with the same name. Anyway, I'm figuring out the job and starting to win over the kids, so that's good." I left out Kyle, *The Underground Stallion*, Adrienne Preston, Ashlyn Lark, and a host of other things. Details, details. I tried to clear them from my head.

"What's the key to winning over people? I feel like I should take notes or something. I'm on the struggle bus with this," he said, shaking his head. According to David's mother, his shyness had always been an issue. Even now, he sometimes found himself in hot water for not talking to the press the way his contract stipulated he needed to. It wasn't malicious or anything; the guy was just hesitant and introverted. But he could rip it up on the basketball court.

"Cookies, David. That's all I got. I make them these cookies," I said, pointing at the plate I had brought over to the living room with me. "They call me the Cookie Lady now. I used to be Boston's private chef to the rich and famous. Now I'm the Cookie Lady."

"You've still got me, Dev. And they're damn good cookies. Did you bring any enchiladas?"

•   •   •

"Hey, what are you up to?" I asked Andrea as I got out of my car outside of Wentworth House. She was sitting on a bench eating an ice cream cone. Raspberry. It looked delicious. My stomach rumbled.

"Georgy Porgy's closes this weekend," she said. "I hear you're an ice cream fan. Better get some while you still can."

"Ugh," I groaned. "When do they open up again?" I had gotten so accustomed to my Vanilla Toffee fix over the past month that I hadn't thought about what I would do during a fall and winter hiatus.

"Usually May first," she said. "Coming back from Boston, I assume? How's David Anders?"

"Good," I said, not wanting to give Andrea any information that could be spread to others at the local watering holes or elsewhere. "It's always nice to see him."

"So, I need some help," she began, and I tried to relax. I quickly learned that leading the dining services involved a lot more than feeding three meals a day to the students and any staff and their families that showed up. There were a million little extra events and needs and things to keep track of. "Did you notice the scaffolding and tarps at the entrance to campus?"

"Yeah, you can't miss them," I said. I had meant to ask the maintenance staff what was going on, but something else always came up, and I was distracted. "What's going on?"

"There is a local artist—actually, he's an alum—named Ward Connelly who is creating an art installation for us. It's his gift to the school, and he's world-renowned, so it's a big deal. It'll be the first thing people see when they drive through the gates of Rockwood. Everyone is very excited about it."

"Cool. So, they're working on this installation under these drapes and stuff until it's ready to be revealed, I'm guessing?" I had worked with a few artists and their families in Boston, plus hosted numerous dinners and receptions for them at restaurants I had worked at, so this wasn't anything new.

"Exactly. And he wants to unveil everything at an event next Friday, weather permitting. Even if there's a bit of rain, we can likely still pull it off with tents. I'd love for you to meet with him to come up with a catering menu. The Board of Trustees will all be in attendance, so we want it to be nice. There will be champagne for adults, so we need to be careful about student access, but I can give you the name of a bartender we've worked with before who will be fine given the circumstances."

"Okay, sounds good," I said. "Email me the details, and I'll figure it out." It was short notice, but it didn't sound like a ton of work.

"I'll tell Ward that you'll meet him at The Barnacle at 9 PM tomorrow then," she said, throwing her napkin and the paper cone wrapper in the trash barrel next to the bench. "So nice this isn't overflowing with cardboard boxes anymore," she mused.

"Um, where's The Barnacle?" I didn't know all the Portsmouth bars and restaurants yet, and this one sounded nautical and interesting. I imagined portholes for windows and lots of life preservers and anchors. Maybe a big whale hanging from the shiplap-covered wall.

"It's right underneath where you work every day," she said with a wink. "Ask Kyle. He'll tell you all about it."

•   •   •

The line at Georgy Porgy's stretched around the side of the little house and past the picnic tables, but I was ready to patiently wait my turn. Besides, I needed to process this new information. I wasn't in the least bit intimidated by taking a meeting with Ward Connelly, the artist, or the prospect of throwing together this event for the most important people in the Rockwood community. No, none of that. What *was* bothering me was the fact that there was apparently a *speakeasy* of all things underneath where I had worked and cooked for over a month. I felt stupid and naïve. I didn't even know where the damn stairs were to reach a lower floor. Or floors. For all I knew, there was a whole underground village at Rockwood.

Kyle and who I presumed to be his daughter Annie, based on the pictures he had shown me, were standing in the halfway point of the line, and he motioned for me to join them. The little boy behind them yelled, "Hey, she's cutting!" and Kyle fished a dollar bill out of his pocket and handed it to him. "Add another scoop, kid. Get espresso chip and stay up all night." The boy and his mother stared at Kyle with their mouths open. I couldn't help but laugh.

"That's my dad," Annie said, shaking her head. "He does this stuff all the time."

"Hi," I said, giving Annie a small wave, not knowing what else to do. "I'm Devon. I went to school with your dad a long time ago."

"I know who you are," she said, pointing her chin up knowingly. "You made the French toast I had for breakfast."

"I wish I had," I said. "But my team did. I was making food to bring to a very hungry basketball player. Do you ever watch the Celtics?"

"When I stay with my dad," she said. "We watch all the sports."

"Well, I cook for David Anders. He's super tall and loves cookies."

"Cool," she said. "Dad, I want to try the Puddin' Pie ice cream tonight."

"They're really playing up the Georgy Porgy theme this year, huh?" Kyle said. "Not sure if they're going nursery rhyme or Toto cult classic song, though."

"Toto sang a song about Georgy Porgy?" I asked. Kyle was an endless font of weird knowledge.

"You bet. You would never know it was the same band that sang 'Africa.'" Kyle looked up at the menu board. "Vanilla Toffee, I assume?" he asked me. "My treat."

I shook my head. "You don't need to," I said. "Especially since I need to get some information from you. I hate to occupy your time with Annie here, but I need a little intel."

"No problem," he said. "We'll go around back to the water where the ducks swim with our ice cream. And yes, I owe you. The food is infinitely better in the dining hall since you took over. Marnie's food really sucked."

I felt bad that everyone was ripping on Marnie left and right, but there wasn't much I could do about it other than change the subject when it happened. She didn't say much to me but did her job well and got along with everyone. I hoped Tam's evergreen quote that "people have short memories" rang true, and eventually, everyone stopped referencing the brief era of terrible boxed meals.

We walked to the water's edge, and Annie meandered down the shore a bit. I pictured her as a toddler, ambling along with her ice cream, babbling to the ducks. She had grown up in St.

George's. Now, at ten, she was a mature only child who had already navigated so much in her decade of life. Although my parents hadn't gotten divorced, I could see myself in her in many ways. She seemed like a person I'd like to know better.

"She's fantastic," I said. "You must be proud."

"I can't take much credit," Kyle said, taking a big bite of cookies and cream. "She's so much like Cora. All her poise, all her smarts. I hope she stays that way."

"Come on, you know about the assassination attempts on all the presidents," I said, trying to keep things light.

"True," he said. "Remind me to tell you more about Warren Harding sometime. So much scandal."

"Deal. So, here's a question for you. Can you please tell me about The Barnacle? Because I didn't know until about thirty minutes ago that I've been cooking above a speakeasy."

"Oh Jesus, I didn't realize I hadn't told you about it yet. Too busy babbling to you last week about Teddy Roosevelt getting shot and still making a speech."

"That was a good story."

"Right? There are so many. Anyway, I'm sorry I didn't tell you about it. It's kinda dumb, at least in my opinion, which doesn't mean a whole lot around here. But it was established early in the school's history by the second Head of School, whose family owned a huge shipbuilding company. I've only been there twice."

"Is it like a normal bar? Do people go there regularly? Is it open every night? How does it all work?" I couldn't help firing questions at him. It was such a strange concept to wrap my head around. A bar in a boarding school full of underage teenagers?

"It's more like a private club for people of legal drinking age who are associated with Rockwood. So, faculty and staff are welcome, but not many use it. You might see a couple of them if you go down there. It tends to be people on the Board and local alumni who like that sort of thing. You have to know it's there, and it's not obvious, which you've already gathered, or else you would've noticed it. You actually can't enter through the dining hall."

"That makes me feel slightly better, then, that I wasn't staring at some staircase for five weeks or something."

"Totally. You go through the back door of the chapel. Hang a left down the hallway. You'll come up to a closed door with a keypad. Type in the code 4-3-2-1."

"Isn't that kind of ridiculous? Everyone must have it figured out."

"Some of the people who come to the club are like ninety. They try to keep it easy. There is an elevator just past the door, or you can walk down the stairs."

"And the students don't know about it?"

"Oh, they know," he said. "It's all locked up at eleven each night, with codes that are presumably tougher to ascertain than 4-3-2-1. You might encounter a couple of them in the chapel, though. Just warning you."

"Why are students in the chapel at night?" I asked, finishing my ice cream cone. "You mean they go there to…" My voice drifted off.

"Sometimes. There are other spots. I once caught kids in the copy room on a Sunday. That seemed really stupid. Teachers are always working on weekends, unfortunately."

"Anyway, why'd you even go to The Barnacle if you think it's dumb?"

Kyle rolled his eyes and polished off the rest of his cone. "Al Holton was on campus, and they paired me up with him as his faculty ambassador, or some bullshit like that. Back when they used to trust me to do things."

"Al Holton?"

"Exactly. They made some big deal about him, but no one knew who he was."

"Who is he? Or was he?"

"He was a senator from Kentucky at the time. His sister was an alum. The dude thought he was hot shit and knew about The Barnacle and wanted to go because it seemed exclusive—you know the type. So, we went. He then lost his re-election to a pro-choice Democrat. In Kentucky. He wasn't very popular."

Kyle's stories were always so much fun. I imagined him in these scenarios and laughed to myself. "And the second time you went?"

He grimaced. "I was lured there by Ryland Dennis."

"When you thought he was having an affair with Cora? That sounds like something out of a movie." I couldn't think of exactly which one. Tam would know.

"Yup, I thought he was going to confess something to me. I was all geared up to, I don't know, do something. I'm not sure what, but something. Instead, we ordered drinks—these two enormous Manhattans with Woodford Reserve—and just shot the breeze. He pretended to talk about soccer, and I attempted to talk about fine literature. Both were out of our element and super awkward, but we were both trying. Then, some guy walked in with a Rockwood security officer and handed me a big envelope. The divorce papers were inside." Kyle shook his head and threw his balled-up napkin into a nearby trash can.

How awful. My body hurt for him, sensing that ache you feel when someone you care about is in pain—or *was* in pain. I couldn't tell how much it bothered him still, but I imagined it was an incident you couldn't easily brush off. I wanted to reach over and hug him, but it would've been super weird with Annie just down the shore and tons of students nearby. Instead, I stood there awkwardly and tried to look sympathetic. "So, Ryland helped set up the whole thing?"

"Yeah, which is why I sit as far across the room from him as I can at all faculty meetings and events. Among other reasons."

"Plus, that, um, paperwork you told me about that requires you to do that."

"That, too. Almost forgot about that," he said with a sly smile. He glanced over at Annie, who was in a one-sided conversation with a duck. "I like being friends with you, just so you know," he said quietly.

My mind flashed back to 2007, to lying on that cramped twin dorm bed with Kyle, listening to Oasis, his hands in my hair, him telling me about a soccer game he wanted to see when he was in England; even that night he had told me many, many stories. Usually, these kinds of thoughts distracted me, but now, I felt myself smile. "Me, too."

9

I felt good about things. Kyle and I were settling into a nice friendship. I had finally met Annie, and although I still felt pangs of attraction to him, for the moment, it seemed like we were doing all the right things. It was tough to tell what the future held, but considering everything that had happened to both of us over the past fifteen years, getting to know and trust each other slowly was the mature thing to do, at least as far as I could tell. I was glad I had steered us toward this course. At least, I thought so. Given my track record with men, I never really knew if I was doing the right thing.

On the night that I was supposed to meet up with Ward Connelly at The Barnacle, we were serving the students dinner on what had been an unseasonably hot October day for northern New England. The leaves were bold and bright, crunching under our every step on the quad, but instead of flannels and jeans, students were in tank tops and some of the shortest shorts I had ever seen. Andrea had sent out an all-campus message that the dress code of khakis and collared shirts was waived for the day, given the extreme heat, and some students took full advantage of the latitude. When a girl came through the line in a string bikini top, I turned to Marnie and said, "I am without words."

She shrugged and said, "I'd wear one if I still could get away with it." That was the most she had said to me in a week, which seemed to be how she approached everyone. I tried not to take it personally.

The boys' soccer team came in from practice, their faces so hot and sweaty they were almost purple. "We should get them some Gatorade," I said to Marnie, who shuffled off to fetch the sports drinks. I got ready to help serve them dinner when I heard a thud, followed by yelling and gasping students. One of the players was lying on the floor, with his teammates surrounding him. I looked around for Kyle but didn't see him anywhere, so I ran over to where everyone was gathered. "Is your coach here?" I asked no one in particular. The boys looked around and shrugged and muttered *no*, so I yelled out to Marnie, "Call 911. He's passed out, but I don't know why." I knelt next to him.

Within seconds, the boy opened his eyes and stared up at me. "You're the one who makes me cookies," he said slowly. His hair was soaking wet, and his uniform was stuck to him. I looked at the other players standing around us, who appeared the same. I guessed that dehydration had been an issue, but the paramedics would have to make that determination.

"Yes, I do make cookies," I said. "What's your name?"

"Jamie. Like the soccer player on *Ted Lasso*."

"Funny," I said. This kid made me smile. "How are you feeling now?"

"I'm okay, I think," he said. "I don't know what happened."

"How we doing over here?" I looked up and saw a tall paramedic standing over us. He had a booming voice and muscles bulging out of his short sleeves. "I'm Heath, with the Portsmouth Fire Department. I'm here with Bill, who's an EMT, and Matt, who drove us. Who's this here?" he asked, crouching down next to me.

I backed up and let Heath and his associates check out Jamie. Finally, I realized I needed to get the students away from the situation and told them to move to the tables or outside. Given how good Heath looked, several of the girls hung back, giggling and whispering. "Seriously," I said to them. "You can sit over there and still look at him." They rolled their eyes at me and plunked down in nearby chairs.

"Okay," Heath said to me, and I felt my heart flutter. He had wavy brown hair and huge ice-blue eyes. He was tan and had a big smile, which I could feel shooting right through me. *This* was something I hadn't felt in a while. Pure magnetic physical attraction. I hadn't even exchanged any real words with him, so it could be based on nothing else. "Jamie's going to be fine, but we're going to bring him to the hospital because he hit his head when he fell. They're going to want to evaluate him in the ER— maybe run a CT. We're going to start an IV of some fluids in the ambulance since, I think more than anything else, this kid's super dehydrated."

"I thought so," I said, really having nothing else to contribute to the conversation.

"Tell that coach of his that they need to remind these guys to drink more electrolytes," he said, winking at me. I wanted to collapse like Jamie had, but hopefully into the strong arms of Heath, the Hot Paramedic. "They're teenagers. They don't even remember their middle names half the time," he said, smiling. I looked down at his hands for a second. They were huge. "You want to come ride in the ambulance with us? Usually, I'd bring the coach, but he doesn't seem to be around, right?"

I hadn't even thought to call Kyle; I just noticed he wasn't there. There wasn't time to do that now, and besides, I had the opportunity to ride in an ambulance with Heath. "Okay, sounds good. I'll be right there."

"We'll be a few minutes getting him set up. See you outside," he said, lightly touching my elbow before he went back to Jamie. *Oh my God.*

I yelled at Marnie that I was leaving and raced out the door. Ashlyn Lark was hanging around outside the ambulance, wearing a crop top and jean cutoffs, talking to Matt, the driver, as Heath and Bill got Jamie into the back of the vehicle. She raised her eyebrows when she saw me. "What are you doing here, Chef?" she asked.

"I could ask the same of you," I said, climbing into the ambulance for the short ride to Portsmouth Regional Hospital.

I helped get Jamie checked in the best I could, but I realized I knew almost nothing about him and had no idea what the protocol was for these situations. I had simply wanted to sit next to Heath in the ambulance, but Matt told me I needed to sit next to him in the passenger seat because it had a seatbelt. The ride had been quick and uneventful, and Heath was, of course, focused on Jamie's care. Now that I was sitting on a plastic chair in a corridor of the ER, trying to fill out a form with very little information, I realized I needed help.

"Hey! Is he okay?" Kyle came running in, disheveled and clearly stressed.

"I was going to call you next," I said. "I don't know how to fill out this form."

"I got it," he said, grabbing the clipboard. "I have access to all the information. I can get it on my phone through the coaches' portal."

"Great. Let me tell the nurse at the desk that you're taking over for me," I said, walking over to the reception area.

When I was done talking to her, Heath was standing next to me. "They're checking him out now," he said. "Kid's going to be fine. Was that the coach who just showed up?"

"Yeah, that's Kyle Holling. He'll take things from here. I guess I'll, um, call an Uber to get back to campus."

"We can give you a ride," he said, flashing that big white smile.

"Just one second," I said, practically running over to Kyle.

"I'm going to go back to school," I told him. "The ambulance guys are giving me a ride. Let me know how Jamie is, okay?"

"You sure you don't want to stay?" he asked. "You can ride back with me later." Kyle eyed Heath, who was clearly waiting for me. Could he tell that I was so excited to just spend a few more minutes in the Hot Paramedic's presence?

"I need to, you know, get ready for that silly meeting at The Barnacle tonight. Of course, I'd rather stay with you. But Andrea would not be pleased if I skipped out on this. This is a really big deal, from what she's told me so far. You know how it goes." It was all true, but I felt like I wasn't being honest with Kyle. *Why am I feeling guilty about any of this?* We were just friends. Still, I felt like a twinge of something, and it didn't feel good.

"Good luck with Connelly," he said. "I need to check on Jamie," he conceded, standing up. "I think about us all the time, just so you know. I know I'm not supposed to, but I do." He walked into the hospital room, leaving me standing there, not sure what to think or feel. I took a breath and turned back toward Heath, who was waiting for me. He bit his bottom lip in the cutest way possible, and I followed him out the door.

•   •   •

I tore my closet apart trying to find something acceptable for a meeting with Ward Connelly at The Barnacle. I had dressed much like the students during my time at Rockwood, mostly because it was easy. Khakis and polos required little thought and, with some wrinkle-release spray, were very little maintenance. I had also eaten an aggressive amount of ice cream since arriving on St George's Island—a lot, even by my standards—so the nicer clothes in my wardrobe were a bit snug. The freshman fifteen were creeping up on me, but I didn't have time to give it much thought. I pulled on a black knee-length dress with no waistband, straightened my hair with my flatiron, and put on more makeup than usual. After the night I had already had, this was the last thing I wanted to do. I'd rather stay in my apartment and watch something cute involving emergency responders. Maybe *Roxanne*.

Walking to the chapel, I replayed the conversation with Heath in my head. When Matt pulled up to Wentworth House, Heath hopped out and walked me to the front door. I was buzzing with all kinds of nervous energy, sensing that he was as interested in me as I was in him, and it was very exciting. I thanked him for the ride and for taking such good care of Jamie. He asked if I was free anytime over the next week or so, and we determined that we were both available the following Saturday. It was the day after the Connelly event, and I deserved a break. Something to look forward to.

"Okay, I'll plan an afternoon of fun for us. We'll have a good time," he had said, smiling big at me again. I couldn't help but stare at his muscular shoulders, arms, and chest and wonder what it all felt like. He was a piece of fine art.

The back door of the chapel was open, just like Kyle said it would be. I listened for any student activity, but it was silent. *Too hot out*, I thought, given that most of the campus didn't have air conditioning. Maintenance staff had been placing fans all over the place, but it hadn't helped much. I hoped for cooler conditions in the subterranean level of the dining hall.

I followed all my instructions, ultimately walking down a long passage that must have been the tunnel from one building to another. Opening the final door led me into The Barnacle. It was dark, with tiny white twinkle lights framing, as I had predicted, portholes, except that these only had fake glowing fish behind them since we were in a basement. There were, indeed, life preservers, mermaids, a big ship's wheel, and, yes, a large whale hanging from the walls. Jimmy Buffett's "Boat Drinks" played softly in the background, presumably so conversations were possible. Not that there were many people there, to begin with.

I noticed Ryland Dennis sitting with a man of about sixty years in large leather armchairs. He waved me over, and I begrudgingly went. *Of course, he's here.* "Hi, Ryland," I said in a flat tone.

"Don't sound so thrilled, Devon," he said with a snark. "Ward, this is Devon Paige, who you are meeting with tonight about the event. Devon, I am the faculty member assigned to Ward for the unveiling reception. Something we do around here at Rockwood."

I thought back to Kyle's story about Al Horton. "Sounds good," I said. "Nice to meet you, Ward," I said, reaching out my hand to shake. He was thin and pale, with gray hair that appeared slicked back but not heavy with gel or another product. He wore glasses with clunky black frames, tight jeans, a thick hunter-green corduroy shirt, and a purple paisley scarf. *In this heat. Ugh.* Luckily for him, The Barnacle did seem to be air-conditioned. If only they had brought the same cooling system to my kitchen above us—another reason to be annoyed by this whole situation.

Ryland snickered; at what, I wasn't sure. "Why don't you go get a drink, Devon, and then I'll leave so you two can talk?"

It always felt like he was telling me what to do or directing me in some way. I didn't like it, but this was not the time to tell him off. I felt like it might be soon. "Sure," I said evenly and walked over to the mahogany bar, where Marnie was drying a wine glass with a towel. "Marnie? You work at The Barnacle?!" I was incredulous. What else didn't I know about Rockwood?

"A few nights here and there," she said. "What can I get you?"

"A whiskey sour, if you don't mind." It all felt strange and like I was somewhere I wasn't supposed to be. "How much do I owe you?"

"There's a tab," she said. "So, nothing. You're on the special events account."

"There's a bar account?" I asked, dumbfounded, while I watched her ream a lemon and add the juice to the shaker.

"Yeah, I guess," she said, shrugging, never one to engage in small talk. She shook up my cocktail, strained it into a glass filled with a large ice cube, and added a cherry. "Here you go."

I dug a ten-dollar bill out of my wallet. "Take this," I said. "Thank you," I whispered, not knowing why I was being quiet. I was so confused about everything that was happening.

Ryland had already moved out of his seat and was talking across the room to some elderly men in sports jackets with canes leaning against the sides of their chairs. I sat down across from Ward Connelly. "So," I began. "We need to plan a reception."

"We do," he said, blinking a few times. "I look forward to my creation being unveiled to the Rockwood community. Rockwood means so much to me. This is my gift to a place that continues to nurture my soul and the Connelly legacy."

A little presumptuous to see yourself as having a legacy, I thought, but I had a job to do and needed to humor him the best I could. "Are you the only alum in your family, or are there others?" I posed.

He chuckled softly. "Many Connellys have graced these floors, these lawns, these halls," he said, taking a significant sip of dark liquor. "This year, especially as my daughter has joined the ranks of the Stallions. That's what my piece is called, by the way. *The Stallion*. Don't tell anyone. I'm letting the scotch speak right now. You're the only one who knows." He put his finger to his lips and gave a smug smile.

"I won't tell," I said. "So, your, um, daughter. Should I include her in the VIP seating area invitation? We'll have an area roped off." Why hadn't Andrea included information about a child who was a current student? So much was left for me to piece together on my own.

"Probably best not to draw attention to that situation," he said, running his hand through his hair. "Like I said, it's the scotch talking. Let's talk food. I like meat."

We spent the next forty-five minutes coming up with some fall appetizers that could easily be enjoyed while standing up and socializing. As we conversed more, there was something familiar I kept noticing about him, and I couldn't put my finger on what it was. Finally, I asked, "You do look awfully familiar to me, Ward. Did you ever have an event at a restaurant I worked at in Boston? I was at Minx for five years, and before that, Bee's Knees and Cardamom."

"I don't believe I have, but I frequent the gardens and galleries of our city to the south quite often. Perhaps we passed by each other once or twice. You never know. Such is life with its fleeting moments." He spoke in such an interesting manner I wondered if it was authentic or a huge heap of bullshit. Regardless, we had a plan for a reception.

When I got back to the fourth floor of Wentworth, I went straight to my laptop, logged into the employee portal, and searched "Connelly." Surely, Ward's daughter would have his last name? Perhaps not. But I was curious.

The only name that emerged was Adrienne's. Adrienne Connelly Preston. *No. There's no way.*

It probably wasn't her. But I needed to find out.

10

"How's Jamie?" I asked, sitting across from Kyle at a picnic table outside the dining hall. I was an absolute mess after a very sweaty breakfast shift in the still-sweltering temperatures, and I was feeling a bit awkward after what he had said to me the previous night in the emergency room, but I knew I needed to check in about Jamie. Plus, avoiding him at Rockwood would be pointless. It was small, I saw almost everyone on campus daily, and he was my only real friend there. I pushed past it all and tried to be an adult.

"He's good," he replied, taking a last bite of his cinnamon roll. "We got back around eight. No serious head injury, luckily. I honestly wasn't prepared for ninety-plus degrees in October, but I should've been better about pushing the fluids with these guys. I think it's going to cool down this weekend." He took a sip out of his Yeti mug. "The cinnamon rolls are killer, Dev. Anything else on your mind this morning?" he probed.

I couldn't escape it. Despite my attempts to shove it all out of my mind, there was plenty I was still thinking about. "When I got back to Norwell senior year that fall, I tried to look for you. I walked by soccer practice, assuming you'd be there. Senior year, you're the goalie, presumably a team captain. I never thought you would have stayed in London. I got to the field, and I saw Ragnar running after a ball. You remember him?"

"Of course. He was a defensive back."

"He was my next-door neighbor freshman year, so I knew him well. Anyway, I called out to him, and he ran over. He asked how DC was, and I said it was enlightening."

Kyle chuckled. I had told him plenty in the past few weeks about my forays into avoiding classes and instead running around shadowing event chefs all around town.

"Then I asked if you were there. He told me that you never came back. That you met a girl in London and were staying." Kyle looked down and nodded. We had already talked through all of this, but I hadn't shared with him how I had found out that he wouldn't be returning for senior year. Or possibly ever. "And that's it. That's how I knew I had to move on from you."

"Did Ragnar say anything else?"

I felt a small smile drift onto my lips, remembering it. "Yeah, he said something along the lines of that you were really fucking them over by not coming back and that the freshman goalie sucked balls. His words, not mine."

"It's true. I did hear that the dude was terrible. Those guys were so pissed at me." He looked around, and most students had gone to class, leaving the outdoor area empty except for us. "What would you have said to me? If I had been there that day at practice?"

"I would have probably ignored you for a while." I forced myself to look at Kyle. It wasn't easy because I felt such a strong bond with him. It was something that spanned years, even if for so many of those years, I didn't see him or talk to him. And now, it was confusing as hell.

"After you looked for me?" he asked, raising an eyebrow.

"Yes."

He smiled and kicked my foot softly. "And then when a while was over? Would you have let me try to explain?"

"Eventually, I think. It was a small school. It gets a little crowded to avoid people."

"But then, maybe? Something more?" Although he was supposed to be talking about over fifteen years ago, I think he was really talking about the present.

"Look, you weren't here—or, um, at Norwell—anyway. I didn't see you again until, well, now."

He sighed. "I need to go to class. I don't want to. I'd rather stay here and talk to you. I'm teaching Calvin Coolidge's presidency today. They called him Silent Cal for a reason. It's not that exciting."

"I'm going to go on a date with the paramedic," I blurted out. "I want you to know that. It's just a date; it might turn out to be nothing, but I owe it to myself. I don't know what the future holds for you and me, but sitting in my apartment alone watching rom-coms probably isn't doing me any good. I need to get out there a little. I'm sorry if this makes things awkward or anything." There. I said it. "And I'm sure you have a way of making Calvin Coolidge's presidency interesting. I'll be overhearing all kinds of chatter from the students later about some great story you told them."

Kyle stood up. "He rode a mechanical horse in the White House for exercise. He had a pet raccoon named Rebecca. Those are my greatest hits for Cal." He started walking but turned around. "Considering everything that has transpired between us, I get it. I'm really sorry. I messed up a long time ago. I hope you can forgive me one of these days. It's been fifteen years."

"I've forgiven you, Kyle, I promise. But for fifteen years, I didn't see or hear from you. So, for me, it's more like it's only been a few months if that makes any sense. It feels very fresh still. I just don't think I'm totally past it yet."

"Okay. Have a good time with the paramedic. That guy's, like, way too good-looking. I don't feel insecure or threatened at all," he said, trying to make a joke out of the situation. I had to give him credit for that. "Oh, and there was a bear."

"What bear? Here?" I knew there were bears in New Hampshire, but the idea of one on the Rockwood campus was terrifying. How did it get there? Did it really walk across the bridge onto the island? Could it climb all the way up my fire escape?

"No, in the Coolidge White House. Briefly. Someone sent him a black bear. Two lion cubs, too."

"See, you're all set for class today," I said, trying to keep things light despite the heaviness I felt.

•   •   •

Ward Connelly and his crew were working on their creation up on scaffolds under a giant canopy, presumably putting the final touches on their work, given that the unveiling was the next day. Rockwood security was stationed by the installation and its equipment twenty-four hours a day, as Andrea was concerned that *The Underground Stallion* would send an intrepid photographer to the scene to get a sneak peek.

"Don't we have an actual student newspaper?" I had asked her. "All I ever hear about or see is the underground paper."

"Yes, but they're way too timid and weak. And their advisor left last year, so they are a bit rudderless at the moment. Oh, it was Cora! You know, Kyle's ex-wife. I think she was so distracted by her emotional affair or whatever you want to call it with Ryland that she didn't do much advising. But you never heard that from me."

I was working with the facilities team to set up tables and chairs and get everything ready for the event the next day. It was grueling work, but it was the kind of thing I had spent my DC semester so many years ago watching people do and helping when they would let me, and it's what had ultimately drawn me into the culinary world. It was my first love when it came to cooking and all that came with it, so there was something that felt good and nostalgic about the plans and the tasks. As I was pushing a podium into place, I noticed a teenage girl watching me from a distance, standing alone. *Adrienne.*

"Hi, Adrienne! Your hair looks different. I like the pink." Her dark, almost black, hair was shiny and straight and hung halfway down her back, but now she had a thick, bright pink streak running down the right side. Not a look I would have chosen for myself, but for a sixteen-year-old girl who had been kicked out of multiple schools and who seemed to hate her parents? Perhaps perfect.

"My roommate helped me with it," she said.

"How's everything going?" I asked. "We haven't talked since that focus group."

"Pretty good," she said. "I like it better here than at the other schools. I mean, school kinda sucks, but I like my history teacher. Mr. Holling. He's funny."

Of course. "He *is* funny. I always found if I had one teacher I liked, it made all the difference, and I could tolerate the others."

"Yeah, something like that. So, what are you doing here?" she asked, gesturing at the tent and everything that was under it.

"Getting ready for the unveiling of the artwork tomorrow," I said, thinking back to my meeting with Ward and his mention of his daughter. I studied Adrienne's face without making it seem intentional. It was tough to tell. Maybe. I thought back to what she had told me about the money being her mother's. It would make sense.

"Oh yeah, The Stallion," she said, shrugging.

"I thought the name of it was a secret?" I posed, wondering how she may have heard about it.

"My stupid English teacher told us," she mumbled. "He's one of the teachers I need to try to tolerate."

"Mr. Dennis, I presume?" Typical of Ryland to tell a class of students privileged information. He probably wanted to try to make himself look cool and important to a bunch of sixteen-year-olds.

"Yep, the one and only," she grumbled. "Can I ask you a favor? It's a weird one."

I had visions of Adrienne asking me to intercede with her father on some issue or something horrible like that. I could just hear it; *"Since you know him so well..."* The last thing I needed to do was interact with Bentley Preston right then. My life was complicated enough. And what could Adrienne even want me to talk to him about? A tattoo? A piercing? Some kind of outlandish trip? I shuddered. "Okay, what can I help you with?" I held my breath.

"I want to learn how to cook."

Oh. "Really?"

"Yeah, I'm addicted to the Food Network, to the cooking shows on Netflix, you know, *Sugar Rush* and things like that. All kinds of YouTube content. And I want to try to do it myself. I always liked your food. Would you be able to help me? I can probably pay you. I just need to tell my parents it's for something else. Because, well, you know."

I certainly did, and there was no way in hell I was going to accept another dime from the Prestons either. "No money needed," I said. "But yes, I'd love to work with you. Why don't you come by next week when you don't have class? We'll make a schedule." As odd as it seemed to spend time with Adrienne, part of me felt like it was penance for what I had put her through. Her mother was awful, but no kid deserved to walk in on what she had.

"Okay, good," she said. "I'll see you later." She started to walk away before I stopped her.

"I have a weird question for you now, Adrienne."

"Sure."

"Do you actually know Ward Connelly? The artist of The Stallion?"

She looked pensive. "I mean, I know of him. But I don't know him personally."

"You've never talked to him."

"No," she said, and I was satisfied with the answer. "But," she continued. "I think he might be my father."

11

Some of this possibility made perfect sense; Julianna had the money, and perhaps some of that could have come through Ward, who was apparently rolling in it. The money allowed her to call the shots where Bentley was concerned, such as shipping him off to Canyon Ranch when she was embarrassed by him (and, let's face it, by me). If he relied on her for financial support, he was much less likely to leave her. And with most schools unwilling to take Adrienne after all the trouble she had gotten into everywhere else, going through Ward was a surefire way to secure a last-minute acceptance at a prestigious place like Rockwood.

Still, things didn't add up. Bentley had never alluded to Adrienne being someone else's biological daughter. He certainly didn't need to tell me any of this, but we had spent a decent amount of time together, and not just in, shall we say, *intimate encounters*. There had been fairly risky lunch dates in the back corners of quiet North End restaurants with plenty of conversation. And, of course, there had been late-night meetings for ice cream when it was so dark out that we wouldn't have been noticed easily. It had felt somewhat cute at the time, even if I didn't have particularly deep feelings for him; I enjoyed the companionship and attention that fit into my hectic schedule. And I'm pretty sure Julianna had known about us; she only appeared to care when Adrienne caught us and then felt humiliated, which I get. It wasn't a good move on either of our parts. But if she had the money and the power, what did she need Bentley for?

For all I knew, Adrienne could be wrong. She had never met Ward, and she just had vague suspicions. "Her office at home is full of his artwork," she told me, which I had never noticed before, probably because I had had no idea who the hell Ward Connelly was until a few days earlier. "And I get this weird gift from him every year," she said. "Last year, it was a birdhouse he made. It had a real taxidermized bird in it. I like strange stuff, but this was too much even for me."

"How does she explain why you're getting a gift from an artist you don't know?" I asked her.

"She says he's an old friend of the family," she replied. "And I just went along with that because there are plenty of people they know who send me things. I'm the only child of a couple that a lot of social climbers want to know," she said, and there was a sadness to her words. These people weren't sending Adrienne gifts because they loved her or were being kind; it was all very transactional. And at sixteen, she knew it.

"What made you think that he's your father then?" I asked as we walked across the campus. I had to get back to the dining hall; she had homework to do, and I definitely did not want Ward to see me talking to Adrienne. It could raise too many suspicions. Unless he had no idea that I had been involved with Bentley—it all depended on how much Julianna confided in Ward. So many questions.

"When I got kicked out of the school in Carlisle, my parents had a very heated conversation in my mom's office," she explained. The door was closed, but it was loud. My dad yelled something about her asking her boyfriend to get me into his school. It was all very sarcastic sounding, like he was mocking her or something. And then she started ridiculing his weight and said it was a good thing you were gone so he couldn't eat fattening food all the time. And she threatened to put him on NutriSystem or something like that. But then she ended up shipping him off to the Berkshires, and I'm here."

"So, you put two and two together that Ward was the boyfriend who could get you in here? Excellent sleuthing." I had to give Adrienne a lot of credit. She was a savvy kid.

"I had a hunch, but I searched online for famous Rockwood alumni. When I saw his name, it was the only one that made any sense. And here I am. A Stallion," she said dryly.

"It's nice here in the fall, though, huh?" I asked as we walked down the path that cut through the center of campus. The leaves had started to turn bold and bright, and the golds, oranges, and reds brought me back to my days on my college campus less than thirty minutes west of where we walked. I wanted to try to find some kind of common ground with Adrienne, but talking about leaves probably wasn't it. Hopefully, cooking would be if she found that she liked it.

"It's okay," she said, stomping on a crinkly brown leaf with her boot. "It's weird that it's been so hot. I like snow, so I'm ready for that."

The weather might not be where we could meet in the middle. "Not my favorite, but I know I have to accept it," I said. "I'm going to get to go to LA in December, though, which should be nice. Do you know I cook for a player on the Celtics?"

"Yeah, some kids were talking about that," she said. "I'm not a big sports fan, but that's cool." She stopped outside of Harris House. "I'll see you tomorrow, um, I don't even know what I'm supposed to call you. Ms. Paige? I know some of the kids call you Chef. Do you like that?"

I shrugged. "I think it's more sarcastic than anything else. Ashlyn and people like her, who I'm pretty sure are making fun of me most of the time, sometimes call me that. But whatever you want. Devon is fine, but I'm not sure what the expectation around Rockwood is for what students should call adults. Yet another thing that was never expressed to me."

"Okay," she said. "I usually don't follow most of the rules anyway. See you later, Devon."

•   •   •

Everything was set and ready to go. The VIP area was roped off, with chairs, a podium, and bottles of water for important guests. A few photographers and reporters from local media outlets were taking pictures and recording the pre-ceremony preparations. There was a general seating area for students, staff, and community members to watch the event. Although students weren't required to attend, it was a Friday after classes, and the weather had returned to ideal autumn conditions—sunny and sixty-five degrees, with a light breeze. Instead of utilizing the folding chairs, many students brought towels and blankets and portable outdoor seats to sit on, filling the small hill adjacent to where the artwork—now shrouded in an enormous white cloth emblazoned with the red outline of a stallion—was to be unveiled. I watched as dozens of local residents walked through the open gates of the campus to be a part of the experience. It made sense that so many wanted to be there; Ward was both an alum and lived among them in the tiny St. George's community.

My team was ready with the snacks and drinks for after the ceremony, and I felt the buzz of nervous energy from them as well as Andrea, who was flitting around checking in on people. It was both her and my first big all-campus event since starting our jobs, and it was a significant one. She introduced me to several members of the Board of Trustees, who expressed their thanks for my acceptance of the job. "And this, Devon, is our newest board member," she said. "Please meet Bentley Preston."

I gasped as Bentley turned to face me. The color drained from his face, while mine likely turned beet red, given how hot it felt. "Um, hello, Devon. Good to see you."

"You, too," I squeaked out, surprised I was able to say any words at all.

"Oh. OH!" exclaimed Andrea. "I totally forgot, really, I did. I'm so sorry. I'm so sorry." As much as Andrea loved good fodder for gossip, judging by the horrified look on her face, I don't think she had connected the dots until she saw our reactions to being introduced to each other.

"It's okay," said Bentley quietly. "Let's not make a big deal about this."

"Is she here?" I whispered, looking around for Julianna.

"Went to the bathroom," he said. "So maybe you might want to −"

It was too late. I smelled the Chanel perfume, so I knew she was standing right next to me. "Well, what a coincidence. I never thought I had to inquire about who was on staff before enrolling my daughter in a boarding school, but apparently, they let just about anyone work here," she muttered.

"Hello, Julianna," I said evenly, trying not to show any emotion or reaction despite the horrible discomfort I was feeling. Andrea watched, wide-eyed, as if she was observing feeding time at the zoo. The kind where you see a lion about to feast on a fresh animal carcass. I was the carcass.

"I'm sure you two can go find a closet to run off to together," she spat out. "I'll be taking my seat now." She walked toward the general seating area and sat down in the front row. The three of us watched in disbelief as she gave the old man next to her a once-over, followed by a dirty look and scowl. He stood up and went to another row.

"She's not nice," I said to myself, forgetting for the moment that Bentley was right next to me.

"No, she's not," he conceded. "I better take a seat with the rest of the Board," he said. "Sorry about all this, Devon. I hope the job is going okay. Other than right now, of course."

I nodded, knowing I had said enough, and retired to the catering station. Andrea stood alone, shocked by everything that had transpired. The chapel bells rang, signaling that it was four o'clock. It was time for the ceremony to begin.

Ward Connelly emerged from the woods in dramatic fashion, wearing tight black jeans, work boots, and a big camel-colored cape. A large cowboy hat sat atop his head. He marched past his creation and through the crowd, causing students and other guests to have to move out of his way. He made his way to the podium, kissed a stunned Andrea on the cheek, and sat down in the front row. I glanced at Julianna, who sat watching him with a knowing, sly smile. *Well, that confirms it,* I thought.

The Chairman of the Board spoke for a few minutes in generic terms about the value of a Rockwood education and the importance of art in our daily lives. Andrea gathered herself together enough to thank the Board for her appointment and to express her excitement about the art installation about to be revealed. "This is the first thing that guests and prospective students and their families will see as they drive through the iron gates of Rockwood," she said. "It will be a symbol of who we are, what we are about, and what we dream about for our future. Simply, it will encompass all that is Rockwood." The crowd clapped, and several students whistled and cheered. "And now, the moment we've all been waiting for, as we've watched Mr. Connelly and his crew escape underneath drapes and tarps over the last few weeks, toiling in sweltering heat to finish their work for our event today. Without further ado, The Stallion!"

A facilities team member pulled a rope, and the cloth was ripped away. Perched high atop a slim black pole was a large charcoal gray, smooth, shiny cylinder, pointed at one end, tilted at an angle, aiming toward the sky. And that was it.

Murmurs shot through the crowd. "What is it?" "Isn't that sort of, *you know...*" "Weeks and weeks for that?" "That's a horse? It doesn't look like a horse." "I thought he was supposed to be good." And finally, a student yelled out, "It looks like a penis!"

From that point on, everything went out of control. Andrea tried to calm everyone down, but the student section was laughing and hooting. Many of the locals were arguing with each other, probably about whether it was good art or not. Countless pictures were snapped of the chaos—and video recorded—and inevitably uploaded to social media. The Board members looked perplexed. And Ward Connelly started to grow furious that he wasn't getting the respect that he seemed to believe he deserved.

A familiar voice boomed through the crowd. "Enough! Come on, students. You can all decide on your own if you like this or not. That's why it's art. It's up to you. Remember the painting 'Washington Crossing the Delaware'? Remember when I told you Mark Twain didn't think it was all that great? Super famous painting still today hanging in the Met in New York, and Mark-fucking-Twain of all people panned it."

"Mr. Holling!" pleaded Andrea. "I know what you're trying to do, but please! Language!" She gestured to the Board of Trustees members, who were watching everything play out before them with a combination of fascination and confusion.

"Sorry, Ms. Lark," Kyle said. "But my point is that you get to decide. But we can't be assholes about it. There I go again. Sorry," he said to Andrea. "Can we end this now? Ms. Paige has some cookies, I know. You all love Ms. Paige's cookies."

"Cookies!" the students started yelling, and soon I was flooded with teenagers grabbing their new favorite treats. I looked over at Andrea, who threw up her hands, and the formal part of the event appeared to be over.

When all the cookies were taken, and I began cleaning up, Kyle walked over to me. "No more cookies, I assume."

"All gone," I said. "There will be more soon, I'm sure."

"Yeah," he said. "Midsy is next week. People will be looking for them then."

I watched as the crew began hauling away chairs, tables, and sound equipment. "What the hell is Midsy?"

"Midway through the first semester. Rockwood has tried to rebrand it over the years as something called Night of a Thousand Laughs, and there are all these comedy performances, improv, that sort of thing. But it's still Midsy. And there are always tons of pranks. We'll see how Andrea deals with it this year. It can be a doozy for the administration."

"Ugh. Another event that no one told me about. I need some recovery time from this one."

"Yeah, this one sucked pretty bad. You did great. But Jesus Christ," he said, gesturing at the sculpture—if you could call it that. Rockwood security, along with an officer from the tiny St. George's police force, were standing guard. They had helped to disperse the crowd, and an additional officer walked Ward home in case anyone harassed him. It had been a bad scene.

"So, all that about judging for yourself was just talk? You think it's a piece of crap?" I looked up at the artwork. It was not my cup of tea, but I didn't know much about art either.

"Oh, people should definitely judge for themselves, that's for sure. Some of them might love it. It might speak to them in some way. Personally, I think it's one of the ugliest things I've ever seen in my life. It's almost embarrassing. And I think Andrea's got a rough road ahead of her with this one. People in town are not happy. The neighbors who live across the street are pissed. This one old lady told me she doesn't want to look at a phallic symbol every time she gets the mail or newspaper."

"Oh my God. Do you really think he intended it to be, well, *that*?"

"Who knows," said Kyle. "I've never talked to the dude. Did you get that impression of him?"

I looked around and didn't see anyone within earshot. "Not really. He was strange, that's for sure. But I did learn something really interesting from Adrienne Preston."

"Adrienne? You talked to her again?"

"Oh yeah," I said. "You want to go have a drink?" I asked, and soon, we walked down to the bridge connecting St. George's to Portsmouth, heading to the little pub on the other side.

12

The Horse was a tiny dive bar on the very edge of Portsmouth, owned and operated by a local Rockwood alumni family. Kyle had gone with me a few times earlier that fall, and I liked it because it tended to be favored by the younger and less elitist Rockwood staff. The older crowd frequented some of the stuffier Portsmouth establishments and, as I had learned, The Barnacle. The Horse was comfortable in the sense that it wasn't snobby or highbrow, but I also didn't risk the whiskey sours there, and Kyle knew it. "Two Jack and gingers, please," he said as we pulled up stools opposite the bartender. "You want to come to Boston with me tomorrow to see Annie in her play? She's actually in a production of *Annie*, believe it or not. But she's not Annie. She's one of the orphans who only has, like, two lines. It's super exciting for her, though."

"That's amazing," I said, taking a sip and almost coughing. "This might have a splash of ginger ale in it. I wish I could. I made some other plans," I said, knowing he could see right through me.

"Oh, this is the date, right? Mr. Muscle Man—who saves people's lives and could probably save the planet from everyone and everything if he decided to, all while looking very handsome and smiling at the adoring ladies throughout his lifesaving mission. Nope, not jealous at all," he mused, knocking back about half his drink.

"Easy there," I chided. "Who knows? Maybe he'll be boring as hell. Or he'll smell bad. Or he'll have some really gross habit. You never know."

"There's no way that dude smells bad. He looks like an Axe commercial. But gross habits ... lots of guys have those. I'm hoping for something super nasty. Maybe he'll pop a zit at the table right in front of you. But I'm guessing he's too good-looking to have zits."

"Or he'll reach over and pop one of mine," I joked. "I get plenty of them from working in the kitchen. You're fixated on his looks, you do realize."

"The guy's like a male Barbie doll."

"That's a Ken," I said. "And you're a very attractive guy since I think you're looking for some kind of compliment or reassurance. There's a reason I started talking to you over watermelon at that dinner, you know. Also, now that I think about it, why were they serving us watermelon in January? Where was this watermelon coming from? I guess I think about these things now that I'm on the other side of the buffet line. Notice it's not January yet, and I'm still not serving watermelon."

"You sure you weren't just looking for a fling before DC, knowing that the guys there wouldn't be so interesting?" he joked, finishing his drink. I had a feeling there would be several, given where this conversation seemed to be going.

"I had no idea at the time that I wouldn't ultimately be attracted to wannabe lobbyists and congressional staffers," I conceded. "And no, I wasn't looking for anything. I thought you were cute and interesting and had a lot to say."

"Because I talk too much," he admitted, signaling to the bartender that he wanted another beverage.

"Not too much," I said carefully. "You are a skilled conversationalist. And I enjoyed that. Among other things." I almost regretted that last line.

"It was a fun night," he said. "We didn't really sleep. And then we went to breakfast, and I remember eating a lot of bacon."

"So much bacon!" I said, remembering the heaping plate we shared, every salty last bite. "And then I had to leave, and that felt weird. I didn't know how to say goodbye to you."

"You kissed me really quickly, I think," he said, swirling the ice around in his glass, not making eye contact.

"I did," I said, thinking about it. Part of me wanted to lean over at that moment and do it again. Just a quick kiss to see if it felt the same. It would have been so self-centered of me to put Kyle in that position given all our conversations, the fact that I was going out with Heath the next day, and because there were likely a few Rockwood eyes on us. Enough people already suspected that something was up between us, despite me telling them regularly that we were just old friends. I decided to stay put and not lunge at him, but it wasn't an easy choice.

He downed the remains in his glass and looked around. I followed his glance, and there were, indeed, several young teachers looking at us. We both waved at them, and Kyle asked me, "You want to go take a walk? Might be good to get out of here."

We walked through the streets of Portsmouth, buzzing with Friday night socializing and merriment. I told him the story of Adrienne and Ward Connelly, as well as my interactions with Bentley and Julianna. He filled me in on his classes, how the soccer team was doing, and his attempts to keep things as normal as possible with Annie and Cora, given the circumstances. "Cora has a new boyfriend," he told me. "He's a lawyer named Gill. And I'm okay with it. Really. I don't know why, but for some reason, I'm not at all jealous. I'm actually kinda happy for her."

"That's good, Kyle," I said. "You must be shifting into a new phase of all this."

"Maybe," he said. "I haven't met the shithead yet, so we'll see how I feel then," he said with a laugh, lightly bumping into me for a moment.

"Right, right, you never know. Should we walk back over the bridge to St. George's?"

"Sure," he said. "Not much longer for these kinds of walks. It'll get cold soon."

"I'm hoping for a mild winter," I replied, happy to only be wearing a light jacket. The thought of my puffy coat and big boots was not appealing. "But I know that's rare."

"Remember how nice out it was that night at Norwell? When we walked around the Loch a million times?"

I thought back to the path that circled Lake MacGavin and how, on that particular January night, it was free of snow and was comfortable to stroll along in just fleece jackets and sneakers. I could almost feel Kyle's hand in mine as I remembered how we walked and talked and got to know each other—over fifteen years earlier. I recalled how we had finally stopped walking and stood facing each other, then held onto both of each other's hands. How our faces had moved toward each other and how our lips met for the very first time. I felt blood rush through my body, and my face flushed just thinking about it.

"You okay, Dev?"

"Oh, yeah, totally. Let's go see what's going on with the sculpture. I wonder if Andrea's keeping security there all night." I had to try to clear those thoughts out of my head.

Sure enough, there were two security guards sitting in a golf cart next to the sculpture. Ashlyn Lark was talking to them, along with one of her followers, a small, shy girl named Jessica. I felt sorry for anyone who was caught up in Ashlyn's whole situation.

Who knew what she was pressured into doing? The whole thing gave me too many flashbacks to mean girls in high school.

"Oh, look who it is?" Ashlyn asked, almost purring. "Mr. Holling, I am going to work all weekend on that paper. I can't wait to learn everything I can about the Guilty Age." Jessica elbowed her and whispered something to her. "I mean, the Gilded Age. Of course. Did you know that I am related to the Rockefellers?"

Kyle nodded and scrunched up his face. "That's fascinating. I'm sure it'll be a wonderful paper. But Ashlyn, would you like some advice?"

"Always, Mr. Holling."

"Be sure to include horizontal integration, muckraking, and Ida Tarbell if you're going to talk about Rockefeller. Also, the gospel of wealth. Like we talked about in class."

Ashlyn looked blankly at Kyle. "Oh, right," she said. "Definitely."

"It's almost curfew. You two should go to your dorms," Kyle said, and we walked away from them toward the quad. Once we were far enough away that they thought we were out of earshot, I heard Ashlyn ask Jessica, "What was he talking about?"

"I'm guessing Ashlyn doesn't pay attention much in class," I said to Kyle as we continued down the path.

"Very little. And I haven't talked about any of those things in class yet," he said with a smirk. "They all have to do with Rockefeller and the Guilty Age, though."

"I have vague recollections of high school history, so I thought so. But I will always think of it as the Guilty Age now," I said. "Where to?"

"One more spot," he said. "Let's go this way."

We veered off the main path and followed a narrower one that curved into the woods. "Where are we?" I asked, grabbing onto Kyle's arm in the dark. "I can barely see."

"There are lights up ahead," he said, moving his hand down to mine and tentatively holding onto it. "Just so you don't trip or anything. I promise that's all."

I felt my heart jump as I got used to my skin against Kyle's again. We had barely touched each other since I moved to Rockwood. It felt both good and strange.

We were soon at the edge of a small pond. The moon was reflected in it, and as Kyle promised, there were several light posts in the vicinity. We stood, staring at the moon in the pond, still holding onto each other's hands. "Wow," I finally said. "This is a beautiful spot. Are we still at Rockwood?"

"We are," he said. "Students hang out over here at night on the weekends all the time, so some of us take turns walking through the area to make sure no one's doing anything they're not supposed to. But it's late now, and they're all supposed to be back in their rooms."

"What about us?" I squeaked out, still staring at the pond, not sure what I was saying. There was something about being back in this kind of setting with Kyle again that was messing with me. I wasn't twenty years old anymore, but for whatever reason, I felt like I was in that moment.

"Are you, well, considering it?" he asked, almost incredulous.

"I don't know," I blurted out. "I know I have this date tomorrow, and I know I want to give that a chance, and I know there are so many reasons why I shouldn't consider anything right now with you, but as for right here, right now..." I took a breath and turned toward him. "Do you ever just want to kiss me and see what happens?" I couldn't believe myself listening to my own question. What was I doing?

He looked at me with intensity and surprise. "Like, all the time. But I want to always respect you, too, Devon. I would never in a million years want to hurt you again. So, that's why I don't do it."

It was both understandable and so Kyle. And so confusing. "But you want to. Right now. You *would* kiss me."

"Of course," he said. "You're Devon. You're luminous."

I was luminous. No one had ever described me as luminous. Still holding his hand with my right hand, I grabbed his shirt with my left hand and pulled him into me. My lips crashed against his and then softened, and I felt myself melting into a kiss from fifteen years earlier. It was exactly like I remembered. And then I saw a flash and pulled back.

"What the hell?" I yelled. I saw two shadows running away.

"You're late for curfew!" Kyle yelled. "If you're in my class, you're getting a zero on your homework! And the one after that!"

"They're gone," I whispered. "Possibly with photographic evidence."

"It's gotta be Ashlyn and her minions, right? The ones behind *The Underground Stallion*? We just saw them," he groaned, pulling at his hair in frustration.

"Probably," I said. "But who's really going to stop a few kids from printing a secret newspaper? No one has any proof it's them. They must have been following us. Are there security cameras out here?"

"Nope," he said. "I know this for a fact. I used to live out here."

"What?" I looked around. "Where?"

"There was a little cabin right over there," he pointed. "I lived there with Cora and Annie. And when I started suspecting something was going on with Ryland, I looked everywhere for cameras. I couldn't find anything. I even went to Chuck in Facilities. He said the wiring would be a nightmare, so they never did it. And I believe him. I hardly had working internet."

"What happened to the house?" Unless my night vision had gone to hell, there didn't appear to be anything in terms of a structure that I could see.

Kyle sighed. "When they moved out, I—by mistake—set it on fire."

I gasped.

"I know the way it sounds. I promise you it was not intentional. I wasn't sleeping, and the doctor in the health center put me on something, and I passed out really quickly one night. I had also started smoking again. I know, I know, gross. Anyway, classic story: I must have dropped a cigarette, and I woke up to the smoke alarm and a few flames. Nothing terrible, luckily, and I was able to run into the kitchen, grab the fire extinguisher, and put it out before the fire department got there. The place was salvageable, but the administration gave me a choice. I could have it fixed, or they would tear it down, and I could move into a dorm. Given the fact that I knew—with the help of my therapist— that it would be healthier for me, in the long run, to move into something else and not have a reminder of my old life, I said they could wreck it. So, I moved into Dalton. They gave me a two- bedroom apartment so Annie would still have a place to stay when she's here. I was very lucky, and most places would have likely fired my ass. No pun intended."

It was a wild story to digest. I also couldn't believe I was hearing another complicated story exposing even more of Kyle's baggage. There was so much damage, both physical and emotional. "I'm glad they didn't," was all I could manage to say.

"I'm a really good teacher," he said. "I think that's why they want me to stay. I suck at a lot of things, but I know I'm good at this. And where would I go, anyway?" he asked. "Are you still going out with him tomorrow, Devon?" He grabbed ahold of my hand again, stroking my fingers a bit.

"I think so," I choked out. "I'm sorry. I just owe it to myself to see. To see what, I don't even know. But I have to."

Kyle swallowed so hard I could hear it. "What was this then? Why did you want to kiss me?"

"I had to know what it was like—if it was the way it was before. And it was. It was still good and felt right, I promise you. Until it was interrupted, of course."

"But it meant nothing, really, if you're still going out with him."

"That's not true," I said, my voice shaking. "It did mean something. This is all very confusing."

"I feel a little used," he admitted, and I couldn't deny any of it. He let go of my hand. "But maybe I deserve it. Maybe this is what I get for what I did when I went to London," he said. "Let's walk back. I'm not going to leave you out here alone."

I followed him silently through the woods, not grabbing onto him this time. When we got to the main path, I said, "Thanks for spending time with me tonight. I had fun until those kids showed up. I'm sorry if you're mad at me."

Kyle shook his head. "I'll see you at Midsy," he said and walked away, leaving me to walk the rest of the way back to Wentworth.

13

I woke to the din of loud voices, someone shouting into a bullhorn, and the clanging and banging of objects outside my window. I ran to the big window in my kitchen and could see a crowd of probably fifty people gathered in the vicinity of The Stallion. I threw open the window and climbed out onto the fire escape to get a better view and to hear what people were saying, or in this case, yelling.

"Hey, Chef! Nice pjs! You having a sleepover?" shouted a voice from the ground below. It was Ashlyn Lark and two of her followers, and they were laughing uncontrollably.

I looked down at myself and realized I was in flannel pajama pants and a t-shirt that read "I like piña coladas" and no bra. I crossed my arms across my chest. "I'm alone!" I yelled and then realized how ridiculous I sounded. Anything I had retorted with would have been stupid.

They kept laughing and walked toward the crowd. I shifted my attention to the swelling group of people who were being asked by police and campus security guards to move back as they hastily set up a barrier around the art installation using stakes and yellow police tape. It looked to be a mix of local residents and students. Some of the people standing behind the line held signs that said things such as, "Your Art is Ugly," "No Porn on St George's," and probably the most pointed of the attacks, "Connelly is a Perv."

I went back inside and closed the window. If Tam didn't know about it yet, she would soon. "I was waiting to hear from you," she said as she answered her cell phone.

"So, I take it you've heard about my place of employment."

"I'm on my way up there right now," she said. "I have a full crew with me. I'm sitting in the back of a van—if you can't tell. Want to be interviewed?"

"Andrea probably wouldn't be thrilled. Are you going to talk to her for your piece?"

"She's still deciding what she wants to do. Off the record, she sounded a bit overwhelmed on the phone when I talked to her about a half hour ago."

"She's always overwhelmed. That, too, is off the record. But yeah, I would imagine this sucks for her." I yawned, making coffee to try to wake myself up. "Anyway, I'm supposed to go on a date this afternoon. I'm thinking of canceling."

"A date?! Dev, that's great. Or is it with Kyle? I mean, that would be good, too. I just want you out there in the world again."

"Not with Kyle," I said. "I kissed Kyle last night. But it's not with him."

"You kissed Kyle," she repeated, obviously trying to understand my situation. Hell, even I didn't understand my situation.

"Yes, and it probably wasn't nice of me to do it. I wanted to try something out. To see if I still had feelings for him."

"And? Devon, do not leave a girl hanging like this."

I sighed. "I do. I liked kissing him … until we were interrupted by these little shits from *The Underground Stallion*. But I'm supposed to go out with Heath this afternoon. And Kyle's pissed at me. So, I'm pretty confused at the moment."

"*The Underground Stallion?* Who is Heath? I swear, someone should follow you around and make a documentary. I might pitch it to my producer. I'll call it The Devon Digest."

"More like The Devon Disasters. Anyway, Heath's the hot paramedic. He showed up when one of Kyle's soccer players passed out in the dining hall from dehydration. But that's another story. *The Underground Stallion* is an underground newspaper, and I think Andrea's horrific niece runs it, but I have no proof. There's a lot of drama here at Rockwood."

"Hot paramedic, huh?" She asked, skipping over the Ashlyn aspect of my reporting. I could feel Tam drift off into romantic comedy land. "I think there was a Hallmark movie with something like this."

"Probably," I replied. "He looks like he belongs in a Hallmark movie. But those tend to be on the wholesome side. I might want to do some very unwholesome things with him. I'm not on speaker-phone with a van full of production crew types listening, right?"

"Nope," she said with a laugh. "Well, good luck with all of it. I do kinda feel sorry for Kyle, though, Dev. I'm sorry to say that because you know I'm always on your side. But that boy must have been so happy to finally kiss you again. He's probably hurting a lot now."

My entire body ached at the thought of Kyle in pain. No matter what he had done fifteen years earlier, I never wanted to inflict suffering on him, and I knew that was exactly what I was doing. I had grown to care about him more than I had realized, which made all of this so confusing. "I am sure," I said. "And I feel awful about it. Which is why I'm thinking about canceling on Heath."

"Ehh, I don't know about *that*," she said. "One date can't hurt. Maybe keep it PG and see how you feel about him, not just what your hormones tell you. But what do I know? Professor Plum is both hot and smart, and I have no self-control around him. I don't have any business telling anyone what to do."

"I need to meet him soon. We need to make this happen." I smiled at the thought of Tam finally settling into a happy relationship. He must be a good one.

"You bet," she said. "Double date, perhaps. With the hot paramedic, or with Kyle, or some guy you meet in line for ice cream. Whatever. Whoever."

"Sounds good," I said, saying goodbye and wandering toward my closet. How does one dress for a Saturday afternoon date in October when you have no idea what you're doing? Or whether you should be going at all?

Eventually, I settled on jeans and a more form-fitting flannel shirt with a lightweight fleece vest. I looked like I had walked out of an L.L. Bean ad. I just needed a golden retriever puppy and a thermos of hot chocolate, and I'd be all set. I met Heath in the parking area adjacent to the dorm and quickly hopped into the front seat of his truck, hoping not many people saw me.

"Hi," he said with a huge, gorgeous smile. I had made the right decision to go on the date. All thoughts of Kyle briefly flew out of my head. "You look very fall-like. Super cute. I like it."

"Why, thank you," I said. "And you, well, you also look great." He did. He was wearing dark-wash jeans and a waffle-knit long-sleeve, charcoal gray shirt that skimmed over his well-muscled physique perfectly. I caught the light scent of some kind of product, and it smelled like he had spent time walking through woodsy paths full of pines. Maybe it was just his deodorant. But it was good. "Sorry about these crowds. We had a controversial unveiling of a new art installation last night. The local community and some of the students aren't very happy with it."

"I heard about it early this morning," he said. "We got an email in case things got out of hand here. I'm glad I have today off. I'd much rather spend it with you doing something fun than potentially deal with angry protestors."

My stomach did a flip-flop. "Same," I said with a smile. "And I mean, really, what could I do to help? Bring them cookies? My cookies are good, but I'm not sure how much they would help in this situation."

"You never know," he said, backing out of his parking space and heading slowly down the main road out of campus and away from the growing crowd of disgruntled people. "Cookies might solve all the world's problems. Maybe tomorrow. Let's go have fun."

We headed south on 1A through Rye and into Hampton Beach. Fall had settled in, and many businesses had signs up announcing that this was their last weekend of the season. It all reminded me a bit of Old Orchard Beach, which was a couple of towns north of where I had grown up in Maine. Motels, seafood shacks, beach shops, arcades, bars, lots of salt and sand. I had been to Hampton a couple of times during college, but it had been many years. Heath pulled into a parking spot adjacent to a mini golf course.

"How about it?" he asked after shifting the truck into park and turning toward me with that huge smile. I think I would have said yes to most things.

"Mini golf? Okay. I haven't played since probably college. I'm going to be terrible."

"Really? You need to get back into it then. It's, like, one of my favorite things to do in the summer," he said.

Huh. Mini golf? "Well, then let's go," I said, trying to keep my voice upbeat. I didn't know what I had expected from this date.

"What do you like to do?" he asked as we picked out our clubs from the rack inside the hut where he had paid our admission fee. There was hardly anyone at the course, and the whole thing felt a little odd. Part of me wanted to be back at Rockwood, taking a walk around the campus and feeling the leaves shatter under my feet. I would say hi to people and be able to scoot away easily when I was ready to move on. Part of me felt like I was becoming a loner and kept everyone—except Kyle, who was mad at me—at arm's length. It probably wasn't healthy. I took a breath and looked up at Heath, who was so darn cute and seemed eager to know me. I needed to at least try.

"These days, I'm pretty busy on campus. I'm still learning the job, and then new things keep getting thrown at me. I had to put together the reception yesterday for the art opening with only a few days' notice. I'm supposed to meet with the Head of School on Monday to talk about something called Midsy. It's a prank night, I guess, that the school has tried to rebrand. But I'm sure I'll be expected to feed people."

Heath set down his green golf ball at the first hole and effortlessly putted it into the hole. "Oh, I know all about Midsy. That's a shitshow," he said with a laugh.

"A hole in one? You took me here so you could make me look bad?" I asked, half-joking.

"Not at all, Devon," he said with a smile and put his arm around me for a second. It felt good, so I tried to relax. "I just thought we could do something fun. But if this sucks, let's go do something else. I'm up for anything."

"No, no," I insisted, my stubborn side peeking out. "I'm not one to give up. I still might kick your ass," I said, lining up my shot. I made it in two, which was still a birdie. Not bad, considering I probably hadn't played mini golf in at least fifteen years.

"That's the spirit!" he said as we walked a few steps to the next hole.

"So, please, tell me why Midsy's such a shitshow. Does the fire department get called to campus?"

"Depends on the year," he said, continuing his streak of greatness with every putt. "See, it took me two shots that time. But yeah, sometimes we have to go, other times it's the police, some years all of us. A hot tub was constructed on the porch of your dorm one year. Then it seeped into the basement and was such a mess. Plus, they had put a keg in the middle of it, which crashed through the boards, and everything had to be rebuilt."

I shook my head as I got ready to putt again. "A keg in a makeshift hot tub? I have no idea how students could get away with that. We have security everywhere."

"That's fairly new," he said. "It used to be there was just one old guy patrolling the campus overnight with a flashlight and a walkie-talkie. Now there are three old guys and a golf cart," he added with a laugh.

"Yeah, so I don't have much of a life these days," I continued, laying it all out there. *I might as well. I'm thirty-five and playing mini golf in fifty-five degrees with a paramedic who appears to be a putting prodigy.* Heath sunk another hole-in-one, and I didn't flinch. "My best friend is in Boston. She's a news reporter and anchor. And I still go down there once a week to deliver food to a client. He's a professional athlete," I added, wondering if it would solicit any reaction. I found myself struggling to find things to talk about, and I realized I hadn't done anything like this in so long. The last guy I had been involved with had been Bentley Preston, which was not a typical situation. Since then, I'd just been hanging out with Kyle. It was like I didn't know how to be "normal" anymore, whatever that was.

"That's cool," he said, perking up beyond his already enthusiastic personality. "Can you tell me who it is? I'm way into Boston sports."

"I am so glad this is the last hole," I said, more to myself than to Heath. I putted the ball, and it plopped right into the dragon's mouth, ending my game. "Finally!" I exclaimed. Heath high-fived me, and we turned in our clubs. "It's David Anders," I said. "You know who he is?"

"So fly!" he whooped, and I didn't know how to react. I couldn't imagine Kyle describing something as "fly," and he was my one recent male frame of reference. "He's really talented," Heath said. "I think he's only going to get better."

"I wish he felt that way," I said, instantly regretting it. I tried not to repeat anything David said to me to anyone else, especially since he kept to himself so much. "But he's a really good guy. Loves my enchiladas and cookies. I bring him other stuff, too, but he always wants those."

"That's awesome," Heath said, seeming really excited about everything I was telling him. "I'd love to meet him sometime if that's ever something that works out. I'm a huge fan."

"Maybe," I said, not knowing how to answer. Even Tam had never met David. He didn't like many people, and I felt very protective of him. "What next, Brooks Kepka? Or whoever your favorite golfer is?"

"He's a good one," he said, smiling at me, tousling the back of my hair in sort of a strange way. I could not figure him out. "Want to get some food? Some beer? Maybe back in Portsmouth?" he asked.

"Oh yeah, sure," I said. I didn't know what to make of this. Maybe I just had not gone out on many traditional "dates" and had no idea what to expect or how to act.

We settled into a brewpub in downtown Portsmouth about twenty-five minutes later. I marveled as Heath ordered six appetizers and a twenty-four-ounce beer. "Can you make a whiskey sour?" I asked the waitress, hoping for the best. I was mostly hoping for something not made with a neon-yellow sour mix, but I knew I couldn't be picky.

"Oh sure," she said. "Jack Daniels okay?"

"That's fine," I answered and glanced back at the bar. There was a bowl of lemons visible, so with any luck, they weren't just for show.

"Whiskey sour, huh? That takes care of the first question I was going to ask you."

"First question?" He was very good-looking, but beyond that, I couldn't tell if we had a true spark between us.

"I was going to suggest we play twenty questions to get to know each other, but maybe twenty is a lot," he said, laughing to himself.

"We could start with five?" Part of me felt like I was on *The Bachelor* or *Love is Blind*, and we were in some sort of pre-scripted situation.

"Perfect," he said, tearing off a piece of the huge sourdough pretzel that had been placed on the table between us. "Okay, question number one. Where did you grow up?"

"Kennebunkport," I said. "But not wealthy. Because I know that's what people think right away. You know, the Bushes, the White Barn Inn, lots of fancy boats at Dock Square, you name it. My mom works odd jobs, mostly because she gets fired all the time. My dad is on disability. He was injured in the Persian Gulf War, but it wasn't a combat injury. It's a long story. How about you?"

"Right near here. Newington, just next door. Your mom sounds like a trip."

"Oh, you can say that," I said, taking a sip from my cocktail. It was definitely a bottled mix, but it tasted like a more natural one. No yellow food dye, luckily. "She's a real pain in the ass, actually. We sort of tolerate each other." I took a bite from a steaming hot mozzarella stick, stretching out a big string of cheese. "This is delicious," I said. "Okay, hit me with another." I figured he might as well find out what he wanted to know, especially since I wasn't sure if there would be a second date.

He laughed and smiled big, and I felt myself melt a little. It was all very confusing. "This should be good since you're a cook. Favorite food?"

"Well, obviously, I enjoy dairy products," I said, gesturing to the mozzarella sticks. "But it's ice cream. I absolutely love it."

"Here's a follow-up. Favorite flavor?"

"Vanilla toffee," I answered, giving a small smile. *Could he connect the dots?*

"Like a Heath bar?" He grinned big, and I couldn't help but smile back. We must have looked ridiculous sitting there, smiling at each other.

"Yes, and I'm not just saying that because I'm sitting across from you. How about you? Favorite food?"

"This stuff," he said, chomping on a chicken wing. "I love good bar food. Especially jalapeno poppers. They used to have really awesome ones here, wrapped in bacon. So bummed they don't have them on the menu anymore."

"And there's dairy in those, so I can appreciate that. And bacon is always good." My mind drifted back to that morning with Kyle, over fifteen years ago, stumbling over to the Norwell dining hall after not sleeping at all, where piles of crispy, fragrant bacon were waiting for us. *Maybe there will be bacon for breakfast," Kyle had said as we walked across campus.* And there was—so much bacon.

"Okay, I'll ask you two more since the ice cream answer had a second part to it," he continued. "What was the last relationship you were in?"

I gulped. I wasn't sure how truthful to be, but all he would need to do was Google my name and find out all kinds of salacious things. Maybe he already had. "I was involved with a married man in Boston. It was not a good thing for me to do at all, and I have all kinds of regrets about it now that I'm removed from the situation." I did. Hearing myself say it made me realize just how badly I felt about it and how much I had buried these feelings. Perhaps seeing Adrienne almost every day as a constant reminder of what I did and how it affected her was making me grasp the gravity of it all.

Heath nodded, but he didn't seem to have a flash of knowing what I was talking about, so maybe he had skipped the Googling for now. "I bet that was tough. I went out with a waitress at the pizza shop across the street for a month or so," he said, pointing toward the window.

"Like, right there?" I turned my head, but of course, all I saw was the busy street behind me.

"Yeah," he said, laughing. "She turned out to have some weird habits, but I didn't pick up on them for a while. Not a good fit, it turned out."

"Come on, you can't just drop that on me. Indulge me with one of those habits. I need something to make me feel more normal." I did.

Heath looked around as if he was worried someone he knew was nearby. Given that he had grown up and now worked in the area, it was a distinct possibility. "I found out in the weirdest way that she chews tobacco," he said softly.

"Really?" I asked, leaning in. "How did you discover this?"

"We went to go see a movie," he said. "*Top Gun Maverick.* Did you see it?"

"I heard it was great. I saw the original when I was younger, but I never saw the sequel."

"It's awesome," he said. "But we're sitting there in the movie theater over by Fox Run Mall, and she's in the aisle seat. I start hearing this noise. I look over, and she's spitting tobacco into the aisle of the theater."

"That is nasty. That's how you found out she did it?"

"Yep. It was the beginning of the end between us," he said. Our faces were much closer now, having shifted in proximity for the story. "Last question," he began. "Who's the last person you've kissed? The married guy?"

I could've lied and said yes, but I had already committed to the truth for the day, and I decided to stick with it. "No, not him. It was Kyle Holling. The soccer coach."

"The guy from the hospital?" Heath asked. "Oh, damn. Are you dating him? I didn't mean to—"

"No, not at all. We have a bit of a complicated past. We went to college together—way back in the day. Something happened then, and we didn't see each other again for over fifteen years.

So, there have been some old feelings to work out. But I am unattached right now." I said it, and I felt good for being honest. I had deceived enough people in Boston. "How about you? Who was the last person you kissed? If it was the waitress, I hope it was before she chewed the tobacco."

He smiled at me and leaned closer. "May I?" he asked.

I nodded, and he closed his eyes and gently touched his lips to mine. The kiss answered the question I had been asking myself all day. Heath was worth pursuing.

"You," he said. "You're the last person I've kissed."

14

"Did you and Kyle have a fight?" Andrea asked as soon as I walked into her office. I hadn't even closed the door behind me.

"Hello to you, too," I said, sitting down in the chair across from her.

"I never see him in the dining hall," she continued. "Only at The Horse."

"I didn't know you frequented The Horse." I certainly didn't those days. When I wasn't working in the dining hall, I was either in my apartment watching the most recent season of *Never Have I Ever* (an excellent show), or I was on a date with Heath. We had gone bowling and to an escape room. We made out behind a set of funhouse mirrors that we stumbled upon. It felt a lot like a high school relationship, except I didn't have to go home to my parents. I wasn't sure what to make of it, but it was a hell of a lot less complicated than dealing with Kyle.

"Once in a while, a girl needs a five-dollar Long Island Iced Tea," Andrea said, tapping a pen absentmindedly on her desk. I shuddered thinking of the quality or lack thereof in those well liquors. "But I hear things."

Of course, she does. "Everything with Kyle and me is complicated. Even when we try not to let it be, it somehow still is."

Andrea pushed a single sheet of paper in front of me. It was the latest copy of *The Underground Stallion*. "Looks like it's gotten more so."

There were side-by-side pictures of me in black and white. The one on the left was the shot of Kyle and me kissing that we knew would emerge eventually, and here it was. On the right was a photo of Heath and me at the pub in Portsmouth. Our very first kiss. *How did someone capture that?* I hadn't seen anyone there who had looked in the least bit familiar, or even anyone under the age of twenty-one. Underneath the images—in bold, all-caps text—it posed the question:

LOVE TRIANGLE?

I didn't bother to read the short article that followed and pushed the paper back at Andrea. "I very recently started seeing a guy who lives in town. A paramedic."

"Yes," she said, pointing back at the article. "Heath Davis."

I grabbed it back off the desk. "They know his last name? I just learned his last name the other day."

"Never underestimate *The Underground Stallion*," she said, taking off her glasses and rubbing her eyes. "Look, you're the least of my worries right now. Things aren't good. As you know, there are people protesting that piece of art day and night. Usually, we get a surge of applications this time of year because people become fed up with their local public schools around October for whatever reason, and I think Admissions has gotten maybe two in the past week. Word has gotten out about all of this, and it's fucking embarrassing." I had never heard Andrea swear like that. The poor woman was *stressed*.

"You gotta wonder about those two who applied, right?" I posed, trying to inject some levity. I turned toward the window, which was cracked open enough that I could hear a woman screeching into a megaphone about neighbors' rights to be free of smut.

"They're probably the next reporters for this rag," Andrea grumbled, balling up the sheet of paper and aiming it at the recycling bin. She missed the shot. "I need your basketball player to teach me how to play."

"Okay, so Midsy," I said, ready to shift gears. "Tell me what you need from me."

Andrea groaned. "First of all, everyone on staff needs to call it by its formal name. It's 'Night of a Thousand Laughs.' We have been trying to keep the humor aspect of the evening but move it away from scandalous pranks. Instead, we will have performances set up around campus that night. The improv troupe will perform in the auditorium. Then everyone will move to the gym for all three a cappella groups, who will entertain us with lighthearted selections."

"Like what?" I asked, imagining Weird "Al" Yankovic or something along those lines.

"I believe the coed group—the Ponies—is planning to sing Harry Nilsson's classic 'Coconut' song."

"Okay," I said with a yawn. I was ready to get to the part where she told me all the things I was responsible for.

She gave me a pointed look and continued. "And then we travel to the amphitheater for the faculty rock band."

"It's going to be maybe forty degrees out."

"We'll be providing hot chocolate and cider, plus we take attendance at each stop," she replied. Which meant *I* would be making these warm refreshments happen. "Besides, I want to keep everyone moving and make them very tired. And then, finally, they will venture to the dining hall for a late breakfast and karaoke."

"That's where I come in. In addition to everything before that."

Andrea put her glasses back on her face and spun her laptop around so I could see it. On the screen were pictures of students very nicely dressed, sitting formally at a meal. "We also have a candlelit dinner to precede all the festivities. This is from last year before all hell broke out on this campus with the leadership. So, a nice dinner, followed by entertainment all around Rockwood with desserts available at each stop, and then a midnight breakfast."

My head was spinning. "I need to serve them dinner and then breakfast like six hours later?"

She nodded. "Yes. We're going to exhaust them. Then stuff their bellies and send them to bed."

"So that they won't terrorize the campus."

"Precisely."

I sat back in my chair and paused. "How well has this plan worked in the past?"

"Not well," Andrea admitted. "But we've added the karaoke and breakfast, plus the faculty rock band. We're hoping this will all add to their fatigue, and they'll be too tired for hijinks."

"Is a faculty rock band that much of a draw?" I couldn't imagine who would be involved in such a thing unless it was made up of the twenty-two-year-old teachers. But given how early it was in the school year, it was unlikely they would even know about this "opportunity," let alone have time to organize and practice.

"Oh, students find them amusing," Andrea said with an air of distance like she was thinking of a million other things. She could have been distracted by the protestors, who were now chanting, "Connelly is a creep. Connelly is a creep." She sifted through some stacks of books and paper until she found an old yearbook. "Here's a picture from a while back. Ryland Dennis is the lead guitarist."

I almost gagged but held back. "Fantastic," I said with as little emotion as possible. "Do you care what I serve them at these meals and various dessert and hot beverage stations? Or should I just come up with something?" My questions hedged on the border of sarcasm, and I knew I was taking a risk. As ridiculous as Andrea could be, she still was my boss, and I didn't have any great employment options at that moment. And up until my schism with Kyle, I kind of was enjoying my time at Rockwood. Minus Ashlyn and the prying cell phone cameras of *The Underground Stallion*, of course. I loved my apartment; the fall had been warm and beautiful, and there was an ease and comfort to living on campus. I just wished Andrea wouldn't keep springing these events on me.

"Whatever you want," she muttered. "Just don't let Marnie put anything in a box."

"She hasn't tried to do that in a while," I replied. "Well, except for the box lunches we sent along on the geology field trip. But those were supposed to be in boxes."

"She's odd, right?" Andrea asked, her glasses slipping down on her nose. It was a strange question for such a quirky person to ask.

"Um, I don't know. She takes me by surprise sometimes. I was not expecting to see her working at The Barnacle."

"She's a mystery. I put her in charge of dining temporarily because she's been here the longest, but I soon regretted that. Just because someone is pushing fifty doesn't mean they'll be a good manager." Andrea sighed when her office phone rang. The light on it had flashed multiple times since I had been meeting with her, but this was the first time her assistant had patched the call through. "Hello, Andrea Lark," she said in a weary voice. "Oh, yes," she continued, sitting up a bit straighter. "That's fine. Tomorrow at ten works for me... I'll see you then." She hung up and stared at me for a moment. Her eyes looked sad and a bit desperate. "That was the *New York Times*. They want to visit the campus and interview me. If I had said no, they would write the article without my input. The last thing I need is for only protestors' voices to be heard. People should get the other side, too." She drummed her fingers on the desk and looked back up at me. "Devon?"

"What would you like me to prepare for the reporter?" I asked, knowing where this was going. "Cookies?"

"*Those* cookies," she said, looking back toward the window and the sounds of the protests. "You know which ones."

•   •   •

"Are you sure this is a good time?" Adrienne asked as she arrived in the kitchen. It was mid-afternoon, lunch was cleaned up, and dinner preparations were starting, but as dining hall operations went, this was one of the quieter times of the day.

"Sure," I said, getting out the ingredients for the cookies. I saw Marnie watching us interact out of the corner of her eye, and I wondered how much she knew. It *was* odd; students who weren't part-time employees didn't frequent the kitchen, and it was known to most people that Adrienne was not a student in need of extra cash. I decided to ignore Marnie and focus on Adrienne the best I could. "I make these cookies a lot, but Ms. Lark requested some for a meeting tomorrow, so I figured that would be a good first project for us to work on together."

"I like these cookies," she said. "I remember you bringing some to my house a few times. My dad liked to put ice cream in the middle of two of them and make sandwiches for us. He sometimes even rolled them in sprinkles for me. That was good."

"Doesn't sound like something your mom would approve of," I said with trepidation. I didn't know where the line was regarding what I could say about Adrienne's parents, so everything felt like a test.

Adrienne scoffed. "He only did that when she was gone. She prefers him to subsist on a kale salad diet—hold the dressing. But enough about them. They make me miserable. How do I make cookies?"

I made myself temporarily forget whose child she was and launched into all of it: why the butter and eggs had been sitting on the counter in advance, why I liked using organic sugar in the recipe, how I had come to the conclusion that both semisweet and white chocolate chips belonged in these cookies, and why I chilled balls of dough on the baking sheets for thirty minutes before popping them into the oven. "I hated my science classes in high school and college, but I love the science behind baking. This makes sense to me," I relayed to her. "And the results are far more delicious than anything I ever made in a lab."

Once the dough was prepared, Adrienne took the small ice cream scoop and began carefully dropping scoops on the parchment-lined cookie sheet. "Does this look okay?" she asked.

"You got it," I said. "What do you want to make next week? It'll be right before Midsy, so it's going to be a little crazy, but if you want to come in for some of the preparations, I'm happy to have you here."

Adrienne shifted a bit on her feet and glanced at me with an air of nervousness. "Could this be an internship?"

I sensed something very uneasy from her. "I hadn't thought of that, but I guess so. I could help you write it up if you want, but I'll be honest: I have no idea what I'm doing. Any particular reason why you want to classify it as an internship?"

Adrienne took a deep breath. "As you know, my high school experience has been, shall we say, disjointed. I have gone to so many schools, and my grades are all over the place. I don't play sports or do activities."

"I thought you rode horses," I said, thinking of her renegade ride to Walden Pond.

"I did, but I hated being told what to do. And the girls at my stable were bitches. So, I quit that. Anyway, I don't have much except a record of getting kicked out of prestigious schools. But

I'm going to try to stay at this one, even though I'm nervous about the whole Connelly thing."

"It's his art, not yours, so please don't worry about this controversy affecting you," I said, trying to reassure her. What a strange boomerang life was, bringing the daughter of my former lover back to my kitchen, seeking an internship from me. "I want to help you, Adrienne. If you can commit to weekly meetings with me where we continue to work through more complex recipes and kitchen skills, I'll be able to write you a kickass recommendation letter. If you want to use that for college or anything else you want to do in life, it should help."

"Thanks," she said. "That's what I was hoping for. The Connelly thing makes me nervous more than anything else. Like I'm constantly feeling dread every time I walk past it or hear the protestors. I don't even know him. I'm not sure why it bothers me."

"It should calm down soon," I said, probably with too much optimism. I had no idea what would actually happen. "But in the meantime, you'll show your motivation and maturity by working with me on a regular basis. It'll help for anything you decide to do. I'm in."

"Thanks, Devon," she said. "No matter what happened with you and my family, I know you're a good person. I heard my dad tell my mom that."

"I'm sure that went over really well."

15

I stumbled into my apartment kitchen at seven on the morning of Midsy, knowing I had to start preparing for what was going to be an exhausting day. The team had already done so much in advance, but given the breadth of this event, we still had more to do. I opened the refrigerator to get the half-and-half out for my coffee, and when I closed it, I caught a glimpse of a face peering at me through the fire escape window. I dropped the carton of cream and saw it was a smiling Heath. I clutched my chest and walked to the window to let him in.

"You just about gave me a heart attack," I told him. "Maybe a stroke, too. Definitely a panic attack."

He wrapped his strong arms around my flannel pajama-clad body. "Good thing I'm an emergency responder," he said, kissing me.

I pulled back and put my hand over my mouth. "I haven't brushed my teeth yet. I'm a hot mess."

"Emphasis on the word *hot*," he said, kissing the back of my hand, followed by my cheek and then the side of my neck. The whole situation was tempting; part of me wanted Heath to keep going with his early morning seduction. But I needed to get to work, and besides, things between us hadn't gone much further than this yet. It was also not the right time, and I definitely didn't want some kind of quickie where I had to run across campus unshowered and with any hint of a sex glow. Marnie would definitely figure me out. And I'd probably run into Ashlyn Lark on my way into the dining hall. Maybe Kyle, too. *Oh God, no.* Heath needed to leave.

I pulled back again. "I am so happy to see you this morning, but I absolutely need to gulp some coffee and get to work. We have Midsy today, as you might already know."

He squeezed my hands and then dropped them to walk back over to the window, pulling a large Dunkin' iced coffee off the fire escape. "I know," he said, handing the coffee to me. "Everyone at the station already got the briefing in case there's an incident. Want me to be here when you get back tonight? I'm not working, which is totally fine by me."

Once again, it felt like bad timing. "I'm not going to be done until at least one in the morning, probably later," I said. "I'll be completely wiped out, I'm sure. I won't be a great person to hang out with at that point."

"Okay," he said with a small smile, but it was clear he was disappointed. "I hope it goes well." He kissed the top of my forehead. "Let me know when you want to hang out again."

I felt terrible about rejecting him. "How about dinner some night this week?"

"Sounds good," he said. "I'll text you my schedule. Bye." He climbed back out the window and headed down the fire escape before I could say anything else.

I ran to the window and yelled down, "Thanks for the coffee!"

"You're welcome!" shouted a group of female students from the grass below in unison. Ashlyn and her friends, yet again, now erupting in laughter.

I slammed the window shut, grabbed my cell phone, and called Tam.

"Well, good morning," she grumbled. I heard a male voice in the background asking who it was.

"I'm so sorry," I said. It was a Saturday morning. Some people sleep in. Apparently, Tam didn't have to be at work, and Professor Plum probably never was needed by anyone early on a weekend morning. "Can you come up here one night this week? I mean, I don't know which night yet. Heath needs to let me know. But I want you to meet him."

"Okay, okay, we can figure it out," she murmured. "Is everything okay? Are you on the verge of marrying him or something? Are you pregnant, Dev?"

"No, not at all. None of the above. I have some kind of mental block toward him. I'm avoiding intimacy with him. And you know me, I'm not one to shy away from things."

"You were caught in a closet with a married man by his teenage daughter. No, you're not one to shy away. Isn't this guy like super hot? Sorry, E."

"Professor Plum's name is E? What does that mean?"

"It's Ellis. I never told you that? He's going to be horribly offended now."

"Does he know we call him Professor Plum?"

"Yes, I told him that on our second date. I decided honesty was an important foundation for a relationship. He rolls his eyes, but he's accepted it."

"So, it's okay for me to call him Professor Plum."

"Yes, Devon, you may. Okay, I will give you two more minutes. I am neglecting this man next to me now that we are both awake much earlier than either of us ever intended. What do you think the issue is?"

I sighed. "I think I feel guilty about Kyle. But I'm trying to figure out if it's that or something about my chemistry with Heath—because that would be ridiculous. And to answer your original question, he *is* super hot."

"Okay, Dev. You let me know your schedule, and I'll figure this out. Can Profes—, I mean Ellis, come, too? It might be helpful to have an outsider perspective, plus I really want you to meet him."

"I'd love it. Get back to, well, whatever. Thanks, Tam."

"Anytime, love."

•   •   •

We got through the formal dinner. My go-to (and Adrienne's favorite) Chicken Milanese, a silky fettuccine alfredo for the vegetarians, and a vegan-friendly stuffed spaghetti squash rounded out the entrées. My team pulled out all the stops, even as Marnie grumbled through the list of dietary restrictions of our students to ensure that everyone had something absolutely delicious to eat that night. "It wasn't like this ten years ago," she muttered as she inspected the label of the vegetable stock I had left for her at her prep station.

"We can make our own veggie stock next time if you'd prefer," I said. "It's not hard, and it's quite tasty, but it'll take a few hours." She didn't say anything in return.

After dinner, as Andrea had specified, students went to the auditorium to begin their travels through the various performances. Each of the entertainment stations had a dessert and beverage table. Given the fact that students would be ingesting food for hours—which made me nervous from a purely biological standpoint—I decided to make all bite-sized desserts. The auditorium where the improv troupe kicked things off featured tiny eclairs, mini cannoli, and itty-bitty crème brûlées, along with lemonade and bottled water. As my team prepared for the late-night breakfast with karaoke, I staffed the table to ensure all went well and, as Andrea had requested, that students weren't spiking the lemonade with vodka.

"What do I do if I see them do that?" I had asked.

"I don't know," she had admitted. "Maybe confiscate it? I'll be there. Bring the student to me." I had the impression she had no idea what she would then do with the kid, but I left it at that.

The improv troupe went through a number of skits and brought a few random students onto the stage to participate, and to Andrea's delight, got many laughs from the audience. Their final skit was called "The Staff of Rockwood," and once I saw a female student come onto the stage in a chef's hat, I knew I was in trouble.

"Guess who I am?" asked the student to the crowd.

"Chef!" "It's her!" "The cook lady." "Devon Paige!" Several students turned to point at me, and my entire body felt like it was on fire.

A male student walked out on the stage, dribbling a soccer ball. He was wearing ripped jeans and a Counting Crows t-shirt, and his hair was a mess. I had to give these kids credit; they were way too clever. "Who am I?" he asked.

"Kyle Holling!" "Coach Holling! "Mr. Holling!" I looked around and didn't see Kyle in the crowd, luckily. I hadn't seen him anywhere on campus since the kiss incident, but I knew he was still teaching his classes. Word was he was a mess in terms of his appearance and barely managed to get through his lessons, but he was showing up. I had wanted to reach out and see if he would talk to me, but I had to get through Midsy first. I was glad he wasn't seeing this.

I caught Andrea's eye from across the room, and she must have noticed the desperation on my face. "Look at the time!" she announced in her best Head of School voice. "We do need to keep to a schedule tonight. Please move to the gym, where we have three delightful a cappella songs awaiting us. And a huge round of applause to our very talented improv troupe!"

I sent thank you vibes in her direction and scooted ahead of the students to make it to the gym to relieve my staff, who were setting up the mini cupcake and sparkling cider station. We even had plastic champagne flutes for the cider, which was quite cute. There was an all-female singing group, followed by an all-male, and then the coed group singing, as Andrea had promised, "Coconut." They called themselves the Ponies, and they were by far the most creative of the three, "riding" out onto the gym floor on hobby horses. One student even juggled coconuts during the song. And best of all, there were no references to Kyle or me in any songs.

The last station before we returned to the dining hall was in the outdoor amphitheater for the faculty rock band. Andrea had yelled at everyone as they were leaving the gym to be sure to grab their coats but also to make sure they were in the amphitheater for attendance in ten minutes, which I knew was not going to happen. Half the students didn't get their jackets for fear of missing the roster check, and the other half who did go back to their dorms were late. I did my best to get hot chocolate to those who appeared cold, but this situation was mostly beyond my control. I heard Ryland Dennis' voice through the speakers and wanted to gag.

"Hey, Stallions! We are the faculty rock band. We're still trying to figure out a name, so if you have any ideas, please let us know!"

"How about the washed-up old dudes?" shouted Shad Wilton, one of the biggest troublemakers on campus. I spotted Andrea strut over to the aisle next to his row and motion for him. The students around Shad hooted and slapped him on the back, and Shad begrudgingly left his seat to talk to Andrea behind the tiered seating.

"On that note," replied Ryland, launching into the Grateful Dead's "Touch of Grey." A few students paid attention and bobbed along with it, but most just turned and talked to each other, ignoring the performance. I stood by a table full of plates of my now infamous cookies, which were devoured in less than ten minutes. I had no idea how these people were going to eat breakfast after this.

"And for our last song tonight, we have a special guest singer. We could definitely use some female vocals, so if any staff are interested in joining us, please reach out," said Ryland. Hardly anyone was listening to him. Students were huddled together, and I spotted two making out under a blanket that they had wrapped around themselves. I looked for Andrea, but she was still chastising Shad, which seemed to be a bit much at this point. "In the meantime," Ryland continued. "We'll take help wherever we can get it. On lead vocals, please welcome student Ashlyn Lark!"

My jaw almost hit the ground as Ashlyn sauntered to the middle of the stage in a slinky cocktail dress and heels. She must have been freezing. Even Andrea stopped lecturing Shad to walk up to the back row and watch her niece perform. My guess was she had no idea this was occurring. "Hello," she crooned. "Jealousy is rampant on the campus these days, whether it be between students or between staff. Sometimes, it involves people who don't even live or work at Rockwood. We thought this was fitting."

The band launched into Natalie Merchant's "Jealousy," which I doubted many of the students knew, but I sure did. *What is Ryland trying to accomplish?* And with Ashlyn as his accomplice, no less. It felt dirty and very inappropriate. Besides, if she had wanted to break up Kyle and his now ex-wife, he succeeded. Was he attempting to stir the pot further between Kyle and me, or was there more to this? *And why does he care?* I could feel Ashlyn looking right at me as she sang, even though her eyes were closed as she was crooning. None of it made any sense, and I wanted to get out of there as soon as possible. Seeing that students were already starting to leave mid-song to head to breakfast, I texted the facilities team that we would be ready for a cookie table clean-up in five minutes and raced over to the dining hall.

I was out of breath and must have looked like a disheveled mess by the time I showed up in the kitchen. "You okay?" asked Marnie in her usual flat tone, which made me feel like she didn't actually care one way or another. I reminded myself that she was like this with everyone and grabbed a glass of water.

"I think so," I said, still gasping a bit. "It's getting cold out. Students are starting to come in. I don't know how much room they're going to have in their stomachs for breakfast, but they'll be here. It looks like karaoke is ready to go?"

"Yeah," she answered. "The Robotics Club said they'd run it for us, so they've been setting up for the last hour. I just sent staff out to serve food. We're fine, Devon. This is the easiest thing we've done all week."

She was right; the formal dinner and all the dessert station logistics were by far much more challenging. "Thank you," I said. "I'll be out there keeping an eye on everything. Let me know if you need anything. You did a great job this week."

"Yeah," she said, nodding. That was about as good as things got between us, and I had to accept it. She was very different from me and a bit of an odd duck to work with, but she did a good job overall.

The students were filling the dining hall, getting food, and sitting at the tables. I noticed many of them were yawning, but a few were signing up for karaoke slots with the Robotics Club members. Within a few minutes, the sounds of students singing filled the cavernous room—lots of Lizzo, Taylor Swift, and Harry Styles. I felt a mix of exhaustion and exhilaration because the students were having fun, and my team had pulled the whole thing off. I had no idea if the students would be up to any antics later, but it was so late, and everyone seemed so tired. Part of me felt like Andrea's plan might work. I walked over to where she was standing in the corner of the room, eating a cinnamon roll.

"Good job, Devon," she said. "Both on the whole thing and this damn cinnamon roll. I can't begin to add up all the things I've eaten tonight, but they've all been amazing. I know I've been asking a lot of you this fall, but you're doing awesome. It means a lot to me."

It was, by far, the nicest thing she had said to me since I had started working at Rockwood. "I appreciate it," I replied. "I also am very excited to have tomorrow off."

"You doing anything fun? Hanging out with that hunky paramedic of yours? He can resuscitate me anytime," she said, and it was so corny I had to laugh despite my exhaustion.

"Maybe," I said. A man walked up to the microphone, and Andrea and I both gasped.

A student was already at the microphone and announced, "Our next performer will be Mr. Holling, and he will be singing Oasis' 'Don't Look Back in Anger.'"

Kyle grabbed the microphone from the boy abruptly and gripped it with both hands, his eyes closed. Like the student depicting him earlier in the improv skit, his hair was a mess. His beard was overgrown, and he was wearing sweatpants and a Manchester United t-shirt that looked like it had been balled up and forgotten in the back corner of a dresser drawer. His big toes poked out of holes in his sneakers. I listened to the words of the song, just as I had listened to them while lying in a cramped twin dorm room bed next to him over fifteen years earlier. As I looked at his stress-worn face, I saw it blurred to a much younger, clean-shaven man, one who had kissed me, held me, and caressed me over many hours that one night. As Kyle belted out the lyrics, I felt them sear into me in multiple places, but especially into my head as I tried to make sense of everything that had happened, as well as my heart, which had grown achy and more confused.

"He's still not over Cora," said Ryland Dennis, who was now standing next to me. "How sad," he smirked. "You know he's singing this about her, right?"

"Oh, sure," I said. There was no way in hell I was going to tell Ryland anything about the significance of this song for Kyle and me.

"Because in case you thought any of this was really about you," he continued. "Cora was where the real magic was. She's an incredible woman. So much beauty, so much style." I felt him give me a once over, and I knew I looked like a mess after working all day and running across campus. I tried to ignore his inspection and took it with a grain of salt. He had very little credibility in my eyes. "You're a distraction," he said, walking away.

"He's an ass," Andrea said. "Don't take him seriously. And you don't see him with Cora now, do you?"

"Nope," I answered, not knowing what else to say. She was absolutely correct, but she also loved her gossip, and I didn't need to feed that anymore that night.

Kyle finished singing and walked out of the room. Students were buzzing and asking each other about the song and what the whole thing meant. "I think it's about her," one student said loudly enough and pointed in my direction. I looked at Andrea and bit my lip.

"You want to try to catch up with him?" she asked. "I'm going to pull the plug on all of this in the next fifteen minutes. These kids need to get some sleep. And then, God willing, they stay there."

I nodded several times and bolted outside, trying to find Kyle. I didn't see him anywhere. I ran to his dorm, but my key wouldn't work on that building. All the students were in the dining hall, so I couldn't plead with anyone to let me in. I looked up to his window, but it was dark. Still, I climbed the cold fire escape in case he had simply gone to bed. I peered in the windows and saw nothing. I knocked on the glass and waited, but there was nothing. It was almost one in the morning; The Horse was closing in a few minutes, and last call had already passed. The rest of the bars in Portsmouth were either closed or about to close, so it wasn't worth heading into town. I checked the parking lot, and I couldn't see his car anywhere. I was out of ideas.

I started walking back to the dining hall, as I figured I might as well help clean up. My phone lit up with a text from Heath.

>*You still up? Everything go okay?*

This was normal. Texting someone you care about is normal. *Why am I resisting this so much?* I felt like I had been fighting with ghosts all night. I texted back.

<*Just finished. We nailed it. Great success.*

I paused for a moment and thought about my car sitting in its spot in front of Wentworth.

<*Want me to come over?*

16

"What's wrong?" Heath rolled over onto his side as I frantically texted Andrea back. I was sitting up in his bed, having woken up due to receiving ten text messages telling me to do just that. I needed to get back to campus.

"It's not good," I said, scooting off the bed and grabbing my jeans from the floor next to me. "Rockwood is trashed. The Head of School's office is a mess. They did all sorts of things to that stupid sculpture. Somehow, they dismantled all the security cameras. The security detail was playing poker all night in their office, and no one knows why. So, that's all part of the investigation now. How these kids managed to get a horse into Andrea's office, I'll never know."

Heath sat up in bed, and admiring his chiseled upper body, I wanted to crawl back in there with him. I had no regrets about going to his place the night before. I had forgotten about Kyle for a few hours, which felt freeing. Spending time with Heath was easy. If I had found Kyle after his karaoke performance, I probably never would have gone over to Heath's apartment, but I had no idea what the right answer to any of it was. All I knew was that I had had fun, and now the fun was over. I needed to go back to reality, and from what I was told, a heavily vandalized fire escape outside my kitchen window.

"They brought a horse into her office? Up those flights of stairs?" Heath asked, shaking his head. "I can't believe I didn't get any kind of notification from the station yet."

"I don't think anyone is hurt, which is good," I said, pulling on my sweatshirt. "The Rye police found a bunch of students at the beach at five in the morning with a bonfire and a ton of champagne."

"Classy," he said. "Hey, I need to work today, but I'll call you later. Can I get a kiss before you leave?"

"Sure," I said, walking over and sitting on the edge of the bed. "This was a good time."

"It was," he said, his hands on my thighs, lightly massaging them. "And I'm excited to meet your friend Tamara this week."

"I'll get in touch with her today now that I know your schedule. We'll figure something out," I said and then kissed him softly.

"I like you a lot, Devon Paige."

•   •   •

"Sorry to interrupt your romp with the paramedic," Andrea said from behind her desk. She gestured at the dark brown horse that was standing and snorting in the corner of her office, its reins connected to what looked like a dog's leash, tethered to the handle of a massive filing cabinet. I gave it a pat, not knowing what else to do. "Animal Control is on its way to get him out of here."

"Looks like he's pretty well-behaved," I said, sitting across from her. Andrea looked awful, both exhausted and with damp yet somewhat greasy-looking hair. There was also a strange smell, but maybe it was coming from the horse. "Are you okay?"

"No. I am not," she said. "I turned on my shower this morning, and guess what happened?"

"I have no idea."

"Beef soup rained down on me. Those fuckers taped beef bouillon cubes onto my shower head."

I suppressed a laugh, feeling both badly for her and impressed by the ingenuity. That was some prank. "They broke into your house? How on earth?" This was a new low. I started connecting the dots in my head and realized who might be able to access the Head of School's house. *Oh.* "I have an idea."

Andrea shook her head. "I guess giving your niece a key to your house isn't a good move."

"And you know she was involved?" As horrific as Ashlyn was, I didn't want to assume anything. But I knew it was likely.

"She was found at the bonfire guzzling a big Yeti mug full of champagne. Taittinger, no less. How do they pull this shit off? I was drinking Korbel until I was at least thirty. If I was lucky."

I wasn't sure what to say, what was appropriate, what would be overreaching. "What are you going to do?"

Andrea sighed, waving to the Animal Control officers who had entered the room. She signed off on the paperwork, bid adieu to the horse, and settled back into her seat across from me. "I wonder what his name was."

"He seemed like a good horse. At least he didn't trash the place."

"Maintenance came through and cleaned up some poop earlier. Luckily, he didn't keep going with that. I am grateful because who needs horseshit on top of everything else? I also wonder where the hell he came from. Even Ashlyn doesn't own a horse."

I thought back to Adrienne's horse stunt at Walden Pond. "Adrienne Preston wasn't in that group at Rye Beach, was she?"

Andrea scrolled through her phone for a few seconds. "No, she's not on the police report. Of course, we don't know for sure if there were others involved, but my guess is this is the core group, given the celebratory nature of the gathering." She passed her phone over to me so I could take a look. Of the student names I knew, they were mostly from the crew that I always saw surrounding Ashlyn. The same kids, I assumed, were involved with *The Underground Stallion*. No big surprises. "We now have to conduct a full investigation. Parents have already been notified. Many have indicated they are hiring lawyers. It should be lots of fun."

"That must have been awkward, you know, calling your brother."

She took off her glasses and wiped them with a cloth. "These keep getting greasy. I need to check the other shower in my house to see if they defiled it, too. I don't think I'll be able to trust mine again for a while. But yes, it was terrible. He and my sister-in-law tend to think Ashlyn can do no wrong, so there were plenty of excuses given despite the fact that they hadn't even spoken to her yet."

I looked at Andrea, who was a combination of sad and angry, her limp hair laden with oily beef soup. She wasn't perfect, but neither were any of us, especially me. She didn't deserve this. "What happens if the investigation yields proof that they did all of it? I saw The Stallion covered in tarps again. I assume they got to it."

"Yes, they spray-painted words labeling it as part of a horse's anatomy, if you know what I mean."

I gasped. "Does Ward Connelly know?"

"That call might have been worse than the call to my brother. Yes, he knows. And to answer your earlier question, the students could be removed. I might be in the position of telling my very own niece that she can no longer attend the school that I oversee. If the Board even keeps me on."

I sat up a bit straighter. "I think you should. Kick her out. She's obviously ungrateful and abusive." This was the overreaching I was worried about, but I felt so badly for Andrea. She was being taken advantage of.

Andrea sighed. "You're probably right. I need to warn you about a few other things. I know it's your day off, so this is just to make you aware of the situation. They ransacked the kitchen. I have no idea how they were still hungry after that breakfast, on top of everything else, but it looks like they grabbed food for their beach celebration. Marnie and I decided that given the circumstances, we would keep the dining hall closed until dinner. We had a boatload of doughnuts delivered and set up a breakfast station outside this morning. It's probably winding down now. We're getting boxed lunches brought in from a deli in Portsmouth. Marnie's idea, of course."

"I'll help them at dinner," I said. "I'll take a night off this week or something." Andrea nodded, looking relieved. "What else should I know?"

"They partied in the library. It's a mess. A sticky keg, books everywhere, so much cleaning is needed. Lots of other classrooms are messed up. We may need to shift classes around a bit until things are back to normal."

I remembered she had mentioned something about my fire escape in her frantic earlier texts. "What about my apartment? Did they break in?"

"No, we checked after we saw your fire escape *decorated,* shall we say? Or it *was* decorated. Not anymore. I had maintenance take everything down after they snapped a bunch of pictures for the record."

I felt a huge pit drop through my stomach as if I had swallowed a bowling ball. "Let me see them."

"Are you sure? Devon, none of it's very kind. And I really need you to stay here," she said, on the verge of tears. "You've been a godsend. I know I don't say it enough, but you've been such a positive force at Rockwood. Don't let the vandalism of a few mean-spirited teenagers drive you out of here. Hell, they'll probably get kicked out anyway."

"Everyone else knows what was there. I need to see it for myself."

Andrea passed her phone over to me. My kitchen window and fire escape were adorned with big cardboard faces. Each was a man I had been involved with at some point in my life. Bentley Preston. Heath. Kyle. Random guys I dated in Boston. A guy I went on one date with during my college semester in Washington, DC. I couldn't even remember his name. My senior prom date. *How had they found these guys?* Perched on the fire escape landing was a waste barrel with the word TRASH emblazoned on it. Affixed to the container was one more cardboard face, and this time it was mine. The message was clear.

"Don't worry, Andrea. I'm not going anywhere." Despite the horror and embarrassment of it all, I felt resolved. And a desire to help make Rockwood better if I could.

"Oh, good," she said with relief. "And I really need to get some more people to help clean this afternoon so we can get the campus back to normal operations tomorrow. I am offering fifty dollars an hour. Do you know anyone who needs cash?"

•　　•　　•

I drove my car the short distance to Wentworth, taking note of the work this defiant group of students had done. Toilet paper filled many of the trees. Signs and flyers of all sizes littered the interiors and exteriors of buildings depicting Andrea's head photoshopped onto a bikini-clad woman's body, straddling The Stallion. I spotted Kyle's car parked on campus. Someone had scrawled *Devon's Boy Toy* on the rear window with what I hoped were washable car markers. These kids had thought of everything.

When I was finally sitting on my couch, still wearing my clothes from the previous night, I stared at my mother's cell phone number in my contacts. Part of me hoped she had another gig that afternoon and would pass. I also knew that fifty dollars an hour was much more money than she ever made, and I could probably find a small, easy task that my dad could handle. They could leave Rockwood that night with perhaps two weeks' salary.

"Oh, I haven't heard from *you* in a long time. Too busy for her mother, I always tell anyone who will listen." This was my mother's greeting when she answered my call.

"Hi, Mom."

"Hello. I can't imagine what this must be about since I never get calls from you. I don't even *try* to call you because you are always so busy doing such *important* things."

I took a breath and counted to three before answering. "Would you like to make some money working at Rockwood this afternoon?" I figured keeping emotion out of it and getting right to the point was the way to go. A businesslike approach with people like her helped keep me somewhat in check.

"At your fancy school? Imagine that. What do you want me to do, scrub toilets? Because I'll do that. I do that all the time."

"I know you do. But it's going to be cleaning some spaces that got vandalized last night. There was a big prank on campus, and we need to get the school ready for classes and a sense of normalcy. You can have dinner here, too, if you want."

"Those kids sound like little shits if they did that. How lucky they are to go to such a fancy place. They don't know how good they have it. I had to drop out of high school to help support my family, as you know. Kids today are so spoiled."

I ignored her tirade and pressed on. "I can probably find something for Dad to do, too," I said. "Nothing too hard on him, I promise. You'll each make fifty dollars an hour."

The woman who never shut up was speechless. After about ten seconds, she finally spoke. "Fifty dollars an hour? Each? That school has that kind of money? I can't imagine how much they've been paying you. I expect a very nice Christmas present, Devon."

I could never win with her. "Would you like to come down here? If not, I'm sure I can find some other people."

"No, no, we'll do it," she said. "We'll clean up after the little shits."

"Mom, if you're coming here, you're going to have to stop referring to them as little shits."

"Okay, okay. For that much money, I can keep my mouth shut."

I had my doubts.

17

My parents' aging Ford Explorer pulled into the parking spot next to my car in front of Wentworth. It felt so strange to welcome them to Rockwood, especially considering the odd circumstances. Although, given my unconventional relationship with them, having a task was probably a good thing.

I opened the passenger door for my dad to help him out. He could walk just fine, but he was slow and careful. He had suffered a traumatic brain injury from a motor vehicle accident while serving as a reservist in the Persian Gulf War. I was only three years old at the time, and given the extent of his injuries, he hadn't been able to return to his job as a postal carrier. His overall condition improved greatly over the years, but beyond puttering in the garden and watching documentaries on TV, he didn't do much—besides make whiskey sours. He loved his whiskey sours, just like I did.

"Hi, Sugar," he said, giving me a somewhat awkward hug. The tension that always existed between my mother and me weighed heavily on everything, and she ultimately overpowered him. It was easier for him to hang back.

"Welcome to Rockwood," I said. "Either of you want anything? Mom, a Diet Coke?" She drank them like most people drank water.

"Got one," she said, holding up her twenty-ounce bottle. "Well, this is *fancy*." Fancy was not a compliment coming from her; it generally meant something she felt was superior to her, and that caused her resentment. I was ready for her reaction and to hear that word *a lot* throughout the day.

"It is," I agreed. It was better to work with her, when I could, than against her. "Dad, anything for you?"

"I'm all set," he said. "Mom brought me some water."

"Okay, we're not here to be tourists," said Mom. "Let's get to work."

We made our way over to the library, as I figured there would be things for both of my parents to do. Adrienne was hauling a very full garbage bag outside when we got to the building.

"Hi, Adrienne," I said. "What are you doing here?" Part of me was still worried that she had been involved in the pranks, and perhaps she was working in a mandatory clean-up crew as a consequence of her actions. But I also knew there was an investigation underway, and my best guess was those students were either confined to their dorms for the time being or had been picked up by their parents. And the last thing I needed was a showdown with Adrienne's mother at that moment. My thoughts were spiraling.

"Ms. Lark put out a call for volunteers to help clean everything up, and it's counting toward our community service hours for graduation. Since I just started here this year, I am a little behind, so I figured I would join in." She looked at my parents, obviously a bit confused. "Hi," she said.

"Oh, my apologies. Adrienne, these are my parents, Camille and Billy Paige. They're going to help today, too."

"That's cool," she said. "Nice to meet you. I'm going to work on the Collections room next. That's where the worst of it is."

Mom perked up. There was no mess too great for her to tackle, and I think she relished the challenge. It was always hard for me to understand. "I'll do that, too," she said. "I'm used to cleaning motel rooms after bachelor parties. This can't be much worse."

"That sounds awful," Adrienne said, holding the door open for her. "Come with me."

I looked at my dad, who softly chuckled and shook his head. "You know your mother. The worse it is, the more she wants to clean it."

"It's strange," I acknowledged. "Okay, Dad, let's go inside. We'll find a project."

There were books strewn everywhere. It made me sad, thinking of the authors who had written these volumes, the editors and publishers who had painstakingly checked every line and formatted every page just right. And now their work was chucked all over a boarding school library because a group of hooligans had decided to trash the place as part of a prank night.

"Hey, Dev." Kyle was picking up a book when we walked into the room. He had a table in front of him where there was a small stack.

"Kyle! I thought you were gone this weekend. I mean, never mind. Kyle, this is my dad, Billy Paige. Dad, this is Kyle Holling. He's a history teacher and soccer coach here. We, um, we went to college together."

My dad reached out his hand to shake Kyle's, and a strange feeling washed over me. I had never once brought a guy—even a platonic one—home to meet my parents, so the idea of introducing one to my dad felt different and incredibly weird. But seeing the ease with which my dad and Kyle launched into small talk filled me with relief.

"History, huh?" Dad asked. "I just finished the Ken Burns documentary about the Dust Bowl. Do you teach that?"

"Every year," Kyle said. "Have you ever seen Dorothea Lange's photographs from it? Incredible work. I always show them to my students."

"I think those are in the documentary." Dad squinted. "I would imagine teaching history is fascinating. I used to just watch shows about war, but I felt like I needed to branch out more. I want to watch the one about jazz next."

"The baseball one is great, too," Kyle said. "Hey, Dev, if you've got work to do, you can leave your dad with me. It's totally fine."

I had told Kyle about my dad's injuries and limitations, but I wasn't sure how much he remembered. I didn't want to embarrass Dad by mentioning anything, so I gave Kyle a look, searching his eyes for any kind of understanding of the situation. He glanced at my dad and then back at me, nodded slightly, and smiled. I felt a rush of warmth envelope me from head to toe from this unspoken communication. I wasn't sure why Kyle and I were as connected as we were, but I felt comfortable leaving. "Okay," I said. "I'm going to go check on dinner preparations and the overall condition of the dining hall. Kyle, text me if you finish or need me to come back. You okay, Dad?"

"You bet, Sugar. So, Kyle, which presidents do you like teaching about the most?"

I suppressed a laugh, knowing Kyle loved nothing more than to go on and on with presidential stories. My dad would be well-entertained.

I couldn't stop smiling on my walk to the dining hall, thinking of Kyle telling my dad the story of Andrew Jackson getting a bullet from an old duel removed at the White House. Then I remembered that I had just left Heath earlier that morning, warm and happy in his bed. *"I like you a lot, Devon Paige,"* he had said. *What am I doing?* My introspection was cut short when I saw a TV crew outside of the administration building and Tam speaking into a microphone while production staff filmed her.

I watched and waited until she broke away and came over to see me. "I was going to text you as soon as I was done recording this piece," she said, giving me a big hug. I had missed the Tam hugs. "This place is so gorgeous, even in November. Some of the leaves are hanging on. Such a great backdrop, I've gotta say."

"How on earth did you hear about last night?" The campus already looked better than it had just a few hours earlier, but there were still remnants of toilet paper in the trees that would likely be there for months.

"We got an anonymous tip, so we followed up with Andrea. I feel so badly for her. She's been through a lot this fall."

"You can say that again," I concurred. "I don't know what she's told you, but I think this is going to be complicated."

Tam nodded. "She didn't give me details, but she did say there are aspects of it that are making it tough for her to deal with. Plus, I would imagine the Connelly aspect isn't helping. He's gotta be pissed. Hey, you don't think Adrienne Preston is involved, do you? Because that definitely gets messy."

I shook my head. "I was worried at first about that possibility, but no, I highly doubt it at this point. She's helping with the library cleanup right now for community service hours, and if she was in trouble, I don't think she'd be doing anything like that. And get this—she's cleaning with *my mom*."

Tam gasped. "They're here? Dev, what's going on? I thought you weren't really seeing them much these days. After you spoke with her amidst all the Bentley fallout..."

I groaned. "And she inquired yet again as to why I hadn't just gone to law school after college instead of doing all this *fancy* cooking. Yeah, I've been staying clear of Camille. But Andrea offered fifty dollars an hour for cleanup help, and I know they always need the money. And let's face it, the grosser the situation, the more my mom wants in. She gets some sort of perverse pleasure out of cleaning the nastiest things. So, giddy up. You get to clean some high school senior's Jägermeisterfilled puke from the corner of the Collections room of the Rockwood library."

Tam laughed, holding her nose. "And your dad? Can he do much to help?"

I couldn't help but smile. "He's helping Kyle reshelve books. It's very cute, actually."

Tam's eyes widened. "Kyle's around? I can finally meet him?"

"Yeah, you can," I replied, looking around to make sure no one else was in earshot. "But it's gotten much muddier." I told her about the karaoke episode from the night before and how I tried to look for him afterward. "And when I couldn't find him, I texted Heath. Remember how I told you that things hadn't progressed much with him?" She nodded. "Well, now they have. And I left him this morning to come back to this mess. And now Kyle is looking adorable and telling my dad historical stories, and I can't stop thinking about how maybe that's where I should be."

"Why shouldn't you be?"

I sat on a bench, and Tam sat next to me. "Everything with Kyle is hard. He's complicated. We're complicated. Everything with Heath is easy."

"Sometimes the hard things are the right things," Tam said.

I shook my head. "I don't know; he didn't even want to talk to me for the last couple of weeks. He was literally hiding from me. And it got to the point where it became too challenging. So, I went with the easy thing. The fun thing. Am I reading too much into all of this?"

"Maybe," Tam acknowledged. "But I think you need a few more opinions, not just mine."

"Yours matters the most."

"Of course it does," Tam laughed. "But I think you know what you need to do."

I thought about the two people who were working in the library, my own flesh and blood, who I had such an unusual relationship with. "Not that. Not them. I've never brought a guy home, not once in my entire life. My prom date picked me up at a friend's house, for God's sake. Why do I care what they think about Heath?"

"You've already commented on your dad interacting with Kyle, and a huge smile came over your whole silly face. I think it would be very revealing to get their take. And then David."

"You think David Anders should weigh in on Heath? Why? We need the Celtics' perspective?"

"I think he knows you better than you realize."

Maybe that was true. "I don't want to hurt Heath. He's a good guy."

"You might not hurt him. But right now, you have no idea what you want."

"Do you know what you want? With Professor Plum?'

"Yeah, I do. He's the one. Hopefully, he'll get off his ass and get me a ring. I want to have little plum babies, and I'm not getting any younger."

"You and me both. What would a little plum baby be called? A plummy?"

"Eww, that sounds like something nasty. I don't want to think about that. Please don't say that ever again."

"We'll come up with something else."

"Definitely. But think about *Sleepless in Seattle*."

"How does that apply here? Walter? Heath is not Walter."

"Okay, what about *You've Got Mail*? I'm trying to think of the right rom-com analogy here. He can be Frank in *You've Got Mail*. Greg Kinnear's character. Meg Ryan—excuse me, Kathleen Kelly—is with a guy, and it's good, and it's fine, and it's comfortable. But then there's Joe Fox..."

"I'm not sure Frank is that great of a guy. He ate all the caviar garnish, remember? Or was it Joe Fox? And you think Kyle's Joe Fox?"

"You're right. It was Joe. How am I getting my characters mixed up? I've only seen this movie a million times. But can I please go meet Kyle?"

I sighed. "Okay, let me just run into the dining hall and make sure we're on track for dinner. I'll be out in five minutes."

After checking in with Marnie and the rest of the staff, I felt comfortable leaving again—for enough time to bring Tam to the library and check on my parents. Tam had met them before, and luckily, my mother kept it together and didn't call her the fancy TV reporter or anything like that. Tam made small talk with Kyle about how she had been Andrea's college classmate and how she and I met in Boston a few years earlier. I had told Kyle plenty about her, and he genuinely seemed excited to meet her. The sullen Kyle from the last few weeks had been replaced by the Kyle I knew, the enthusiastic, all-in Kyle. It made me both happy and even more confused.

As I walked Tam back to the news van, she linked arms with me and said, "I really like him, Dev. I know I'm meeting Heath this week, and I'm excited about that. But there's a way that he looks at you out of the corner of his eye... I can't describe it. It's just there. Know that it's there, and I see it."

"I love you," I said, giving her a hug. "Thank you for being here today, even if it's for work. You have no idea how much I needed you."

"And anytime your campus is trashed by spoiled brats, I'll be here."

18

"Are you sure you don't want to stay for dinner?" I asked my parents. "You're skipping my free and quite excellent dinner for a ten-dollar turkey dinner at a congregational church. Even under these current circumstances, we're eating delicious sesame chicken and vegetable lo mein tonight. You love Chinese food!" I could not understand some of their life choices.

"Sounds fancy," my mom said, and I rolled my eyes. "We already bought the tickets."

I looked toward my dad, and he sheepishly shrugged his shoulders. "I'll save you a fortune cookie," I said to him, giving him a hug. "They go great with whiskey sours." My mom had already gotten into the car, never one for much affection. "I'll come up to see you soon," I directed toward her through the open car door.

"To what do we owe this honor?" she asked, turning the key in the ignition.

"It's been a long time, that's all. I miss the cat. I'll be in touch." I shut the door behind my dad and walked up the path to where Kyle was standing.

"They are brutal," I said to him, shaking my head. "Well, she is. He's fine. He can't get a word in edgewise."

"I really enjoyed hanging out with him. The guy knows his military history. And just history in general. I learned a lot."

"Thanks for doing that," I said. "He doesn't really have people to talk like that with. She couldn't care less about history."

"Your mom works hard, it seems."

We were walking now along the campus path, but with no real direction or purpose, it seemed. "It's funny," I replied. "She doesn't mind getting dirty. I mean, bachelor parties at local motels? Nasty. But she's abrasive and judgmental and pisses people off, so she gets fired. And then gets hired somewhere else because it's so tough to find workers who are willing to do what she does. It's an endless cycle. It's been like this most of my life."

"You're nothing like her," he said, and I was so relieved he could see that.

"Well, thank God. I mean, I've got some spunk in me," I said, and Kyle laughed. "But I never got terminated from a job. Until the most recent one, but well, you know what those circumstances were. I can't believe my mom spent the whole afternoon with Adrienne Preston," I said, smacking my hand against my forehead.

"Adrienne's a good kid. I doubt she said anything." He took a turn toward the wooded path that went to the pond where we had walked just weeks earlier and shared the ill-fated kiss. That wasn't happening this time, but I felt okay continuing the walk. The conversation felt healing and comfortable, which I think we both needed.

"I was glad to see her," I said, meandering through the crunchy leaves along the way and spotting the water on the other side. "I was worried she got caught up in the hijinks."

"Why would you think that? Pressure to fit in as a new kid?"

"I was thinking more about the horse that ended up in Andrea's office." I filled him in on the Walden Pond incident that ultimately brought Adrienne to Rockwood.

"Wow," he said, shaking his head as we began to walk around the pond. "I never would've thought."

I took a breath. "I've missed hanging out with you."

"Me, too."

"Where were you last night?" *How was that only last night?* I felt like I had lived a week during the previous twenty-four or so hours.

"Singing Oasis and making a damn fool out of myself," he said, not making eye contact with me. "I'm sorry if that made you uncomfortable at all. It's been a rough stretch for me, and all I could think about was what we listened to that night. Why I felt compelled to croon into a microphone in front of all of Rockwood is beyond me." He still wasn't looking at me, and I didn't dare try to initiate even a quick look for fear of where it would lead. I had been down this literal path just weeks before.

"Ryland came up to me and said you were singing about Cora."

"He's an idiot."

"Preaching to the choir there. Those were good songs we listened to that night. And I'm sorry for anything I've done wrong. I never want to hurt you." We were on our second lap around the pond. Stopping could mean trouble, so we kept going.

"I know that. Deep down, I know that."

"I looked for you after you sang. I couldn't find you, but I was worried about you." I allowed myself a glance his way and saw his face soften.

"You did?"

"Of course."

He sighed. "I got right into my car and drove to the beach. I needed to be at the ocean, even though it was too dark to really see it. I could hear it and feel it, though. What is it about the ocean? Anyway, then I drove to Boston and slept in my car until Annie was awake so I could take her to breakfast. I looked and probably smelled awesome. I don't think Cora has any regrets, trust me."

I laughed. "And then you came back to all of this fabulousness."

"The flyers of Andrea in the bikini riding The Stallion might be my favorite."

"They are ridiculous. I feel terrible for her, but good lord, I can't stop laughing when I see them. How did your car get written on if you were gone?"

"No clue. It must have happened after I got back this morning. Maybe after the criminals came back to campus?"

"That's terrible. Did you hear what they did to Ryland?" I figured this would cheer him up a bit.

"No! Give me the dirt!" It felt like earlier that fall when we would walk and chat and tell stories.

"Someone got into his apartment and plastic-wrapped his toilet. Apparently, he got hit by a big ol' spray. From himself."

"Ugh! I love it! How did you hear about this?"

"The kitchen staff was talking about it when I went in there to check on things a little while ago. Marnie found out somehow."

"That is amazing," he said, shaking his head.

"Okay, I'm starving," I said. "Want some sesame chicken? I can assure you it's better than the ten-dollar turkey dinner my parents are eating."

"Sure," he said, and we walked back toward the woods. "Just so you know, all the songs from, you know, that night? I was making them into a CD that day in London—when Lila came into the room for the first time. I was going to send it to you in DC. I know you thought I had forgotten about you, but I hadn't."

Back in those days, making a CD for someone was a time-consuming and somewhat intimate gesture. *Why is he just telling me this now?* "What did you do with the CD?" I asked as we came out of the woods and reached the main campus path just as students were walking to dinner. "Throw it out? Lose it?"

He shook his head. "I brought it back from London when I moved back. It's in my parents' house in Connecticut somewhere. I have a few bins of old stuff. But it's there. I still have it.

Kids started walking past us, several turning their heads to look at us, a few saying hi. It all felt like slow motion as I took it in that the CD was made up of those songs, the ones that we listened to as we sat in an anonymous dorm room that belonged to neither of us, talking and then not talking, on a night that would forever connect us, over fifteen years earlier. And that it still lived in a basement Rubbermaid tub, likely amidst soccer trophies, old goalie gloves, and perhaps some term papers that were once worth saving, now yellowed and faded. I watched Kyle banter with his students in his quirky way, and more than anything, I wanted to reach for him.

19

"You like this guy." David had been planking for what felt like a ridiculous amount of time. I was sweating just watching him.

"What makes you think that?" I asked, putting away the containers of enchiladas, twice-baked potatoes, and everything he would need for a killer steak sandwich in the refrigerator. And cookies. There were always cookies.

"You want me to meet him. When have I ever met one of your dudes?"

"There haven't been that many dudes since I've known you, David. Just Bentley Preston, really, and I wasn't exactly going to bring him over here."

"You took him to the freaking Celtics game, Dev. Courtesy of me."

"I just said two tickets! I didn't tell you who I was bringing. And we were sort of disguised. Those were terrible tickets, by the way."

"You said you wanted something out of the way, lady. So, that's what I gave you. Obstructed view," he drawled in his southern accent. "Besides, he had to show an ID with you when you picked up the tickets. I have my ways. I asked who you brought."

I had to laugh. "You went all FBI on me? Why'd you want to know so badly who I was bringing?"

"Okay, Dev, you ask for tickets somewhere kinda hidden. That is not normal. Even this hermit of a basketball boy knows that," he said, shifting into downward dog. "I've taken up yoga, baby! It's changed my life."

Yoga might be a good idea for him, I thought to myself as I pulled together the ingredients for a smoothie. I had started doing this on my weekly visits, and he slurped it right down without saying a word. I knew his mother was entrusting him to me, and I felt almost maternal toward him. Or perhaps like an overprotective older sister. "Yoga can be very grounding, or so I hear," I said. "I've never had enough patience for it, but maybe I'll try again."

"Bring ambulance boy down here for some yoga," he said, pulling back into child's pose. "You still haven't answered my question about Rich Man Preston, but I'll move on."

I rolled my eyes, knowing that David probably had as much disposable income as Bentley did.

"Why should I meet this guy? The candy one?"

"Heath? Tam thinks you are a good judge of who is a match for me."

"Ha!" he said, standing up and taking the smoothie out of my hand. "That's funny. I've never met her, but I watch her on TV. Tamara Sparks is one interesting lady." He took a big glug from the glass. "But maybe she's right. Maybe, just maybe, I see things from a different perspective. Like, I know you in a unique way. And I'll be more objective."

"She said something along those lines."

"But here's my question, Dev," he said, putting the glass down on an end table and sliding down into the cobra position. "Why all these opinions? Why don't you just go out with him and see where it goes? Something's holding you back."

"You know, David, if you were this open and talkative with the press, they'd say much nicer things about you." It was true; they only labeled him as a sullen and standoffish individual, and with good reason, considering how he acted toward them. Hardly anyone saw the David I knew.

"You're avoiding the question again, Dev. What's going on?" He sat cross-legged, which made me smile as I watched him contort his very long legs into a seated position favored by preschoolers.

I sighed. He probably needed to know the whole story. "There's a teacher at the school," I began.

"I knew it!" he exclaimed, throwing his hands up in the air. "I knew there was more to this story!"

"He's also a soccer coach—was a soccer player when I first met him in college. I'm not sure what your thoughts are on soccer."

"Soccer is a respectable sport," he replied. "What position did he play?"

"Goalie."

"That's cerebral, ya know?" he posed, tapping the side of his head. "So, he's a thinker. Probably smart."

"Very smart. Could tell you anything you ever wanted to know about any president. He also talks a ridiculous amount. It can be exhausting—charming, but exhausting."

"Well, I can't relate to that because, as you know, I don't say much. Only to you." I rolled my eyes and laughed. "But you knew him in college? Don't take this the wrong way—because you're not old at all—but that's a long time ago."

"Yeah, I know, I know," I said. "We had a one-night *encounter*—if you know what I mean. But after we had talked for like a million hours. It was almost like one of those pods on *Love is Blind*, where they spend forever talking to each other." He nodded; I knew that David secretly loved watching dating shows on TV even though he never dated anyone. "And then we both left the next morning, me for DC, him for London. And we never saw each other again, not until this fall."

"And how was that? Did you hop right back in the sack again?"

I swatted his arm. "No, no, we did not. We talked about everything that happened and slowly got to know each other again. Hung out as friends. It was really nice, actually. He's a good guy to hang out with—an interesting person who sincerely cares about me. He's divorced with an amazing ten-year-old daughter, so he's got some past stuff going on. And it's more than that. He ditched me once before, so many years ago, as you pointed out. I tried to get in touch with him when he was in London, but he got involved with someone there almost immediately. So that's always in the back of my mind, sort of a trust issue. But he's a great guy."

"So, why don't you just go out with him? Sounds like you enjoy his company and all that. The London stuff was forever ago. Hell, I was only nine if it was fifteen years ago!"

I looked at the extremely tall adult basketball player sitting before me and imagined him as a nine-year-old shooting hoops in his Georgia driveway. "You're right. It *was* a long time ago. And if I hadn't met Heath, you and I may be having a very different conversation right now."

"You want me to meet Heath and tell you what I think."

"Yes, David. I do."

"And do I get to meet soccer boy, too?"

"Let's focus on the paramedic for now."

•   •   •

"Professor Plum, I presume?" I extended my hand to the tall man in wire-rimmed glasses standing in front of me.

"I aspire to look like Christopher Lloyd circa 1985," he responded, shaking my hand.

"He's seen the movie?" I asked Tam as he and Heath introduced themselves.

"My complete indoctrination of him into all things eighties and nineties movies is almost complete. We watched *Clue* last month," she said. "Heath?"

"Yeah, nice to meet you," he said with his warm, easy manner, and I couldn't help but smile at the handsome specimen of a man I had brought with me to dinner in Newburyport. Since my strange but thought-provoking conversation with David a few days earlier, I still didn't know what to think, but I had decided not to stress about it for the time being. Heath was fun to hang out with and even better to look at, so I tried not to put too much pressure on myself.

"It's very nice to meet you," said Tam. "Shall we sit?"

Agave was a good spot for us to gather, as I always found that tacos were common ground for many people. You could usually find a variety to meet your personal tastes and dietary needs. Tam was a vegetarian and had suggested it both for the food and the midpoint location for us to meet, and I loved the idea of something not too stuffy. Tacos it was.

"So, Professor Plum, or Ellis, I should say, what do you teach?" I asked as we settled into our table.

"I'm in the history department. My area of focus is the twentieth-century American presidency."

All I could think of was Kyle and how much he would enjoy this. Instead, I was sitting next to someone who did amazing things all day—he saved people's lives, for God's sake—but he probably would not have as much to talk to a history professor about. I felt an uneasiness that I quickly tried to shake off. "Very cool," I said.

"I don't know how cool it is. Some people think history is super boring. I try to convince them otherwise, but I'm not sure how good of a job I do at it."

"I heard a really good story once about Calvin Coolidge's pets," I said. "That people kept sending him random animals. Like a bear, a bobcat, some lion cubs."

"He and his wife kept the raccoon!" Ellis exclaimed, obviously glad someone seemed interested in what he loved.

"That's right. The raccoon was named Rebecca."

Tam shook her head and took a sip from her margarita. "How on earth did you know all this?" she asked me.

"I have a friend at Rockwood who teaches history," I said flatly, trying not to give anything away, even though I knew Tam saw right through me.

She made a face and shifted her attention toward Heath. "So, Heath. Can you tell us a good paramedic story? I'm sure a lot is confidential, but there's got to be something you can share."

Heath took a swig of his Dos Equis. "Oh, yeah, how's this one? We get a call that a twenty-eight-year-old female named Trixie is about to give birth in the kitchen of her house. We race over there, and it's a chocolate lab. We end up assisting with a litter of six puppies."

"Twenty-eight-years-old?" Ellis asks.

"In dog years," Heath answers. "She was really four."

"That's amazing," said Tam. "Were the dogs okay?"

"They were adorable," he said. "Let me find a picture." He scrolled through his phone for a moment and then showed us a few photos of firefighters and paramedics with cute little puppies. "This is when we went back to visit them a few weeks later. Two of them were adopted by firefighters." I watched Tam's heart melt into a puddle at images of good-looking men and little fur babies.

"Exactly my point," said Ellis with a chuckle. "History professor telling Calvin Coolidge stories versus hunky emergency responders cradling adorable puppies. I'm boring."

Heath reached across the table to fist-bump Ellis. "Thanks for the compliment, bro," he said, and everyone laughed.

After we had finished eating, Tam and I retreated to the bathroom; I was dying to hear her thoughts on the evening.

"I really like him," she said from the next stall over. "He's so cute and has a sweet way about him. He looks at you with a mix of admiration and awe. It's refreshing to see a man so smitten."

"Professor Plum seems to like him, too. And I'm a fan, by the way. This is a good match for you. I mean, anyone who can get you to stop discarding men the way I go through bags of chocolate chips in the dining hall kitchen..."

"Noted," she said while washing her hands at the sink. "But we're focusing on you right now since it seems to be urgent. I agree; Plum loves him. I think they really are going to a hockey game together, and Ellis doesn't even like sports that much."

"But," I began, not finishing my thought as I took out lipstick from my purse.

She sighed. "So, back to my weird, *You've Got Mail* and *Sleepless in Seattle* analogies because I can't give those up. You're right. He's not a Frank. Definitely more of a Walter," she said, referring once again to Meg Ryan's love interest played by Bill Pullman.

"He luckily doesn't sleep with a big noisy humidifier on the nightstand."

"It's not technically winter yet. You never know." She applied lip gloss and then turned to me. "You're not in love with him, Devon. Professor Plum might be, but I don't think you are."

"We just started dating a few weeks ago. It's very early. How long did it take you to know Plum was the one?"

Tam opened the door to the restaurant. "I went back to my old apartment in the Seaport after our date and couldn't sleep, so I watched *Love Actually*."

"One of your favorites. Even if it's from the early 2000s."

"I do prefer the eighties and nineties. But I got such Jamie vibes from Ellis."

"Colin Firth's character. The author. I love it when his pages end up in the pond. Who would let that happen? But so charming."

"Yes. Then, I started craving every scene in all my movies where the characters realize they need to be together. So, I got onto YouTube and watched them all. *When Harry Met Sally*, *Notting Hill*, *While You Were Sleeping*, you name it. I still couldn't sleep. By then, it was four in the morning."

We stood by the front door to the restaurant and saw the men waiting for us outside on the sidewalk. "What did you do then?" I asked.

"I had been searching high and low for the perfect romantic moments when I realized I could live my own. Finally. So, I took a shower and figured out where he lived and bought sticky buns from Flour."

"Those are incredible." My mouth watered at the thought of the Boston-area bakery favorite.

"They are. And I got on the red line and took it to Porter Square and walked through the rain for like five blocks. I pressed the buzzer, and luckily, he was home."

"Probably because it was like six in the morning."

"Seven. Flour in Beacon Hill didn't open until six-thirty."

"Okay, continue."

"And I met him outside his apartment, soaking wet. Because my life has become a rom-com. And I said, 'I thought you might want breakfast.'"

I clutched my chest, somewhat joking but also loving this story. "I'm guessing that was it for both of you. Because this is, indeed, a rom-com."

"We've spent every night together since."

We opened the door and said our goodbyes, with Heath and Ellis promising to be in touch about future plans. And then Heath took my hand, and we silently walked to his truck. As I opened the door, I could have sworn I saw the flash of a camera.

20

"What do you know about *The Underground Stallion*?" I asked Adrienne as we assembled the pans of spinach gratin before their trip into the oven. I had planned a steakhouse night with a wide assortment of savory vegetarian side dishes. The captain of the boys' hockey team had approached me with a sincere request for more steak, and I was finally starting to feel like I was connecting better with the students. I wanted to make it a good dinner in hopes of hearing more such wishes. The longer I cooked for other people, the more I realized the importance of food as a connecting point, and I knew that things like this were going to make all the difference in my relationship with Rockwood. I was trying.

"It's a secret newspaper," she replied with a shrug. "I know there are kids involved in it, but I'm not sure who they are or what their aim is. Maybe they're just disruptors? Our regular newspaper is almost nonexistent, so they get to dominate the scene. I'm just happy they've left me alone so far." She sprinkled a mix of gruyère and parmesan on top of her pan full of spinach, cream, onions, and more cheese. "Why do you ask?"

"Come on, I know you've seen their issues. I am often the focus." I opened the ovens, and we loaded our creations inside. "I can't go anywhere without someone scurrying behind a tree or snapping a picture. It's creepy and unnerving. Are things so boring here that they feel compelled to spend their time stalking me? Notice they didn't run anything on Midsy. I bet they were all involved in it."

"Possibly," she said, washing her hands. "Or else they're just scared of the pranksters. Ashlyn and her crew are pretty powerful on this campus. I avoid them at all costs."

"I always assumed Ashlyn was in charge or at least involved with the paper," I said. I noticed Marnie in the far corner of the kitchen, clearly eavesdropping as she began to peel potatoes. "Hey, Marnie! There's more heavy cream over here if you need it once you get to that point."

"Sounds good," she said in her typically flat tone.

I gave Adrienne a small smile, and her eyes lit up in recognition. I knew she thought Marnie was a bit strange; most people did. "Anyway, I'm trying not to let them get to me, but having your adult social life be the central feature of a student newspaper is weird. Given everything you know about me already, I'm sure it's not improving your opinion of me," I said quietly in hopes Marnie didn't hear, but I had to say it. Part of me worried that Adrienne thought I was just an old tramp. I knew she was enjoying her kitchen internship with me, and I wasn't sure why I cared so much about what she thought, but I did.

She sighed. "It's fine. I honestly keep forgetting about you and my dad. Or maybe I just compartmentalize it. Does that make any sense to you?"

Despite some of her past decisions, Adrienne was very mature—perhaps more mature than most adults I knew. "It does. I'm glad you feel that way."

Adrienne's phone buzzed, and she paused to look at it. "My roommate. She said my mom's outside by the sculpture screaming at Ward Connelly. A crowd is gathering." She stuffed her phone in her pocket. "Why is my family such a sideshow?" she posed while slinging her backpack over her shoulder. "I gotta go."

"I'm coming with you," I said and ran after her. As much as I didn't want to deal with Julianna, Adrienne shouldn't have to face this situation—whatever it was—alone. It wasn't until we were outside the dining hall that I realized we both still had our aprons on.

We heard Julianna Preston long before we saw her. Words like "charlatan," "huckster," "grifter," "scammer," "cheater," and perhaps most damning, "terrible lover" were thrown around while Ward Connelly stood before her with his arms crossed, wearing a huge purple cape and an eye patch, his gray hair tied back into a low ponytail. It was early December and long past Halloween; this was just another day in Connelly's clothing choices. Julianna looked like she had come straight from the Pilates studio, wearing probably at least five hundred dollars in high-end workout gear. *What on earth is so urgent that it brought her an hour up to Rockwood in such a frenzied state?*

"Are you done?" he asked in a gruff voice. "You're making a fool out of yourself, Julianna. All these people. Your daughter now, too," he said, gesturing toward Adrienne who was standing next to me, both of us spattered with flour from the roux we made.

"*My* daughter?" she demanded, throwing her hands into the air. "Take a little responsibility, Ward Connelly. Besides just throwing your money and influence around. Have you even *talked* to Adrienne?"

Adrienne looked mortified, her eyes growing bigger by the second. "Stop, Mom! This is ridiculous. Take your lovers' spat off my campus."

"Not anymore!" Julianna proclaimed, and the crowd that had gathered darted their eyes back and forth between her and Adrienne. "Now that he's taken up with *kitchen staff*!"

Everyone immediately turned to me. "Not me!" I shouted. "Definitely not." *Yuck*.

"Thank God," muttered Adrienne. "Please, Mom, let me live my life. If you have problems with people, please don't be so fucking public."

"I'm leaving," Julianna announced. "I'll see you at Christmas, Adrienne." Everyone watched in silence as she stormed off and got into her Mercedes.

Ward turned to the audience. "I trust you all will have a pleasant evening," he announced to the small crowd that had gathered. He then climbed up a scaffold to a small landing, where he started adjusting what appeared to be a security camera on the trunk of a tree.

I patted Adrienne on the back a couple of times. "I'm really sorry that just happened."

She shrugged. "The price I pay for a dysfunctional family. Thanks for being here. I'm going back to my dorm now. I want to change clothes before my delicious steak dinner tonight."

"Sounds good," I said. "I'm going to head back there and make some sautéed mushrooms. What do you think about those?"

"I like them with thyme," she said, somewhat shyly.

"Thyme it is," I said. "Excellent suggestion."

As we were about to leave, a woman ran by us and started climbing up the scaffolding. When she got to the top, Ward turned and faced her, and they embraced and began passionately kissing. She had a wool cap on that covered her hair and a big winter coat, which disguised her appearance. Hanging out the bottom of her coat, however, was a white apron string.

Adrienne and I looked at each, wide-eyed, and both mouthed "no!" at the same time.

•   •   •

"Let me get this straight," said Heath, sitting in the passenger seat of my Jeep. "Marnie works with you in the kitchen. She was the temporary head of dining until you got there."

"Yes," I answered as we drove up the Maine Turnpike. I had just told Heath the story of the scene that took place at The Stallion the previous afternoon, which would confuse the hell out of anyone who didn't know these people. I knew all of them and was still perplexed by what I witnessed.

"And she's a weirdo."

"Definitely a strange person. Not much personality from what I've seen, and I've worked with her almost every day for over three months now. She also enjoys serving food in cardboard boxes, but that's a whole different story."

"And she's also a bartender?"

"At The Barnacle, which is the secret campus bar under the dining hall kitchen. No one told me about it until I had been working above it for about a month. Did you know there was a speakeasy at Rockwood?"

"No clue, but maybe some of the old timers know. I'll have to ask around."

"My guess is that's how she met Connelly. I had a meeting with him there before the unveiling of the sculpture. I get the impression he goes there a lot. But it's a strange pairing, especially since he's obviously had something going for years with Julianna Preston."

"And she's a lot different from Marnie?"

I laughed, imagining Marnie going to one of the elite fundraisers or charity balls Julianna and Bentley frequented. "Night and day. Julianna barely eats. By the end of my time there, she only wanted vegetable broth. Marnie eats a ham and cheese sandwich that she dips in a cup of mayonnaise for an afternoon snack. A snack, mind you. In between her lunch and dinner."

Heath shuddered. "I can't stand mayo."

"Ehh, I see it as a necessary ingredient in certain recipes, but I could never eat it straight up the way she does. But noted. I won't make you anything mayo-centric."

"Awesome," he said, giving me a quick kiss on the cheek, which made me smile. Heath was so sweet, and I really did enjoy hanging out with him. As I had tried to explain to Tam on the phone the night before, I had started to realize some of my issues with relationships.

"I don't trust myself when it comes to men," I had explained to her. "I tend to make terrible decisions."

"Things change, times change, circumstances change," she said. "So many people believe in you, Dev. You need to believe in yourself."

Which is why I proceeded with my promise to introduce Heath to my parents, despite my deep reservations about Tam's plan for me.

"You're bringing who? Are you engaged, Devon?" my mom had asked on the phone the night before.

"No, Mom, I just started dating him not too long ago and thought you should meet him. I'll bring you dinner."

"Nothing fancy," she said. Of course she did.

Heath seemed to be trying to put all the information together. "So, you think Julianna somehow found out about Marnie and Connelly, and that's why she drove up to campus and made a scene?"

"That's the most I can determine," I conceded. "Adrienne knew nothing and was as shocked as I was. Ward still hasn't talked to her, even though it seems to be well-established now that he's her father and is paying for her to be there. Or at least got her admitted despite her track record at other schools. I feel bad for her. She has a tough situation despite all her money."

"It sounds like she enjoys hanging out with you," he said. "Whoa, that house is killer."

"I think she likes learning how to cook. She is seriously considering a culinary college program, like Johnson and Wales. Which will not go over well with her parents."

"Some of us didn't even go to college," he said, patting my knee.

"And that's totally fine," I said. "Okay, I know you see some amazing houses. I will warn you that the house we are going to does not look like any of them. It's tiny."

"All good, Devon. I'm just happy to spend the day with you."

We pulled up to the corner lot where I grew up. The little yellow house hadn't changed since I had been there last, which was close to a year ago, with the exception of a bit more peeling paint. My dad's gardens were trimmed back for the winter, and part of me wished I was bringing Heath there in the summer when they were brimming with flowers and tomatoes and green beans and butterflies. Instead, the sky was cold and gray, with snow in the forecast within the next week.

My dad ventured out of the house onto the front step with his cane, waving with his free hand. "He's a good man," I told Heath. "I wish he had more of a life. But he loves his history documentaries. And his garden in the summer. Best tomatoes ever. I should've come up here and grabbed some to make sauce, but this summer was chaotic." I was rambling and avoiding what was ahead.

"It's okay, Devon," he said. "Don't be nervous. They're your parents."

"It's just a whole dynamic," I explained and sighed. "You'll see." I grabbed the cooler from the backseat. "Okay, let's go."

"Hi, Dad," I said, giving him a gentle hug. "This is Heath. Heath Davis."

My dad extended his hand to shake. "Billy Paige. I hear you're a paramedic. I've certainly had my share of ambulance rides. You are good people."

"Thank you, sir," said Heath, doing all the right things. This was the easy part; my dad was mild-mannered and agreeable. Nothing like the tropical storm that was waiting for us inside.

"Shall we?" asked my dad as we ventured into the house, which was really just a room with a small living area that blended right into the kitchen, with two bedrooms and a bathroom upstairs. I wondered if my bedroom had changed at all. My mother was always threatening to do something different with it, and I continued to tell her to go ahead and do whatever. She never actually followed through with any of it.

"Hi, Mom," I said, unloading the cooler almost immediately. It was always good to have a task, something to do to keep me occupied and not standing there idle. The downtime was when we tended to argue about the stupidest things.

"What's in there?" she asked, not saying hello or introducing herself to Heath.

"Chicken pot pie. I know you like it." I went through my recipes to find the most classic New England winter dishes I could. *Nothing fancy*, she had told me.

She caught my eye. "I like the frozen one I buy at Hannaford." She knew exactly how to antagonize me.

"Well, maybe you'll like this one, too," I replied, determined not to let her get to me that afternoon. "Mom, this is Heath Davis. Heath, meet Camille Paige."

"Ma'am, so nice to meet you," he said, shaking her hand.

"Aren't you handsome?" she asked, and I groaned audibly. "Well, he is. I don't think anyone can argue with that. He must know he's handsome. Don't you, honey?"

"Um, thank you for having us over," he said, looking at me with wide eyes. I silently conveyed the message *I told you so* with my expression back to him.

"Devon brought the food," she said. "Always so fancy, this one. I bet she added all kinds of herbs and wine to it."

I had. "It'll be fine," I said. "Let's turn on the oven so we can heat it up." I didn't want to spend any more time there than I needed to.

"Whiskey sours?" my dad asked. He had already taken out the well-bourbon he used and the bottled sour mix. I had tried bringing the good stuff with me one time years ago, and it wasn't particularly well-received. My dad was polite about it, but he liked what he liked. I could imbibe some neon yellow mixer every now and then for the good of the relationship.

"Of course," I answered. "Heath?"

"Yes, absolutely." I'm sure he could have used twelve drinks, given the situation I had brought him into.

When we eventually sat down to eat, Mom launched right in. "When Devon said she was bringing someone to meet us, we assumed she was engaged," she said, taking a forkful of chicken pot pie and examining it.

"*You* thought that," Dad said, shaking his head. "I was just glad to spend time with you and to meet your friend." It was about the most he would ever push back on her, but I was grateful for whatever I could get.

"Anyway," I said, taking a sip of water. "Heath and I have been spending time together for the past six weeks or so. We're still getting to know each other. We met at Rockwood when a soccer player passed out in the dining hall due to dehydration."

"Isn't Kyle the soccer coach?" asked my dad, draining the last sips of his third whiskey sour.

"They know Kyle?" asked Heath with a nervous tremble in his voice. Heath didn't know much about the Kyle situation—only the most basic details—but my parents knowing him would add another dimension and more depth to everything between him and me.

"My dad cleaned up the library with him after Midsy last weekend. They met then. Remember I told you how they came down to work that day?" I tried to keep everything nonchalant and low-key.

"That's right," Heath said.

"Yes, Dad, Kyle is the soccer coach. Anyway, I rode in the ambulance with Jamie, the boy who needed to get checked out at the hospital. And Heath, of course. He ended up driving me back to Rockwood. We went out for the first time soon after that." I took another bite of my creation. Despite my mother's criticisms, it was delicious.

"This needs salt," Mom said, shaking an excessive amount across her plate.

"Dad, what do you think?" I asked, ignoring her.

"I love this crust," he said. "So different from what I'm used to."

I smiled, and I felt Heath's foot tap mine under the table. "It's the same pie crust I use for lots of things. Let me know if you want a fruit pie next time."

"It's not really pie season anymore, Devon," my mother said, now gobbling up her sodium-enriched dinner.

"Apple pie tastes good any time of year," I said, rolling my eyes. "I'm making about twenty of them this week."

We only lasted another forty-five minutes when I fibbed and told my parents I had to return to campus for a meeting with the kitchen staff in preparation for the week ahead. We said our goodbyes, and I could've sworn my mother patted Heath's backside on our way out of the house.

"I'm so sorry," I said to him once we started driving.

"Why are you sorry?" he asked. "You warned me about everything. Your dad is very nice. Your mother is a handful and should appreciate you more. It is what it is. Don't be so tough on yourself, Devon. I'm glad I got to meet them."

"You're a very good person, Heath," I said. He was. I wasn't sure if having him meet my parents changed anything about how I felt about Heath, except it cemented in my mind that fact even more than it already was: from everything I had seen up to that point, Heath was a good guy.

I dropped him off at his apartment and headed back to Rockwood. Sitting in the parking lot outside Wentworth, I pulled up my email on my phone. There was one waiting for me from my dad.

Thanks for coming by today. Loved the pot pie.
He's not the one for you.
Love, Dad
P.S. Mom liked him.

I wasn't sure whether to laugh or cry, so I did both.

21

"What are you making?"

I was layering flat noodles, marinara sauce, and a blend of cheeses and herbs into large pans for the dinner service that night. "Lasagna," I replied to Ashlyn Lark, whom I had never spotted in the kitchen of the dining hall before. Since the Midsy incident and her pending disciplinary hearing, I had barely seen her anywhere. "Can I help you with anything, Ashlyn?"

"Not really," she said, opening the refrigerator and snooping around. I decided to ignore her unless her actions became too egregious, even though I wanted to pull her out of my workplace by the ponytail. "I know you told my aunt that she should kick me out." I didn't answer her and continued with my lasagna assembly. "I also know what happened between you and Mr. Holling."

I put my wooden spoon down on the counter so that I wouldn't be tempted to throw it at her. Or smack her with it. "What are you talking about?"

She smiled, almost in a sneer. "That you had some kind of fling in college. And then he went to London and didn't come back. Because he met someone there; she must have been quite the catch not to come back to you," she said, her voice dripping in sarcasm with the last sentence.

I took a breath and paused. "How would you know anything about any of this?"

"People talk to me. Must be my magnetic personality."

I couldn't contain my rage any longer. Every single mean girl who had ever made fun of my house, my mother, or anything else about me in high school was standing in front of me, and my anger had bubbled to the surface and was about to boil over. "Maybe it's because you scare the shit out of them, you little bitch. I hope that you *do* get kicked out of here. It would be a much happier campus."

Unfazed, Ashlyn laughed. "Has someone told you that you're not supposed to talk to teenagers that way? If not, it's kind of a thing." She whipped out her cell phone and flashed it in my face. "Got exactly what I needed. A lot easier than I anticipated. Thanks, *Devon*."

The familiarity with which she said my name bristled me like nothing else I could imagine. I also knew I would not skate through this one easily if I didn't do something immediately. I snagged her phone out of her hand and dropped it into the bubbling pot of sauce on the stove.

"What the fuck?!" she shrieked, and I couldn't help but laugh. I knew my actions wouldn't do me any favors, but it was still better than a recording of me calling the niece of the Head of School a bitch.

"You would've done the same thing," I said, taking care to slowly stir the sauce with my wooden spoon, clanking the phone around in the stockpot. I knew I couldn't use the sauce anymore since it was contaminated, but I had plenty of backup Rao's marinara in the pantry.

"True," she conceded, and we both stood in silence for at least twenty seconds. "I need to go to the Apple Store to get a new phone, I guess."

"I think Manchester's the closest. Mall of New Hampshire."

"Okay," she said. I couldn't believe I had defeated Ashlyn Lark, at least for the moment. She turned toward the door and started walking away.

"One quick question," I said, and she stopped.

"Yeah?"

"Do you run *The Underground Stallion*?" I figured I had nothing to lose by asking the question that had stumped me ever since I got to Rockwood.

"I'm not even involved," she scowled. "Takes too much time. I have better things to do."

"Who is, then?"

"It shouldn't really surprise you," she said, leaving the kitchen. Ashlyn owed me nothing, and I didn't blame her for not telling me. The sauce sputtered and hit me in the nose as if her phone still had something to say.

•   •   •

"What's he like?" Heath asked as we drove into the Seaport.

"Quiet. Moody. But with me, he's kinda goofy. High-fives me a lot. He reminds me of some of the Rockwood kids. Acts really young compared to the other Celtics, even the ones who are younger than him."

"Yeah, a lot of those guys have kids and stuff."

"Exactly. David is such an introvert, but with his mom or with me, he's just a kid. Even with his trainer or the housekeeper, he doesn't say much. Once they're out of earshot, it's a different story." I sighed, pulling up to the valet. "I hope one of these days he'll break out of his shell."

"He's such a good player. I used to watch him when he played for Villanova."

"He is. I just think if he had more confidence, he could be incredible."

We carried the coolers to the front desk, where Heath presented his driver's license and got a visitor's badge before heading with me to the elevator. "How did you end up working for him?" he asked as I pushed the button for the penthouse.

"His mom is a big-deal doctor in Atlanta. She was in Boston for a conference, and he had just moved here to start playing for the Celtics. I guess he was a mess, and she was trying to figure out how to make it all better. You know, what *good* moms do."

Heath laughed at my less-than-subtle dig at my own mother.

"One of the doctors she knew who lived here was a new client of mine. They made the connection, and here we are. The Boston doctor dropped me when my scandal hit, along with everyone except for David and his mom. He's my last client."

"Besides the four hundred students of Rockwood."

"And their teachers. And anyone else who stops by," I said, thinking of Ashlyn's phone. I had finally dug it out of the pot with some tongs, and luckily, it was dead as a doornail. I hadn't heard from Andrea about it yet, but I did jump a bit every time I felt my phone buzz in my pocket.

"Okay," I said to Heath as we stood outside of David's door. "You ready to meet David Anders?"

"I guess so," he said. "Although I have no idea what I'm doing here."

"It's the boyfriend tour," I said. "Everyone has to meet David."

"All the boyfriends, huh?" he asked. He leaned down and kissed me softly, and I breathed in. He always smelled good, like a pine-scented deodorant or some other basic man product. "Is that what I am now? Because we hadn't really talked about it."

I dropped my cooler bag next to me and looped my hands onto the belt that encircled the waist of his jeans. He *was* sexy. "Would you like to be my boyfriend?" I asked as I felt his mouth on the edge of my jaw, making its way to my neck. My mind flashed to Kyle making that exact move in that dorm bed over fifteen years earlier, and I wanted to wipe my memory clean. I wanted to be in the moment, to be present with Heath. I fought through it and made myself turn my face until my lips found his. Our kiss deepened until the door opened, and David stood before us, all six foot seven of him, making even Heath seem small.

"What the hell, Dev?" he asked. "Save it for later."

"Hi, David," I said, extricating myself from Heath. "This is Heath Davis. Heath, David Anders."

"Davis, David," said David, whooping a laugh. "How ya doing?" he asked, shaking Heath's hand.

"Good to meet you," said Heath. "Nice game last night."

"Wish Coach would've left me in," David lamented, crashing backward into his couch and absentmindedly picking up a PlayStation controller. "I bet I could've had twenty easy."

"You got ten," I said, unloading the coolers and showing Heath where to put everything. "Good to get into double digits consistently again."

"I just know I can do so much better," he said, furiously playing a soccer game on the enormous flatscreen in front of him. "All that soccer talk last time you were here got me thinking I needed to try FIFA. Turns out I'm better at this than playing the thing I'm actually paid to do in person every day."

"Dude, anyone can play a video game," I said, throwing his smoothie ingredients into the blender and trying to ignore the soccer reference. The last thing I needed was for Heath to know that David and I had discussed Kyle when I had been there the previous week. "Do you realize how lucky you are to have these gifts? And do I have to tell you this every time I see you?"

"Probably," he said with a sly smile. He turned to Heath briefly and then redirected his attention to the screen. "I just like the attention."

"Anyway," I said, handing him the drink. "Think about what you want to eat next week in LA. You know I can't pull off the enchiladas there."

"The struggle is real," he replied, still maneuvering a soccer player on the field. "Didn't you do a steak wrap one time? Where were we? Phoenix?"

"I think that was Houston. But yes, that wasn't too hard. Okay, I'll plan for that. I'll get the usual road stuff for LA. And your mom is meeting you in Denver. I only can manage to do this occasionally."

"I wish it was all the time," he muttered. "Why don't you leave the school and come back to Boston, Dev? I could probably get you some other Celtics to cook for."

"You'd have to talk to them first, David," I said, rolling my eyes while I washed the blender.

"I talk to them!" he announced across the room. "I just don't hang out with them and go to Contessa and shit."

"Contessa's good, dude. You should go out with them for dinner here and there."

"I've got enchiladas," he grumbled. "And cookies!" He turned to Heath. "Have you had her cookies?"

"Um, I don't think so."

"You've never had one of my cookies?" I asked, dumbfounded. I hadn't given him my famous cookies. Kyle probably had eaten two hundred that fall alone.

"Nope. I think the only thing I've had that you've made is that chicken pot pie we had at your parents' house."

The whole thing felt so strange; I was a cook. It was my livelihood, the center of my life. And the guy who I sort of considered my boyfriend had barely tried anything I had created. I hadn't even *thought* of it. "Well, then, I guess you need one. Take two," I said, holding out a plate toward him and David.

"Good, huh?" asked David, his mouth full of chocolate chips.

"These are great," Heath said, clearly enjoying them.

"You should come to LA with Dev," David said, not shifting his eyes from the screen.

"Really?" Heath asked and then looked up at me. I shrugged my shoulders. I didn't know what to think.

"It would be cool," David said. "You'll get floor seats to see us play the Clippers. I'll pay for your plane ticket, too."

"Um, can you get time off from work?" I asked. Part of me wanted him to say no, and the other part of me had no idea what I wanted.

"Probably," he said. "I never take vacation."

"It'll be quick," I said. "We're only going to be gone for three days total, with the first and third days mostly for travel. And as soon as we land in LA and drop our bags at the hotel, we need to start food prep right away. And we have to stay at a hotel with a kitchen, so it's not the super posh hotel the team stays at. It's a whole thing. It's definitely not a vacation."

"I'd be with you," he said with a wink. "Plus, like David said, floor seats."

"Yes, bro," David said, high-fiving him.

"Okay, so I guess we'll see you in LA," I said, bringing the cooler bags to the door. "Heath, would you mind running down and asking the valet to get the car? I just need to work out some payment stuff with David."

"No problem," he said, standing up and shaking David's hand before grabbing the bags to bring to the Jeep. "I'll be watching you on TV until then."

"You got it. I'll try to get more than ten tomorrow night."

As soon as Heath was in the elevator, I gave David a dirty look. He pursed his lips and shook his head at me.

"Really?" First, my dad, now David.

"Nope," he said with a shrug.

"Why not?"

"I like him, Dev. He's a good guy. But no. Not for you."

"Why the hell did you invite him to go to LA with me then?"

"I just told you I like him! I wanted to give him floor seats."

"You could've done that for tomorrow night here at freaking TD Garden."

David laughed. "I guess you're right."

"Ugh!" I growled, throwing my hands up in the air before I pressed the elevator button.

22

A snowflake landed on my nose as I walked back to my apartment from the dining hall. I looked up at the gray sky and pondered how cold it was in New Hampshire and that it would be about forty degrees warmer in Los Angeles twenty-four hours from then. Not feeling motivated to pack yet, I pulled out my phone and called Tam.

"You're procrastinating about packing for your trip, aren't you?" she asked upon answering.

"How'd you guess?" A few more snowflakes filled the air. "It's snowing here."

"You don't like winter," she retorted. "Go pack your sunny California clothes. It'll be a welcome break from reality."

"I don't know about any of this, Tam." I sighed. "Where are you? You love winter. Is it snowing there?"

"Not yet. Hopefully later. I just got on the T at Charles Street. I'm heading to Professor Plum's place. I want to snuggle up by his fireplace."

"Plum has a real fireplace? He's definitely a catch."

"Wood-burning. His place is so cool," she said. "I love Porter Square."

"Am I making a big mistake, Tam?"

"Going to LA with Heath or going with him instead of Kyle?"

"Both." I could hear the rumble of the subway and knew the call might cut out soon. "What do you think?"

"Okay, I've given this some thought," she rattled off. "Maybe you're like Harry and Sally. You should rewatch that tonight for some further guidance."

"But they didn't talk after they slept together—except for that awkward dinner where they ate those big leafy salads and didn't really say anything. Kyle and I talk all the time. Except for those couple of weeks before his karaoke performance. But you know what I mean."

"You two didn't talk for over fifteen years," she responded.

"Well, this is different. Considering us, I think—"

"What, Dev? The call keeps cutting out. I just need to move in with this man and stop all this public transit back and forth. What did you say?"

I practically whispered, "I said, *considering us.*"

"So?"

"He always says that. Kyle. Or at least he did, back when we used to talk about us and what we were going to do."

"I think you know, Devon."

Kyle was walking up the path, his sweatpants jammed into L.L. Bean boots, oversized flannel shirt, no coat despite the weather, his beard overgrown, and his hair sticking up everywhere. "I gotta go, Tam," I said, ending the call.

"Hey," I said as he approached.

"Hi," he said. "Such a good dinner tonight. I loved that chicken shawarma. I can't begin to tell you how much better the food is this year. That sauce with the dill. Yum."

"I'm so glad," I said, looking at Kyle and noticing crumbs stuck on the collar of his shirt. "Have some cookies at dinner, too?" I asked, lightly brushing them off onto the sidewalk that was now frosted with snow.

"I think four or five," he said with a smile. "Oh, I've been meaning to tell you, I did a whole thing in U.S. History today about presidents and their favorite comfort foods. I figured with winter and the holidays it would break things up a bit and keep them entertained. And you're in good company. Not only does Joe Biden love ice cream, but James Madison was a big fan."

"Wasn't he tiny? I would think he was more of a veggie guy."

"A hundred pounds, but he loved the ice cream, just like you do."

"Sweet. What's the grossest thing you told the kids?"

"Oh, that's easy. Nixon. Cottage cheese and ketchup."

"You're making this up." I loved bantering with Kyle. There was always something for us to talk about.

"Not at all. Nasty, right?"

"Totally." It was getting dark, and I had an early flight with Heath out of Boston. "I better go," I said. "I'll be gone for a few days. I need to go out to LA with David."

"Clippers game. Should be good. I'll try to watch it."

"I'll be home the next night. His mom is able to meet him in Denver."

"Have fun."

"It's hectic and a lot of work and not much sleep, but getting the chance to see him play is always great," I said, shifting on my feet back and forth. I found myself looking down more than I was looking up, and I felt it. *He knew.*

"You're taking the paramedic with you, aren't you?" he asked quietly.

"I am," I replied and cleared my throat. "Okay, I really need to pack. The food should be all right with me gone. Marnie's following my menu." I started walking away, not knowing what else to say, until he interrupted me.

"You know, when I was making that CD for you in London, I put the best songs on it that we listened to that night," he said.

"It was a lot of songs," I squeaked out.

"It was. So, I had to cull it. I picked out the most fitting ones."

"Oasis. 'Don't Look Back in Anger.'"

"You knew that already. Counting Crows, too."

"Which one? We listened to a few, I think. 'Anna Begins'?"

"Definitely. And Guster. 'Rocketship.'"

I closed my eyes, feeling the nonexistent music for a moment. "2007. But those were older songs, even for then."

"It was our soundtrack."

"I need to go, Kyle," I said. I turned from him again and then turned back, giving him an awkward and unexpected hug. Even outside in the snow, there was such a difference in him compared to Heath. Heath smelled exactly like you expected him to—the pine-scented deodorant, maybe Old Spice, a touch of hair gel, some fairly neutral aftershave. Clean, manly, strong. Kyle was more of a mess. Sweat from running late to class or taking his goalie through reps at practice, coffee that he had guzzled all day and perhaps spilled on himself, cookies from the crumbs still stuck to his clothes. Cookies that I had made. "I'll see you in a few days," I grunted, pulling myself away and running back to Wentworth.

$$\bullet \quad \bullet \quad \bullet$$

The last time I traveled with anyone was in 2007 when I flew back to Boston from Washington DC with the students from my semester there. I hadn't connected particularly well with anyone from Norwell in my program and had spent much of my time shadowing event planners and cooks across the executive branch of the U.S. government. I remember sitting next to a guy on the plane who was droning on and on about how he wanted to be a lobbyist for the EPA after college, and I ended up crafting a makeshift whiskey sour with Jim Beam, two lemon wedges, and a sugar packet on the forty-five-minute flight as a coping mechanism.

Now, I found myself about to take off from Boston with Heath sitting next to me. The plane was still parked on the taxiway at Logan, but he had his earbuds in, and his eyes were already closed. It was early; he had picked me up at five in the morning for a seven-thirty departure. Still, I felt antsy; I wasn't used to anyone else accompanying me on these trips to support David. And I couldn't help but think how different it would be if Kyle was sitting next to me in row fourteen. He would likely be talking my ear off—even at this early hour—probably telling me a story about which president was the first to fly in an airplane. *I need to remember to ask him who it was*, I thought. I couldn't shake him, even as we raced down the runway and ascended into the sky. As we broke through the clouds, Heath started snoring.

"Can I get you anything to drink?" the flight attendant asked me twenty minutes later once we had reached a safe cruising altitude.

"Jim Beam, two lemon wedges, sugar packet," I recited. "I know it's early." I gestured to the snoring man next to me.

"Oh, I get it," she said. "No judgment. I have one of those at home." She swiped my credit card and handed me the ingredients for my concoction. "You think he wants anything?"

"Nah," I answered. "I bet he's okay."

Almost seven hours later, we began our descent into LAX. I had watched two movies plus a holiday cookie-baking television show through the airline's entertainment system, as well as drank two more of my weird cocktails. Heath's body shook a few times, and he opened his eyes. "Hey," he said with a yawn.

"Good afternoon," I said. "We'll be on the ground in ten minutes or so."

He smacked his lips a few times. "You got any water?"

"Here," I said, handing him a bottle from my bag. He had barely said anything at all throughout the day so far, but he was annoying the shit out of me.

"What do we do when we get there? Go to the beach?"

I tried not to roll my eyes. "I'm here for work. Plus, we're going to be in downtown LA at a Residence Inn close to where the Clippers play. Nowhere near the beach. I need to check into the hotel and check to make sure all the food is there."

"They bring you the food?" Heath picked up a magazine out of the seat pocket and began flipping through it, and I wanted to grab it out of his big hands and maybe smack him on the top of his head with it, Dorothy-on-*Golden-Girls*-style. Heath had never irritated me before. *Why now?*

"Yes, I pay the hotel staff. Really, David's mom does—and they stock the refrigerator and cabinets before I get there. Or they are supposed to. It doesn't always work out perfectly. That's why I go early enough to check, and then I can always run over to Whole Foods if necessary. David won't get in with the team until late, but the staff at his hotel knows to expect me. I drop off something in his fridge for when he gets there, and then I go back tomorrow with what he needs before the game."

"Pretty high maintenance," Heath said, putting several pieces of gum into his mouth and then chewing loudly. What *was* this? It was like I was sitting next to a stranger.

"I've been working for wealthy people for a while now," I said as evenly as I could. "I try not to judge and instead focus on doing what is needed to keep them happy."

"Like that other client you had?" he asked with a laugh, and I could not believe my ears. *Is he referring to Bentley Preston? He is!*

"That had nothing to do with money," I said, now seething. "How dare you bring him or that situation up! I don't bring up women you've dated. That tobacco-chewing waitress sounded like a real catch."

"Easy, easy," he said. "Don't get all weird on me."

"I'm anything but weird," I said, standing up after the flight attendant pressed the chime to signal it was time to deplane.

"The only reason you're here right now or going to a basketball game on the freaking floor is because of me."

He put his hand on my lower back, and I flinched. I really didn't want him touching me. "Sorry, Devon. I'm just tired. I shouldn't have said that."

"Tired? You slept for almost seven hours!" I grabbed my bag from the overhead compartment and walked down the aisle to the jet bridge, not caring if he joined me or not. Of course, he did.

Everything was ready for us at the hotel except for the tortillas for David's steak wrap. The staff shopper had left rice paper wraps like someone would use to make spring rolls. We needed to go to the store.

"Can't we just use these instead?" Heath asked, examining the package.

"They'll fall apart. David doesn't want a delicate appetizer. He wants steak and peppers and onions and provolone in a sturdy tortilla. Trust me."

"That's how it goes, right? Devon's way or no way at all, huh?" Heath was already in his swim trunks and sunglasses, and I realized he wasn't there to help me or be my partner in anything I was doing. He was taking his vacation in California, and that's how he was treating the time. I had completely overestimated him.

"I don't hop into an ambulance and tell people what to do. That's your job, and this is mine," I said. "Go to the pool. Enjoy yourself. I'm going to the grocery, and then I'm coming back and making David the late-night food he wants after a flight. And then I'm going over to the Ritz-Carlton and dropping everything off. I'll probably get something to eat for myself after that. You're welcome to go off on your own and do whatever. I don't care."

"I'm not sure who you are, but you're not the fun Devon I knew back in New Hampshire," he said, running his hand through his hair. "What's gotten into you?"

"I guess you're seeing the real me," I conceded. "Take it or leave it." He didn't say anything in response, so I grabbed my purse and the hotel key. "See you later," I said, walking out the door and heading directly to the elevator. He didn't try to stop me.

23

Hotel bars are a rare guilty pleasure for me. The last time I had ducked into one was, of course, right after Bentley and I got caught, and everything changed, but before then, I enjoyed the occasional pop into the Charles Hotel in Harvard Square or the Fairmont Copley. There is something about being somewhat anonymous in an upscale setting that has always felt exciting. When it's just me, sitting at the bar, sipping a drink, chatting a bit with the bartender or a fellow bar patron, I can be whoever I want to be. After an early morning and my disastrous day of flying and dealing with Heath, followed by preparing a meal for David to eat when he eventually got to the hotel, there was nothing I wanted more than to be whoever I felt like being perched atop a gorgeous barstool at the Ritz-Carlton.

I must have been perusing the cocktail menu for a long time because I soon felt eyes on me from behind the bar. I looked up and saw an older, gray-haired gentleman—my best guess was mid-sixties—drying a rocks glass with a bar towel and smiling gently. "What do you enjoy drinking?" he asked in a way that seemed genuine and almost loving.

Just the way he said it, I felt cared for in a way I hadn't been in so long. Tam always gave me that sense of home and understanding, but I hadn't found it in many other places. I knew it was the bartender's job, and part of working in an upscale place was talking to customers on a personal level—I had done the same thing for years in restaurants—but at that moment, he appeared in front of me like some sort of guardian angel. It overwhelmed me to the point that I fought back tears. I had no idea what had come over me.

"Um, well, this is going to sound really basic," I said, pushing the menu back toward him.

He smiled again. "I've heard everything, Devon."

Taken aback, I stared at him, searching his face for any recognition. *Who is this guy?* "How did you know my name is Devon?"

He gestured to my ID badge that was connected to a lanyard that I had tossed onto the bar counter when I sat down. I wore it whenever I did anything on the road for David. His mom had it made early in our arrangement to make me look official—and so fewer people would question a woman delivering a home fry and bacon skillet to a basketball player's hotel room for when he got off his flight. "Oh yeah. That's me." I looked back at the smiling face on the badge and barely recognized her. It felt like a lifetime since I took that picture. Way too much had happened in my life. "I love whiskey sours," I said, scrunching up my mouth in a bit of embarrassment. The cocktail menu was full of complex concoctions featuring things like green chartreuse, falernum, absinthe, and rums of various degrees of aging and levels of spice. I felt like I was ordering a fuzzy navel at Buckingham Palace or something like that.

"I got you," he said, deftly grabbing a bottle of Angel's Envy. It brought me right back to another Ritz, 3,000 miles away, when I drank a whiskey sour with the same exact liquor after Adrienne had walked in on Bentley and me. *What had I even been thinking?* Adrienne was now an important presence in my life. I hated that I had done that to her.

A few minutes later, the bartender handed me the drink. "I'm Charlie, by the way. I hope this works for you."

"My mom always said I would be Charlie if I had been a boy," I said, taking a sip. "Oh, this is really good. There's something slightly different. What'd you do?" I detected a slight variation from the flavor profile I was used to when I made them myself, even with fresh lemon juice, homemade simple syrup, and good bourbon like this.

"Two things," he said, holding up two fingers. "Meyer lemon juice, which mellows the acid a bit, and a rich demerara syrup instead of just simple. You looked like you needed something better than what you're used to."

Given everything that had happened that day, I couldn't have imagined a better choice of words. "You are correct, sir." I took another sip. "Your name's really Charlie?" I thought back to my mother crowing about sons, about how her son Charlie wouldn't have ever complained about taking out the trash and why she shouldn't have to do it after a day of disposing of other people's garbage. Maybe she was right—I probably should've just done it—but I wasn't so sure a son named Charlie would've been so eager to take out the trash, either.

"Yes, Charlie Donelan from Charlestown, Massachusetts. That's a neighborhood of Boston. Did you detect the accent?"

"You're from Boston," I said, not even asking the question. It was a statement. Because I should have just known—this was the guy I needed to talk to that night.

"Yes, I moved here two years ago when my partner Connor passed away. It was time for a change—couldn't be more different from Boston! Where do you live, Devon?"

"Up until late August, it was Boston. For thirteen years! I'm sure we crossed paths at some point. I worked in a number of restaurants for a while there. Did you bartend? And I'm sorry about your partner."

"He was sick for a long time," Charlie replied. "Thank you. Without him, Boston wasn't Boston for me anymore. I was a bartender for Barbara Lynch, Lydia Shire, Jamie Bissonnette, and many of the greats. Where were you?"

"Gosh, Minx, Bee's Knees, Cardamom. And then I was a private chef. We definitely overlapped as guests in each other's establishments, no doubt." I sighed. "And now I run dining services at a boarding school called Rockwood on St. George's Island near Portsmouth. Adjacent to New Castle if you know the area."

"We used to go to Wentworth by the Sea for our anniversary each year," Charlie said, mixing a Manhattan for an order that a waiter handed him. "Connor liked to play golf by the ocean, and I liked to drink by it."

"Perfect place to go then."

"Are you hungry, Devon? Would you like some dinner?" Once again, Charlie wasn't someone taking my order. There was a concern, an eagerness to take care of me that I couldn't put my finger on.

"Yes, actually, I've been up since four East Coast time. So, that would be like one in the morning LA time." I yawned as if by suggestion. "I know this is the Ritz, and I'm sure there are amazing things on your menu, but do you, by chance, have a burger?"

"Of course we do," he replied. "Is there anything you would like on it? Caramelized onion jam? That's my favorite."

"That would be lovely." I thought back to the morning after with Kyle over fifteen years earlier. "Could you add some bacon?"

"I think that would go so well with the jam. I'll have to try that next time. Coming right up."

Digging into the juiciest, most flavorful hamburger perhaps of my life, I realized that I couldn't remember the last time I had eaten something that I hadn't cooked or had at least been part of the production. Those tacos with Tam and Plum, maybe? But this was simple enjoyment of someone else nourishing me, and it tasted great. "Thanks so much, Charlie," I said, my mouth probably way too full to be talking in a place like the Ritz.

"So, Devon, do you mind me asking what you're in town for? You're far from New Hampshire."

"I work for a player on the Celtics in a very part-time capacity," I answered. "I typically feed him once a week, and his mom usually joins him for road games, but she has a medical conference she needs to attend. She's a doctor in Atlanta. So, I occasionally help out on the road." I realized I had probably said too much; I never knew where the line was when talking to others about David. There was something about Charlie that made me want to spill it all out and tell him every detail about my life and, even more so, for him to tell me what the hell to do about all of it.

"David Anders," Charlie replied. "I remember some buzz about his mom being at his away games from some commentators, but there was no way Anders was going to give any information about anything to the media," he said with a laugh. "I'm sure he's different in private."

"He is," I agreed. "He's a lovely person." I ate a perfectly crispy French fry and sighed. I was enjoying this food so much; maybe I was just so overtired that I was delirious, but it was good. "Do you watch a lot of basketball? You must, if know about David's surliness with reporters."

"I used to go to a lot of Celtics games at the Garden," he said. "I don't get to see them much anymore since they are rarely in town, and the tickets are always so expensive when a good team like them comes here."

"Are you going tomorrow night? Or do you have to work?" I asked, taking the last bite of the burger. It had been huge, and I ate it all.

"No, I'll probably watch it at a local bar, but I bet I'm one of the only Boston fans there," he said with a wink.

"Want to go? I can get you a ticket." David's mom always reminded me that I should let her know if I had a friend who wanted to see a game, and I rarely took her up on the offer. This would be the time to do it. Charlie was a quality human being.

"Are you sure?"

"You bet. Charlie Donelan, right? I'll send David's mom an email right now. It's late in Atlanta, or else I'd text her."

"That's so kind of you, Devon."

"You have been very good to me tonight, Charlie. I can't tell you how much it's meant to me." I examined my empty plate. "And obviously, I needed someone to take care of me. Your ticket will be at Will Call."

"Can I get you some dessert? Ice cream?"

"How'd you know?"

"A guess. Sounds like I made the right one."

I was full, but I managed to put a dent in the most gorgeous parfait I could have imagined. The layers of ice cream, sauces, and cookie crumbles were heavenly and complemented each other so well. There were no Heath bar pieces to be seen, and for once, I was grateful. I needed a break from toffee.

"I have a question for you, Charlie," I said, pushing the half-eaten parfait glass forward. I couldn't eat another spoonful. "Is fifteen years too late to rekindle a one-night stand?"

"It depends," he said, taking my glass away and, without me asking, refilling my ice water. "Are the two people involved better suited for each other now than they were then?"

I thought about the two people in 2007 who had started talking in a dinner line, both going for the same slice of watermelon. We were barely adults then, about to embark on big adventures in cities we had never visited, about to meet new people, some of whom would change the direction of our lives. Yet we ended up back in the same place, different people we had been then, but yes, perhaps better suited for each other than we once had been. And I couldn't help but ponder if, back in 2007, our trips had both been canceled at the last minute that morning when we ate bacon together. Would we have become a couple? And if we had tried to start a relationship based on walks around a pond and hours of talking and listening to Oasis and Counting Crows and Guster in a too-small bed and an initial electric physical chemistry, would it have lasted? Would it have been enough? Did we have a better shot at it now?

"We might be," I said, sliding my credit card over to him. "You helped me to answer my question."

Once I reached the hotel lobby, I realized I had left my badge on the bar. I ran back in, and it was gone. I didn't see Charlie anywhere, but there was a woman still working behind the counter. "Did you see an ID badge? I left it on the bar by accident. It says Devon Paige on it. I can show you my driver's license if you need it."

"No worries," she said, handing it to me. "Charlie told me to make sure you got it. He just left. He stayed an hour after his shift ended tonight. Such a good guy."

He stayed to talk and take care of me. There weren't many people in my life who would have done that, certainly not Heath. *Kyle would. If I needed him, Kyle would stay.*

Frustrated with being in LA with Heath but finally seeing clarity, I went back to my hotel. I had never been so grateful that David's mom always booked me the two-bedroom suite at the Residence Inn. Heath was snoring loudly from the room with the king bed in it, leaving me with the room appointed with a queen bed. *Of course.*

24

"Where'd you go last night?" asked Heath as he walked into the small kitchen area of the hotel suite.

I didn't look up, continuing to sauté peppers and onions in a pan. "I had to deliver the food to David's room and then finally got something to eat. I figured when I didn't hear from you that you were all set on your own." I finally glanced at him, and he was unshaven and disheveled, fresh out of bed. *Kyle looks like this most of the time*, I thought, but on him, it was endearing. On Heath, I found it annoying. Everything he did now was irritating to me.

"I thought you would have at least crawled into bed with me," he muttered. "That's why I chose the king bed."

"Oh," I replied, not knowing what else to say. "You were snoring pretty loudly when I got back here, so I thought it was better if we both got a decent night's sleep." Had Heath snored the one time I had slept at his apartment? Or the two times he had slept at mine? I hadn't noticed it.

"I do that when I'm overtired," he said. *He slept for an entire transcontinental flight and went to bed before I did. How could he be so exhausted? Whatever.* "What're you up to now?"

"Food for David for before the game. I need to bring this over to him this morning. And usually, he wants me to hang out for a bit before he goes over to the arena. You might want to plan to meet me at the game. I'll make sure your ticket is at Will Call."

"Still on the floor, right?" he pressed, and I tried not to roll my eyes.

"Yes, you and I will be seated together on the floor," I answered. I wished I didn't have to sit next to him, but there was nothing I could do at this point. I kept thinking back to everything Charlie had said the night before. He actually hadn't said much at all—he was just very good to me when I needed it the most—but it was the question he asked in reply to my initial question that kept coming back to me. *Are the two people involved better suited for each other now than they were then?* I looked over at Heath, who was scrounging through the groceries in the refrigerator. *I'm here with the wrong guy*, I thought.

I got ready for the game, knowing there was no way in hell I was coming back to the hotel and dealing with Heath any more than was necessary that day. As I walked across the street to the Ritz, I got a text from David's mom, alerting me that he was having a rough morning and if I could go see him soon, that would be great. I picked up the pace and made my way past the security guard whom I had met the day before. I took a deep breath and knocked on David's door.

"It's me," I announced. "Devon."

The door opened, and David was standing before me, phone pressed to his ear, tears streaming down his face. "Okay, Mom, Devon's here... Yeah, I think so... See you tomorrow night... Love you." He threw the phone on the bed, and I put down my bags so I could hug him. I felt his long, muscular arms around me and squeezed him back as tightly as a woman of average height and build could, but hugging him always felt a bit strange. He towered over me.

"What's going on?" I asked. I had experienced this with him a few other times over the years, but it was certainly stressful. I felt a huge responsibility to get him past whatever was bothering him so that he could play in the game that night. "Let's sit."

We sat down on the small couch, and I pulled a box of tissues closer. He took one and blew his nose before grabbing both sides of his head with his big hands and dropping his elbows to his knees. "I watched that show on the Sports News Now channel this morning."

"The one where they go through all the players who should be traded? David, I told you to stop watching that shit. It messes with your head every time."

"I know, I know, I can't help myself. It's there on the TV, I know it's on, and I know they're gonna talk smack about me. Why are they always talking about me?" The tears were streaming again, and I grabbed a tissue and wiped his cheeks.

"They talk about a lot of players, not just you. Who else did they mention?"

"I don't know. I shut it off once they were done, saying that I was underperforming and probably should be with a less prestigious program so I could grow as a player. What if that's true? What if I get traded? I have a hard enough time with the only team I've known since college. You know change is tough for me."

"Of course; I know that. Your mom knows that. Your agent knows that. And we'll always help you figure it out. Are you still talking to that sports psychologist?"

He pulled one of my cooler bags over to him and opened it, finding one of the steak wraps, removing the foil, and biting into it with a vengeance. "She told me I have imposter syndrome. That I'm worried I'm not as good as other players and that I think I'm a fraud."

"Sounds about right, but I've been telling you this for the whole time I've known you. Can you hand me one of those wraps? I didn't have breakfast."

"Yeah, here you go. It's good. Thanks, Dev. And yeah, I know. I probably don't need a shrink to tell me the same shit you've been telling me for years."

I took a bite. "This tastes great. Well, hopefully, she can give you better tools for getting through it. I don't know how useful I am with coping mechanisms. I just feed you things."

"Good things, Dev. I don't know what I'd do without you." He dug through the cooler and found a tumbler packed in ice. "Is this what I think it is?"

"I made sure there was a blender in my room. Enjoy your smoothie."

"You're the best," he said, taking a drink. "I think that's part of it," he said quietly. "If I get traded, say, to, like, Oklahoma City, what happens? I don't think you're going to move to the middle of the country. You've got a real job, and now you've got this ambulance dude."

I sighed. "First of all, I'm ready to kick 'ambulance dude' to the curb. He's not who I thought he was. I can't believe you got him to come out here."

"Don't blame me," he said, gently pushing my shoulder. "You could've told me no. Or brought Tam or something."

"You put me in an awkward situation," I conceded. "But I'm dealing with it. And don't worry about any of the rest of it. We'll cross those bridges when we get there. I'm not making any promises to anyone about anything work-wise right now. One day at a time. I think you should try to do the same, but what do I know? I'm not the sports psychologist."

"You're a lot smarter than her, I think," he said, polishing off his wrap. "And my guess is she can't cook for shit."

"We'll probably never know the truth where that's concerned." I stood up and opened the shades in the room, letting the LA sunshine in. "You've got a game to get ready for."

•   •   •

The arena was packed, with plenty of Boston fans in green sprinkled among the red and blue colors of Clippers supporters. I took my seat next to Heath, having waited until the last possible minute to join him. He was drinking a beer and eating a pulled pork sandwich when I arrived.

"Hey," he said. "You were right when you said you'd be busy. I thought you would just be dropping food with him and leaving. What did you do all this time?"

I left out the details about spending two hours drinking cappuccino in the lobby of the Ritz, followed by aimlessly wandering through a nearby shopping area. "There's lots of stuff for me to do pregame to help David," I lied. *Well, there were plenty of things, but it didn't take eight hours.* I wanted to get through the game and then maybe investigate changing flights and hopping on the red eye instead of going back the next day. I could easily make up an excuse for something that I suddenly needed to do the next day at Rockwood.

I scoured the area where David's mom assured me Charlie would have a seat. I spotted him sitting and watching the players warm up, sipping a beer. He saw me looking his way and waved. I waved back and smiled, forgetting for a moment that Heath was next to me.

"Who's that?" he asked, gesturing to Charlie.

"An old friend," I answered. "Looks like they're about to get underway," I said, eager to change the subject.

David was never in the starting five, so I split my time between watching the action on the court and glancing at him as he nervously waited from the bench for the coach to signal that it was time. I felt his anxiousness surge through my body, and I wondered if this was normal or even healthy. I did worry that David depended too much on me and that I took on too many of his emotions as my own, but maybe this was what family was. *Yes, David is my family now.* As an only child, I didn't know what having a sibling felt like, and perhaps this was it. I cared about his happiness as much as I worked toward my own.

He finally checked into the game. From that point, everything changed. The crowd marveled, howled, and yelped as he took control, hitting virtually every shot, getting fouled as Clippers players attempted to block his moves and steal the ball from him, failing at almost all their efforts. I marveled as the Celtics' coach beamed with excitement, watching his perhaps most misunderstood player finally break out. He subbed David out when he looked spent, soaked from head to socks in sweat, but he was eager to return to the court, and that he did. By the time the game-ending buzzer rang while David nailed his final three-pointer, he had scored fifty-eight points. The Celtics crushed their opponent by thirty.

The Boston fans in attendance erupted, and David ran off the court to where I was sitting. He scooped me off the ground and threw me over his sweaty shoulder, and I was laughing and crying with abandon, all while clinging to his jersey so I wouldn't slide off. When he finally put me back down, he grabbed me by the shoulders and yelled, "We did it, Devon!"

"You did it!" I shouted back. "David, it was all you!"

Reporters flooded the floor, with most crowding around him and a few pulling me aside. "Who are you?" one man with a microphone asked.

"I cook for him," I said simply, enjoying every minute of watching David rip out of his shell and finally open himself up to the media. He was glowing, and I still felt all his feelings. This time, though, it was pure magic.

"Oh, you're the woman who in Boston—" the reporter continued, and I knew where this was going.

"Excuse me," I said, running out of the arena through a pair of heavy doors to an empty stairwell. I pulled out my phone and called Kyle.

"Dev!" he exclaimed. "Oh my God!"

"Kyle! Did you see it?"

"It was amazing! And I saw you afterward. Everyone on the broadcast was trying to figure out who you were. Like if you were his girlfriend or something. And then—"

"Yeah, I'm sure someone knew who I was. It happened here, too. Whatever. Kyle, he finally did it! I knew he could."

"Everything's going to change now for him. I feel it."

"I feel it, too," I said, and then we were silent until a crowd of spectators opened the doors and descended onto my hiding place to rush down the stairs and out of the arena to head home or to the bars or wherever they were going. "I gotta go, Kyle!" I shouted, not sure if he could hear me over the sudden din.

"What?" he asked.

"Bye!" I stood there as people rushed past me, and I realized that I needed to keep moving so I wouldn't get trampled. I followed them down the stairs until I reached an exit and stepped outside into the warm December Southern California air. I stood in the middle of the street and took a big breath. Disappointed Clippers fans walked past me while the scattered Boston supporters fist-bumped each other and celebrated David's amazing night.

When I walked back into our hotel suite, Heath was standing on the other side of the doorway with his suitcase. "You're going home?" I asked.

"Oh yeah," he answered. "You didn't even notice me leave."

"When did you leave?"

He shook his head. "I saw you bolt out of there and go into that stairwell. I followed you, and then I saw your face. Your face said it all. I knew you were talking to Kyle."

"Heath, I don't know –"

"No worries, Devon. I got the message." He walked past me into the hallway. "Best of luck to David. He had the game of his life." And with that, he wheeled his bag toward the elevator.

I closed the door behind him and looked around. There was a bit of a mess in the kitchen, but it wasn't too bad. I had barely unpacked, so there wasn't much stuff out in the queen bedroom or adjacent bathroom. I lay down on the bed for a few minutes, staring up at the white ceiling. I thought back to my phone conversation with Kyle in the stairway and smiled. I was so glad he had watched the game and could understand everything I was so excited about. *Kyle.* I bolted up from the bed and began throwing everything into my suitcase. I dragged it into the kitchen and living area and grabbed the things I needed to bring back with me, leaving the rest. I hated not cleaning everything up, but I had to get to the airport. I fished a twenty out of my wallet, threw it on the counter, and left.

In the cab on the way to LAX, I realized there were four different airlines I could choose from, but I wanted to avoid being on a flight back to Boston with Heath. The challenge was that the four possible airlines were in four distinct terminals, so I didn't dare book anything yet. The first terminal that was a possibility was Terminal Three, so I asked the driver to drop me off there. I ran to the check-in area and spotted Heath's hoodie sweatshirt from behind at a Delta kiosk, so I dashed back outside and hopped on the first shuttle bus I saw. Then I realized it was for the rental car facility.

"Is there any way you can drop me at Terminal Four? Or Five? Or Seven? Any of them would be fine," I said to the driver.

"You forgot Six," he said gruffly. "Fine. Here's Four."

"Thank you!" I cooed as I sailed down the bus stairs and scurried into the American Airlines Terminal.

Once I was inside, I realized that I could finally just open the app on my phone and book the flight. I knew there were seats available; I had checked all that en route to the airport. Within minutes, I was booked and heading through security on my way back to what I hoped could possibly be home.

25

I couldn't text Tam because it was ridiculously late—the middle
of the night—on the East Coast. I paid for Wi-Fi on the plane but
didn't know what to do with it. I finally opened my email and
tapped out a quick note to her.

*If you didn't watch the game, I'm sure you know by now.
Amazing. I'm on the red-eye home (alone). Hope Kyle will still
want me. Feels more like Jerry Maguire than Harry and Sally.
But I'm fidgety Tom Hanks trying to get to Jonah in NY in
Sleepless in Seattle on this plane. xo me*

There wasn't anyone else I was ready to talk to about any of
it, and I had already spoken to David's mom from LAX after she
landed in Denver. I knew that I should try to sleep, but my
attempts were fruitless. I ended up watching two seasons of *The
Office*, remembering that it was one of the few shows Kyle
enjoyed. Maybe we had a little of Pam and Jim in us, too. I had
to hope for the best.

Once I landed at Logan just after eight o'clock in the morning,
I felt like I was running in slow motion. My legs couldn't possibly
get me through the terminal any faster. By the time I finally made
it to the elevator to go to the parking garage, I realized I didn't
have my car since Heath had driven me to the airport.

"That fucker!" I exclaimed as the door to the elevator opened, just in time for a family with two young children to stare back at me. "I'm so sorry," I said, holding the door open for them. "It's a guy with a car." The woman nodded in reply and shuffled her kids away from me as quickly as she could.

I would either have to rent a car that I would have to figure out how to return somewhere or take another form of transportation. I pulled up the Amtrak app and saw there was a train departing in twenty minutes that could get me to Durham on the University of New Hampshire campus. *Right near Norwell*, I thought. I dashed outside and threw myself in a cab. "North Station! Please!" I shouted at the driver, who must have had immediate regrets for letting me into his car.

I sprinted through the train station and into an Amtrak Downeaster car as the doors were about to close. The ride was over an hour long, so I walked to the café car and bought a hot coffee and a whoopie pie. I couldn't remember the last time I had eaten anything. As I devoured the cream-filled chocolate cake sandwich, my phone rang. Tam must have read my email.

"Hey," I said with a muffled voice, my mouth full of whoopie pie.

"You sound weird. Where on earth are you?"

"Eating a whoopie pie on the Amtrak Downeaster," I said, taking a sip of coffee to clear my voice a bit. "We're about to pull into Haverhill."

"Okay, weird, but I'll excuse it for now. Devon, oh my God! I feel like so much has happened since you left two days ago."

"It has," I agreed as a few new passengers boarded the train. "First of all, David was unreal. It finally happened. You can't tell anyone this, but he was an absolute mess before the game." I looked around to see if anyone was watching me, and luckily, they were either sleeping or staring at their phones with their headphones on.

"Ooh, that must have been awful. Sounds like you got him through it. You two are a good team."

"I think so. It all made me very grateful to have him in my life—if that makes any sense. He feels like family now. Like you."

"Aww, I love that. Speaking of family, I moved in with Professor Plum."

"Tam! That's the best news! I'm so happy for you. I really dig him."

"Thank God because he's here to stay. And I love your place, but the wood-burning fireplace won out."

"I get it." My condo was now empty. I had a lot to decide where that was concerned, but it could wait. I had much bigger issues to deal with. "So, about Kyle," I began.

"And Heath! Darling, you went out there with the handsome paramedic, and you came home alone? And somehow, you're now on a train? What happened?"

I sighed, looking out the window as we crossed into New Hampshire. *Soon, Kyle.* "It's a long story that involves snoring and someone who was not what he seemed, and the most wonderful bartender named Charlie, who used to live in Charlestown and who we probably got drinks from at some point but now lives in LA. But it all made me see that Kyle's the one. I just hope he still wants to be with me."

"So, you're heading there now?"

"I've got to figure out how to get from UNH to Rockwood, but yes, that's the plan."

When I got off the train in Durham, I found someone who looked like a student and might not be totally freaked by a person asking transportation questions. "Do you have any idea how I can get to Portsmouth from here?" I posed, trying to seem as normal as possible.

"There's a bus," she said, giving me the once over. Considering my lack of sleep and a recent shower, I may have looked worse than I realized.

"Awesome!" I exclaimed. "When?"

"Not till noon," she said with a shrug. Which was almost two hours away, yet it seemed like an eternity. "Sometimes Uber will do it. I usually ask a friend for a ride," she said, walking away from the unstable stranger asking strange questions.

Ask a friend for a ride. I dug out my phone and called Andrea.

•   •   •

"I can't thank you enough," I said to Andrea, closing the passenger door behind me as I settled into the front seat of her Volvo sedan.

"I needed to unload some hot gossip on someone, so your call came at a great time," she said, pulling her car away from the curb. She gave me a quick glance. "But seriously, what the hell happened to you? You look a little, well, thrown around. Like you've been on a bender or something. I saw the basketball game last night. That was some exciting shit, but it didn't end here until after midnight. I wasn't expecting to pick you up at a train station less than twelve hours later."

"Heath-the-paramedic and I are through," I said, checking myself out in the car's visor mirror. *Rough.* I threw a stick of gum in my mouth and dug through my purse for a hairbrush and some lip gloss. "It took a cross-country flight that he slept—and snored—through and very minimal interaction once we got there for me to realize that he is not the guy for me. And once that game was over, I couldn't wait to get back here." I had left out quite a bit of the story—Charlie the bartender, David's pre-game near-collapse, my post-game phone call with Kyle—but I knew who I was talking to. Anything I told Andrea could easily be repeated at The Horse later that night or to any random staffer she happened to run into walking from her house to her office.

But Andrea knew better. "You couldn't wait to get back here to Kyle, huh?"

"Time will tell," I said, dropping Visine into my bloodshot eyes. "I'm sure you'll find out."

"Likely," she said with a laugh. "All right, gossip time. Wait until you hear this one."

"Lay it on me," I said. "We have approximately twenty-five minutes until we are back on campus."

She cleared her throat and almost whispered, "I know who's behind *The Underground Stallion*."

"No way! I thought it was your niece until the other day, and I point-blank asked her. Not sure if you heard about that," I said.

"You know, I always suspected her, too. The perfect way to say eff off to your aunt, you know? Anyway, it's not her. It's a team effort. A partnership. Are you ready for this?"

"You're killing me, Andrea."

"Ryland Dennis and Marnie."

"*Marnie? My Marnie?*" My jaw was probably scraping the floorboards of Andrea's car at that point. *What the hell was Marnie doing running an underground newspaper? And with Ryland, of all people? A faculty member?*

"Well, she's sort of his Marnie, to be honest, but from everything I can tell, they're not involved sexually. I think it's more of the fucked-up kind of thing he had with Kyle's ex-wife Cora. He gets wrapped up in these weird, co-dependent, emotionally obsessed relationships. And then there's the Ward Connelly situation. That's who she's actually banging from what I can ascertain. You know about that, right?"

"I do. I spotted them making out on the scaffold. She was disguised, but we figured out who it was. How do *you* know?"

She sighed. "Julianna Preston called me one day screaming about it. I guess he's done with Julianna, at least for now, and told her that he found a woman who serves him meals in tiny, inspired, beautiful boxes."

I burst out laughing.

She nodded. "Right? You couldn't make any of this up. I should just leave Rockwood and write a damn book."

"So, it's sort of a love triangle, but not really? And why did Julianna call you? What on earth would you do about it?"

"She wanted me to fire Marnie. I'm not sure what impact that would really have. Ward has plenty of money. Marnie would be fine, provided they stayed together. I think Julianna was desperate because she was losing her sugar daddy."

I tried to process all of this. "She wanted you to fire Marnie for sleeping with her longtime lover, who is the actual father of her child, while she stays married to Bentley." I realized what I had said while thinking out loud. "Oh my God! I didn't mean to say that."

Andrea patted my knee. "You don't think I figured out the paternity of Adrienne a long time ago? Ward basically told me without telling me when he called to beg me to admit her after she got kicked out of her most recent school."

"The Walden Pond horse incident."

"Exactly. But I think she's a good kid."

"So do I," I said, smiling, thinking of my kitchen apprentice. "But that still doesn't answer the original question. Why *The Underground Stallion*? How do Marnie and Ryland benefit from any of this? And who's doing the grunt work? It's definitely not them running around snapping pictures."

Andrea groaned. "That's how I found out that they were behind it. A small group of students came to see me at my house yesterday afternoon. No one has ever shown up at my house, so I knew something strange was going on. Two of the kids were crying. Ryland has been putting pressure on these students of his to do all the investigative work. It's wrong on so many levels. They're worried they're going to get bad grades in his class if they don't comply."

"That's atrocious. Sounds like you have a human resources nightmare on your hands. I'm sorry, Andrea." I did feel bad. She had dealt with one mess after another since she became Head of School.

"It's okay," she said. "Definitely a little housekeeping in order, but we'll get through it. It's a good school. I can still say that."

"What about Marnie?"

"There will be an investigation. Obviously, Ryland's involvement is worse since these were his students. And he's just a big asshole who wanted to spy on people and make their lives miserable when it comes right down to it. Just to fuck with them, I think. But I do want to better understand Marnie's motives more than anything else. I'm not sure, however, if she is to be trusted anymore. I mean, she worked for you, but the newspaper still spent much of the fall trying to slut shame you. Sorry for the brash terminology, Devon."

"No, I agree, it was a rough way to start a new job, that's for sure." I was so tired I had no idea what to make of it. "Whatever you decide, Andrea. You're the boss."

"Yes, yes, I am," she said, pulling into Portsmouth. "Look at this, all decorated for the holidays. I've been so distracted I've barely paid any attention. It's December, for God's sake."

"Indeed, it is." I looked at the pretty shops on Market Street, all decked out in lights and bows and sparkles. "I'm so glad to be back here. Thanks for coming to get me."

"Anytime, Devon. I am very grateful to have you at Rockwood," she said, turning onto the road that would lead us to St. George's Island and Rockwood. We were quiet for that stretch of the drive, and I pressed my forehead against the window to take it all in. I noticed every tree, bush, curve of the road, and glimpse of the ocean as if I was seeing it for the first time. We passed by The Horse and onto the island, hanging a right into the campus. There, waiting for us, was Ward Connelly's infamous sculpture, *The Stallion*, now adorned with huge cutouts of Celtics shamrocks and basketballs, plus a gigantic poster with my face on it and the words, "It must have been the cookies."

"What?" I asked as Andrea slowed the car so I could see all of it. "How did this happen? There are security cameras. I'm so confused."

Andrea smiled. "I can turn off the cameras whenever I want. There was a student watch party for the game last night, and Adrienne Preston suggested we do something for your arrival home. Glad they got it done then because you're back a little earlier than we expected." She shrugged her shoulders. "Kinda feels like home now, huh?"

I nodded, taking it all in, still floored by what I was seeing. "I think so."

26

I climbed the four flights up to the top of Wentworth and tried to figure out my plan. I would quickly shower, make myself look presentable, and then track down Kyle. It was a Sunday, so unless he was in Boston visiting Annie, he would probably be in his apartment or in the library grading papers or reading. Once I found him, I wasn't exactly sure what I was going to say, but maybe I wouldn't have to say much. I might just be able to get away with kissing him, at least as a conversation starter. The very thought of Kyle's lips against mine made me happy and anxious at the same time. What if that wasn't what he wanted anymore? I hoped I wasn't too late.

I turned the key and opened my door, hearing a clang as the door hit something inside my foyer. I walked in and bent down, finding a clear square case on the floor. I picked it up and discovered it was a CD. *What is this? Could it be ... the CD?* I glanced around, not knowing what to do.

I heard knocking on the window above the fire escape. I ran into the kitchen, CD in hand, and saw Kyle perched on the landing, bundled in his down jacket and wool hat. I unlatched the window and threw it open, grabbing his hand to pull him into the kitchen. We stood in my kitchen, staring at each other, cold air billowing into the room from the outside, until I finally held up the CD and searched Kyle's face for the answer I hoped I would get.

"You know," he said. "In case you're still considering us."

"Considering us—you say that a lot," I said, swallowing hard, trying to keep my composure despite my shaking voice. "You say a lot of things a lot."

Kyle reached behind him and shut my window. Then he put both of his hands on the sides of my face and looked into my eyes while gently stroking my cheekbones with his thumbs, almost like he was checking to make sure all of this was okay. We had been through so much, and maybe now the time was right. I placed the CD case on the kitchen counter and wrapped my arms around his waist. "It's not too late for us, right?" I asked.

"It's not too late," he said, and finally, after all our mishaps and mixed connections, we kissed. It wasn't the kiss of two young adults who barely knew each other from almost sixteen years earlier or the confused kiss by the pond that had been interrupted by Ryland's students earlier in the fall. It was soft and deep and slow. It was everything I had been hoping for once I realized this was exactly what I wanted. Kyle was the one.

"I have a question," I whispered, pulling back slowly. "How did you get the CD? I thought it was in Connecticut at your parents' house."

"It was," he said, pushing me gently against the kitchen counter and sliding his hands around to my lower back. He was still wearing his jacket. I would have to do something about that. "I drove down there after I talked to you last night."

"You drove to Connecticut after midnight," I said. "Let me help you take off the jacket." I unzipped it and slid it off his shoulders.

"You can remove anything you'd like, Dev," he said. "Yes, I got there at around three-thirty in the morning. I decided not to scare the shit out of them, so I slept in my car in front of their house, which seemed like a reasonable plan at the time, until that scared the shit out of their next-door neighbor, who called the police. So, I was awoken at five by a Mystic police officer and my mother in her bathrobe."

I cracked up. "That's ridiculous."

"It was. And then I had to explain that I was there to dig through some bins for a CD and would be leaving immediately after I found it. My parents were really worried about me after Cora left, but now I think they've given up completely on any hopes for normalcy."

"And you found it."

"Normalcy? I'm working on that."

"No, I mean the CD."

"Yeah, I got scared I wouldn't, but here it is. I listened to it in the car on the way back up here. Good thing my car is old and still has a player in it."

"The Jeep still has one, too. I haven't used it in years." I picked the case up again. "I want to listen to it." Kyle kissed me again, this time with more urgency, and I felt the blood rush through my body. "We can go listen to it later in the car. Plenty of other things we can do before then," I said, feeling his body against mine.

"What do you want to do?" he murmured, and I knew what I had to say.

"I really need a shower," I said. "I'm sure I just killed the mood or something, but I have been traveling for so long. It was like something out of *Planes, Trains, and Automobiles*."

"Is that a movie? I love your movie references."

"John Candy? Steve Martin? Seriously, Kyle. It's a John Hughes film, for God's sake."

"I have a lot of movie-catching-up to do," he admitted. "Don't you have some amazing clawfoot tub in that bathroom of yours? Am I just imagining this? You know you've got the best apartment on campus."

"I do have a clawfoot tub. Are you suggesting we use it? I've never gone in there with anyone else before. You think there'll be enough room?"

"It's worth a try," he said. "It's Sunday afternoon, and we have nowhere else to be. What do you say?"

I opened the cabinet above my head. "Whiskey sours?"

"This bath is sounding better all the time."

•   •   •

A few hours later, we were in the Jeep headed west to Norwell. Neither of us had been there in years, despite Kyle living so close for so long. We needed to drive somewhere to listen to the CD, which still sounded pretty good after years of sitting in a Rubbermaid bin in the Hollings' basement.

"This is a really amazing piece of our history, despite the circumstances in which it was made," I said.

"Oh, you mean that it was abandoned because I met a British woman who turned out to be a complete waste of time, and how I should have told her I was busy and kept making the CD? And sent you the blasted thing?"

"I still don't know if our timing would've been right that fall," I said, turning into the campus. "What would it have been like for us to reunite right here in late August 2007? What do you think would've happened?"

"Oh, I have a good idea what would have happened," he said. "Something like what happened a couple of hours ago."

I laughed. "Probably. But would that have been enough in the long run? I wonder. Maybe we needed to go through all the experiences we've had to get to this point." I pulled into a visitor parking space. "And there's one very important person we're forgetting."

"Annie," he said quietly. "I can't wait for you to spend more time with her. She's going to love you."

"I'm excited, too. Do you think she'll like baking cookies and stuff like that? I'm not very theatrical, but we can watch all the movies. And I already know she likes ice cream."

"She does. I know it's freezing out, but I miss Georgy Porgy's. May is way too far away."

"It is. You know I don't enjoy this weather." I pulled on my hat and gloves. "You ready to walk around the Loch again?"

As we had in January 2007 on a much warmer night, we walked around the body of water that was so small that calling it a lake was a stretch. Hand in hand, we told each other stories of our classes, parties we had attended, and people we knew. We mused about sending in a class note to our alumni magazine about our reuniting to give our classmates a shock. We stopped and kissed at the point where we were almost positive we had done the same years earlier. It was all very sweet and nostalgic and very, very cold.

"I can't feel my toes or my nose," I said. "I was in LA this time yesterday. I think I've confused my body. Plus, it thinks I don't sleep anymore."

"I only sleep in driveways now," he said. "Let's go."

We walked across the quad as students were heading to the dining hall for dinner, and it seemed so strange to be at Norwell watching the same kind of scene we were a part of almost every evening at Rockwood, just with younger people. We stopped and sat on a bench and watched them shuffle past us, laughing and talking, some couples holding hands, a few smoking cigarettes, many with big backpacks, clearly heading to the library as soon as dinner was over.

"They've got finals soon, I bet," I said, leaning into Kyle as we observed the Norwell world unnoticed.

"I wonder how many of our professors are still here," he pondered. "Most of them seemed so old. They were probably our age."

"We're only thirty-five, goofy," I said. "Were any college professors later presidents?"

"Why do you ask?"

"I figured I should learn something since we're back at college."

"Well," he began, taking my hand and pulling me up to stand. "John Quincy Adams taught at Harvard and Brown. Taft taught at Yale Law School after he lost reelection and before he became a Supreme Court justice."

"He was a justice after he was president?"

"Yep, the only one in our history. He didn't really want to be president. Teddy Roosevelt talked him into it. And then ran against him four years later."

"That's right. That's how Wilson was elected. It's all coming back to me now."

"You got it. After he was president of Princeton," he said as we got to the Jeep. "Ice cream near me," he said, speaking into his cell phone.

"You really want some? It's maybe thirty degrees out."

"For you, anything. You still on a toffee kick? Not sure if this place has it," he said, scrolling through the results.

"No more Heath for me," I answered. "What looks good?"

"Caramel Oreo Swirl? I bet you would like that one."

"Oh, definitely." My stomach growled as if by suggestion.

"Did you know that Barack and Michelle Obama had their first kiss while getting ice cream?" he asked.

"You didn't read that in a history book." I laughed, imagining Kyle pouring over presidential romance stories.

"No, it was an interview with Oprah."

"Even better."

27

"You should just move in here," I said, lying in bed in my apartment with Kyle, feeling like I was finally where I was supposed to be. I was somewhat kicking myself for not linking up with him right away once I got to Rockwood like he had seemed so fully ready to, but part of me knew that I hadn't been all there. The trust we had built over the past few months, the getting-to-know-each-other aspect of it all, the slow burn of seeing each other practically every day and almost never touching each other, plus my ill-fated relationship with Heath ... maybe that's the way it all needed to happen. I would never know for sure, but in this moment, sprawled out in a sea of sheets and blankets and pillows on a December morning, all was right in the world.

"Us shacking up. Now, that would be something for *The Underground Stallion*," he said, running his hands through my hair, getting caught in the inevitable knots from a mane that needed a thorough scrubbing. Our bath together the day before had been less of a cleaning experience and more of one of laughing, splashing, and, for lack of a better term, foreplay. I definitely needed a good long shower.

"Does the paper even exist anymore? Can I stop worrying that someone is lurking behind a tree, ready to take my picture? I can't believe Ryland and Marnie were the brains behind it, and I use the word *brains* loosely," I said. "What will happen to them? I don't envy Andrea's job at all."

"He's certainly not teaching this week," said Kyle. "The buzz among the faculty on the group chat is that he told his classes to read a book of their choosing this week and send him a paragraph review of it. That's it. And then we'll hit the holiday break, so who knows when the investigation will conclude. Then, the disciplinary hearing will take place at some point. Couldn't have happened to a nicer guy," he said, his voice dripping with sarcasm.

"I love that you have a group chat. Karma can be a real bitch," I said, lying with my head on his chest like I had so many years ago. "Andrea let me decide whether or not Marnie could work this week. I said she could stay for now, but we would see what the investigation yields. In my mind, what Ryland did was far worse since it involved the manipulation of students. Plus, I'd need to either hire a replacement or see if one of the workers on my team is ready for this kind of role. There's a lot to think about. But like Andrea said, trusting her is an issue. I need to talk to her."

"For whatever reason, Ryland is able to work these women. I saw it with Cora. I don't get it, but I'm just a straight guy. What do you think? Is he all that appealing? Is he some kind of sexy beast?"

"He's gross," I retorted. "I don't understand the magnetic pull they feel to him at all, even though it doesn't seem overtly sexual. More like mind games and manipulation."

"Anyway, enough about him. We don't need to waste our time talking about that asswipe. Back to the issue at hand—do you really think I should move into your apartment?" he asked, pulling me on top of him and grabbing the backs of my thighs in a way that was just so sexy.

I melted over his body and sighed. "Maybe eventually," I said. "We probably have to give everyone a chance to get used to us as a full-fledged couple. This is what we are now, right?" I hoped so. For once, I was sure.

"That's what I want if that's what you want," he said, gently lifting my face up so I was looking at him. "I love you, Devon. I realize I haven't said that yet. I should've said it yesterday. I was just so excited that all of this was finally happening that I forgot to say it. But I have felt it the whole time. I love you and have loved you since the day you got here, and I brought you those Coors Light cans."

I felt a rush of emotion and bliss. "I want all of it. I love you, Kyle. I think I always have. I never forgot you, but I pushed you to the very back of my brain for all those years because it hurt so much. I never want to let you go again." We kissed, and I felt tears drop from my face onto his, which I wiped away. "Promise me you'll never go to London again, okay?"

"If I go, you're coming with me," he said, hugging me closer to him.

"I think I need to go to work," I grumbled, looking at the clock on the wall. "I'm sorry. Don't you have to teach a class today or something?"

"Maybe. But I'm also really hungry," he said. "Maybe there will be bacon for breakfast?" he asked hopefully, and my mind drifted back to us posing the same question before we were separated from each other so many years earlier.

"Luckily, I know who's in charge of the kitchen," I said, rolling over to grab my phone. "Oh my God. Charlie sent me a message on Instagram."

"Who's Charlie? Is this another emergency responder you've connected with?" Kyle asked, kissing my shoulder.

"He's a bartender in Los Angeles who is old enough to be my father and prefers spending his time in the company of men, so you have nothing to be concerned about." I showed him the screen so we could read the message together.

Dearest Devon – I hope you don't mind that I reached out to you here since you have a private Instagram account. I wanted to thank you for the Celtics ticket and the chance to witness one of the most memorable games I've ever seen, particularly since I knew David had been struggling to achieve this level of success. Well, he did it, and I know you must be so proud.

As for the other topic you and I spoke about late into the evening, I hope you are seeing the clarity you were seeking. You, Devon, will be a gift to whoever is lucky enough to land you. I wish you well and hope you will connect when you return to LA.

With all the best everything, Charlie

I cleared my throat as I felt so much gratitude wash over me. "Do you believe in guardian angels?" I asked Kyle, putting my phone down. "Like people who appear in your life just when you need them?"

"Absolutely," he said. "This guy's smart, by the way. You are a gift." We were now lying on our sides again, facing each other, and despite the fact that I really needed to go to the dining hall and he needed to teach, I wanted to stay in bed with him all day.

"Have you ever encountered one? A guardian angel?" I asked, surprised by his answer. Kyle was a scholar and an intellectual and crossed the line into cynicism at times. A guardian angel seemed like a stretch for him.

"I have," he said, kissing the tip of my nose. "You."

"What?"

"You showed up right when I needed you. I was trying to come back from everything awful that had happened to me. I was on the slow road to better days, but from the moment I saw you that day when you visited campus, everything felt better."

"Even when it didn't? It hasn't exactly been smooth sailing."

"I think I always knew," he said, kissing my lips this time. "I knew that somehow, we would end up like this again. And I would finally get to say all the things I needed to say to you. Just in a more comfortable bed this time."

"That dorm bed sucked," I said with a laugh. "And I think we're better at all of this now anyway."

"You've always been amazing," he said, kissing the top of my hand. "What else did you and Charlie talk about? He said you were seeking clarity. Was it about Heath?"

"It was more about you," I explained. "I asked him if fifteen years was too late to rekindle a one-night stand. Although we're closer to sixteen years now, I guess. But you get the idea."

"What did he say?"

"He answered me with a question of his own. He asked me if the two people involved were better suited for each other now than they were then."

"I think we've answered that question over the last almost twenty-four hours," he said, pulling me to him again. "I never want this to end, Dev."

"Me neither. I'm all yours now." I kissed him again and groaned as I rolled out of bed. "You ready to shock the hell out of the campus community and walk down the steps of Wentworth together and across campus to the dining hall?"

"But will they be all that shocked?" he asked. "I think most of them will be relieved. A lot of them have been very concerned about my well-being since the karaoke incident. There have been many inquiries and concerns."

"It shows how beloved you are here," I said, pulling on my jeans. "I doubt anyone is missing Ryland Dennis right now. Let's go get some bacon."

•   •   •

The sun came out that afternoon and warmed things up a bit, and I took an hour-long break before getting ready for the dinner service. Sitting on my favorite bench, still exhausted from a general lack of sleep over the previous few nights, I was giddy at everything that had transpired since returning to Rockwood. Kyle found me there after he taught his last class of the day, and we got a kick out of talking to people who passed by us, many of whom seemed surprised by how casually we were hanging out together after being somewhat guarded and covert about even being friendly with each other for so many months. It felt good not to care what anyone thought anymore. One female student even point-blank asked us, "So, are you two like, you know, a couple now?"

"Something like that," Kyle said, putting his arm around me. "How could I not like the cookie lady?"

"She probably has access to basketball tickets," said one male student, as if I wasn't sitting right there.

"That's true, I do," I said. "That's definitely why he's hanging out with me."

There was a commotion building around a black Sprinter van in the adjacent parking lot. "What's going over there?" I asked Kyle, and the students we had been talking to walked over to see what was going on. The small crowd parted, and we watched Ashlyn Lark emerge from nearby Browning Hall, wearing sunglasses and her Canada Goose down jacket, carrying her cell phone and a large purse. Two men pushed luggage carts filled with suitcases and other belongings to the Sprinter.

"She's actually leaving? Andrea finally kicked her out?" Kyle asked, his eyes huge with shock.

"That's a new cell phone she's holding," I mused.

"How do you know?" he asked.

"It's a good story," I said. "Let's save it for later. I want to savor every moment of watching her leave." And we did.

Soon after the Sprinter pulled away and Kyle and I gave each other a fist-bump, a shiny white Land Rover pulled up at the same parking lot, and I watched as Bentley and Julianna Preston got out of the still-running car, along with a driver who I didn't recognize. The driver hustled over to Adrienne's dorm, and I felt panic creep into my body.

"No, no, not Adrienne. She didn't do anything. I'm positive she was not involved in Midsy. Oh shit, Kyle. She can't get kicked out of another school." I looked over at Julianna and Bentley, who had noticed me sitting there watching the scene unfold. Julianna started walking in my direction. "Ugh. I think she wants to talk to me."

"Want me to stay with you?" he asked. "She probably won't say much with a witness."

"You don't know this woman," I said. "She's malnourished and quite hangry. I'll deal with her. You shouldn't be subjected to this." I stood up and walked in her direction.

"Julianna," I said.

"Devon, hello," she replied.

"Is everything all right? Is Adrienne—" I didn't know how to even ask the question.

"We came up to take Adrienne out to dinner," she said, and I instantly felt relieved. "As you likely know, our relationship with her is often strained, and we need to have some interactions with her that are lower stakes. In other words, not just special occasions." She sighed. "This is all at the suggestion of a therapist. I'm sure you know I wouldn't be able to come up with these ideas on my own. I'm a lot of things, but an empathetic human isn't often one of them."

I didn't know what to say and needed to be careful not to insult her, so I decided to stick to Adrienne. "I've gotten to know her a bit this fall. She's a lovely person. You have much to be proud of."

She nodded. "I'm not sure how much credit I can take for any of who or how she is, but I thank you for that. I wasn't thrilled when she said she was cooking with you, but I recognize that until now, she didn't have any significant interests or anything she was even slightly considering doing after high school. We had our sights set on the Ivy League for her, but if culinary school is where she ends up, so be it." Her face looked pained saying these words, but knowing her as I did, I recognized that getting to this point of acceptance was huge progress.

"Well, that's great," I said. "I hope you have a good dinner."

"Thanks, Devon. You know about Ward, right?"

"That he's..." I didn't want to say it. I hoped she would finish the sentence for me.

"Yes, who he is to Adrienne and to me," she said mercifully. *Whew.* "Well, he's not much to me anymore, but I'm glad Adrienne is here. In weird ways, she occasionally spends time with him, at least from what they tell me."

"I saw her helping him with lights on the scaffold the other day," I volunteered and then instantly regretted it. Julianna probably hated the idea of Adrienne doing grunt work like that.

She rolled her eyes. "Whatever. It's something. I am moving on from him, I guess, with my own husband. Imagine that," she said with a short laugh, gesturing toward him. Bentley was still standing against the Land Rover, probably perplexed as to what on earth Julianna and I could be talking about. "He's okay," she said. "You know that already."

"Um, yes," I replied awkwardly. "Well, good luck with all of it."

Adrienne and the driver walked toward us, relieving me of this incredibly bizarre conversation. "Hi, Devon," she said. "Okay, Mom, I'm starving. Let's go eat." She was wearing a long corduroy skirt and Doc Martens, and I knew Julianna was doing everything in her power not to make the *"are you really going to wear that?"* comment. I silently applauded her for not saying a word. More progress.

I said goodbye and caught Bentley's eye, giving him a wave. He waved back, and I settled back next to Kyle on the bench. "This has been a very long day," I said. "A good day, but a lot has taken place."

He kissed my cheek. I could get used to this. "Don't forget the Celtics are on tonight. We need to see if David can do it again. There's another watch party in the student lounge again if you're interested. Or we can go to The Horse. They'll have it on there. Or, of course, there's always The Barnacle. Marnie can mix you a drink. Hang out with Ward Connelly. That sort of thing," he said with a laugh.

I yawned. "Or we can light a fire and watch it from the best apartment on campus."

"The whiskey sours are really good there. That's definitely where I want to be."

28

David had a forty-five-point game in Denver, followed by a fifty-two-point night in Houston two days later. When his mom texted me to see if I could meet her for coffee when I came down to Boston once he was back, I knew something was up. She would have usually flown straight home to Atlanta.

"I think I might be getting fired today," I told Kyle as I packed up David's enchiladas, cookies, and smoothie ingredients.

"I doubt it," he said, handing me the most beautiful peppermint mocha. His Nespresso machine had made its way from his apartment to mine, and it felt like the slow migration of many things like that. I wasn't complaining; it was freezing out, and not having to make my own less-than-inspiring coffee or venture to the student-run coffee shop was lovely. Plus, Kyle's handcrafted mochas almost evoked ice cream feelings in me, so I was happy. "She may just want you to be present more since it had such a positive effect on David. Which, of course, may be tricky for you to figure out. But I'm sure Andrea will be flexible. She loves you. Look what you've done to this place. Cookies," he said, grabbing one out of the food storage container just before I was going to shut it.

"Someone else is paying for those cookies," I said. "But yeah, I guess I need to hear what she has to say. There's nothing else I can do right now."

There was a knock at my door, and Kyle and I looked at each other. Being alone on the fourth floor, students and the other staff who lived in the rest of the building rarely came up to my apartment.

"Do you want me to go out the fire escape?" he asked.

"No, no, I'm sick of all that. Everyone needs to get used to us. It'll be fine," I said, walking over to the door and opening it.

It was Marnie. "Hi. I hope it's okay that I'm here." It was the first time she had ever visited my apartment. She was in her usual attire of stretchy black pants and a tunic, and she was still wearing her apron from the breakfast shift, which seemed strange, but it was Marnie. Not much surprised me about her anymore; I was used to all her quirks.

"Sure," I said, opening the door and gesturing for her to come in. "You obviously know Kyle."

Marnie stared at him and didn't say anything. Kyle slung his backpack over his shoulder and took another cookie. And then he grabbed me by the waist and planted a dramatic smooch on my lips, likely to shock the hell out of Marnie. "See you later," he said to me and then waved at her. "Bye, Marnie."

I closed the door behind him and decided not to attempt any explanation of what just happened; it was easier that way. "Why don't we sit on the couch?" I asked her. Once we were seated, I knew I would have to break the ice because she wasn't likely to. "Is everything all right with you?"

She nodded. "I know there's a lot going on right now, and I'm not sure what I'm allowed to talk about and what I can't. First, I want to thank you for letting me continue to work right now. I know you could have kept me out of the kitchen. I like cooking, and things would be more stressful for me if I couldn't."

"Oh, well, that's good, Marnie. I'm glad I could help. I just don't understand why—"

"I'm giving Andrea my resignation this afternoon," she blurted out.

"You're what?" Of all the things I was preparing to hear that day, those words certainly were not it.

She looked down and shook her head. "This is tough to explain, but maybe you'll understand. I know you've had some relationship struggles in your past."

That was the understatement of the year. "Yes, I have. Are you okay?"

She nodded. "Oh, yes, I'm really good. I just know it sounds strange. I'm in love with Ward Connelly."

I couldn't help but smile. It was one of the oddest pairings, and he probably had around twenty-five years on her, but love was love. "That's great, Marnie. Is he nice to you? Because that's really the most important thing."

"So nice. He's teaching me to paint. He likes the food I cook for him. We have a good time together. Which is why I'm going to Arizona with him."

"What's in Arizona?" I had been once—with David for a matchup against the Suns—and loved it. I tried to imagine Marnie in the desert surrounded by cacti while Ward made some sort of sculpture out of red clay.

"He was asked to teach a one-year course in Sedona to a group of artists with different specialties. Some are visual, so they paint, sculpt, that sort of thing. Others are writers. A few are musicians. One is an actor. So, he'll be one of the instructors, but there are others. And they need some kitchen help. I love southwestern food, so I figured this was a good chance to learn more. The pictures look beautiful, and I haven't traveled much. The students explore the world around them as they create their art, and we send food along with them on their day trips."

"Marnie, this sounds like a great opportunity for you." I couldn't help but think of Marnie getting to serve boxed lunches and things like that to the students. It was a perfect match. I did feel a little wistful that Adrienne wouldn't see much of Ward for a while, but it was all so new and sporadic, even with him living down the street. Hopefully, they would keep in touch. In the big picture, this seemed like a good thing. "I'm really happy for you."

"Me too. Thanks for understanding. Sorry to leave you, but I'm sure you'll find someone else. A few of the staff might be interested in the job. You're a good person to work for."

"I appreciate that," I said. "I'll deal with it after the break. We've got some time to figure it all out." I glanced at my watch, realizing I needed to stop by the dining hall on my way to Boston to make sure everything was okay, especially if Marnie wasn't likely to be working. "Just one more question while you're here. Why *The Underground Stallion*? And getting wrapped up in things with Ryland. I don't understand it."

She squirmed a bit and crackled her knuckles, causing me to shudder at the sound. "I don't know. He convinced me that there were power shifts happening on campus and that something was needed to keep people in check. He was worried about your arrival here and insisted that you were jockeying for Andrea's job and that some pictures and articles would keep you in your place, as he always said. And you know he hates Kyle."

"The feeling is mutual," I muttered. "He thought I wanted to be Head of School? Ha! That's ridiculous. I barely know how to do this."

"The stuff with the paramedic and you," she continued. "That was to get Kyle upset—to get under his skin. It seemed to work. I felt bad about that. He was a mess at Midsy with the karaoke."

I nodded. "Yes, it was a rough night. You all weren't involved with the Midsy pranks?" I had visions of Ryland creeping into Andrea's shower to implant the bouillon cubes.

She shook her head furiously. "Absolutely not. That was all Ashlyn and her friends. They bribed the security guards with a new poker set, too. Well, those guys didn't know they were being bribed, but I saw it that way." She sighed, shaking her head. "Who knows? Ryland was the one who told me about that, so maybe he *was* involved. I didn't put two and two together until now." She cracked her knuckles again, and I tried not to wince. "You know Ashlyn was sent home, right?"

"Andrea finally did it."

"Which makes me nervous she'll do the same thing to me, so it's time for me to resign."

"But you should anyway," I insisted. "Arizona will be great." I stood up, and Marnie did the same. "All right, my friend, I need to make sure lunch is ready to go before I head to a meeting in Boston. Are you coming, or are you going to try to catch Andrea now?"

"It's grilled cheese and tomato soup day," she said.

"It is. I'm going to ask the team to stuff bacon in some of them," I replied, thinking of Kyle.

"I'll try to see her after that. Let's go cook." And for one last time, we did.

●　　●　　●

I felt a pit in my stomach as I pulled up to David's building, even though I had been there countless times. The valet took my car, and I brought the usual bags up the elevator to the penthouse. When I walked into David's condo, Dr. Anders was sitting on the couch, typing on her laptop.

"Devon," she said, not looking up. "Just give me a moment more, and then I'm all yours."

"It's no problem," I said. "There's plenty to put away. Is David here? I can make him a smoothie."

"He had practice," she said. "Just leave everything in the fridge. I can make him one later." Her nails clicked against the keys while I unloaded and stored everything I brought. "Okay, that's done. Want to walk over to Caffé Nero? We don't have it in Atlanta yet. I could go for that caramel latté they have."

We braced for the cold December weather and plodded across the street to the coffee shop. Once we had our hot drinks and were seated, I decided that this would be a very different approach from sitting with Marnie earlier. I waited for Dr. Anders to speak, and she eventually did.

"Thanks so much for taking the time to meet with me, Devon. I want you to know how much I appreciate everything you've done for David."

She's definitely firing me. Kyle wasn't right this time. "I've loved working with him," I said, swallowing hard and trying to keep my composure. "And I'm so excited about how things are going for him right now. It's good to see his hard work paying off."

She nodded. "Hopefully, it continues. I know he's happy about it. Did you see his press conference after Houston? The reporters can't believe he's actually engaging now. As you know, this is a big change. You deserve a lot of the credit for this. You've been a constant in his life, and you've also been able to gently build his confidence. We've all known he was capable of greatness this whole time. He just needed to believe in himself. I think he does now."

"Well, thank you. It's an amazing thing to witness. I'm very proud of him." I sipped my latté, trying to channel my focus to the sweetness of the caramel and the smoothness of the milk as it blended with the espresso in my cup. It was better than thinking of where this conversation was inevitably going.

"Devon, I know this isn't easy. You're working full time at Rockwood, plus cooking for David and coming down here every week. And I'm sure going to LA was a challenge for you."

"A lot of good came out of that trip, though," I interjected. "Thanks for the extra ticket, by the way. My friend was very grateful."

"You are very welcome. I'll always help with that when I can. Anyway, as I was saying, I know working for us hasn't been without its difficulties. It's emotional to deal with David, as I know all too well. But now that he's reaching the kind of success he has been striving for, we need more consistent assistance here in Boston."

There it is. "Thanks for everything these last few years," I said, keeping my voice as even as possible. "It's been an honor. I'm happy to help train whoever you decide to hire. Just let me know what you need."

Dr. Anders shook her head. "I think you've read me all wrong, Devon. I'd like to make you an offer."

•   •   •

The Jeep drove back to Rockwood as if it was on autopilot. I mulled over every single word Dr. Anders and I discussed, all the possibilities, all the angles, all the praise she gave me for everything I had done for David. I thought of my sweet little condo in Beacon Hill, waiting for me, now sitting empty since Tam had moved in with Professor Plum in Cambridge. I thought of the things that Dr. Anders offered me, opportunities I had always wanted but never quite knew how I would make happen. I also racked my brain going through the possibilities of David being traded to various teams in cities across the country, which could ultimately happen at any time and which would upend the whole plan. It was so much to consider.

Andrea was sitting on the front steps of Wentworth when I walked up to my dorm. She was dunking a triangle of grilled cheese sandwich into a paper cup of tomato soup. "Marnie brought me this," she said. "And then she quit."

"What are your thoughts on that?" I asked, sitting next to her. "It's cold out here. You can come inside if you want."

"But there will be kids around listening to our conversation if we sit in the lounge," she said. "And I'm not hauling my ass up to the fourth floor, even if your apartment is nicer than my house." She took the last bite of her sandwich. "I don't know what to think of it. I know this sandwich is good, even though the soup is cold now. She brought the one with bacon in it."

"That's how I like it," I said. "You don't have to investigate her or hold a hearing for her now. That's something."

"True," she said. "I just know it's a major pain in the ass for you now to reshuffle your staff and find someone who you can leave in charge so you can have a day off or something."

"Look, Andrea, I need to be transparent with you," I began. "I just came from Boston. David Anders' mother made me an incredible offer so I can be more available to him. She wants to buy me a restaurant. I'd hire the staff and get the whole thing off the ground, with the idea that eventually, it would pretty much run itself. And then I could be there to support David and probably travel with him more."

She frowned. "That sounds like a dream come true for someone like you," she said. "I've loved having you here, Devon. Really, I have. I don't want you to leave. But I understand it." She slurped the rest of the soup down. "You're probably going to take Kyle with you, too, aren't you? It's a good thing all the chaos over that stupid sculpture has calmed down. Now kids just decorate the damn thing, and Ward's gotten over it. Well, sort of. He still has those cameras, but he'll be in Arizona soon and likely will stop obsessing over it. Anyway, I can hire people. They won't be you and Kyle, but I'll learn to live with them." She sighed and lobbed the soup cup into a nearby trash can.

"I told her no, Andrea."

"What? Why? Are you crazy?"

"Maybe. But it's not so cut and dry. David will likely get traded at some point. Then what? I'm not moving to Oregon or something. Or I could, and then he gets traded again a year later. That's not the life I'm looking for right now."

Andrea looked relieved. "What kind of life *are* you looking for?"

"Something like this," I said. "At least for now. And I'll still keep working for David, and I promised to train someone else so we can tag team a bit. It'll be fine, maybe for a little while. I'll figure it out." I looked at my watch. "Sorry, Andrea, I need to go see someone. I'll see you later." I stood up and started walking before I stopped and turned back. "There will be sliders at dinner tonight. I've come up with an incredible caramelized onion bacon jam for them, based on something I just had in LA."

"I wouldn't miss it."

29

"Hey," I said, getting out of my Jeep at the fire station.

"I never thought I'd ever see you again," Heath said, standing against the ambulance. He was in a gray hoodie sweatshirt and athletic pants and looked very hot, but not what I wanted or needed. What I wanted and needed was sitting at my kitchen table, cursing the lack of capitalization in a student's essay about the Teapot Dome scandal and its impact on Warren Harding's presidential legacy while waiting for me to come home so we could go get a drink at The Horse. I couldn't wait.

"I wanted to clear the air about a few things. I feel like I owe you that much," I said.

He crossed his arms across his chest. "Okay, I'm all ears."

I took a breath. "I'm really sorry about how it all went down. You know, dragging you to LA and everything."

He gave a short laugh. "Hey, you didn't drag me anywhere. I was a guest of David Anders."

"That's true. But I'm sorry."

"You were different on that trip," he said.

"So were you."

He sighed. "Maybe we both needed to see that in each other. Deep down, Devon, I think I knew the whole time. You and Kyle, it was going to happen one way or another. I just got caught in the crosshairs of it."

He was right. "You didn't deserve that."

He shrugged. "It happens. At least you weren't spitting tobacco into the aisles of a movie theater." We both laughed, which felt good considering how badly we had ended things. "But I appreciate you coming over to talk to me, Dev. Most girls wouldn't have bothered."

I smiled. "I figured you might show up on my campus at some point again, and it always helps to be on the good side of emergency responders."

"Generally, a solid plan," he agreed. "Have a great life, Devon."

"You, too, Heath." I meant it.

· · ·

"I just graded the worst paper of my life," Kyle said from my kitchen table as I walked in the door. "Somehow, the kid confused FDR with TR but then mixed JFK in there. I don't know what's going on. Was my use of acronyms in class that confusing? I need a drink."

I leaned down and kissed him, savoring that I was finally home with him.

"How was your day?" he asked. "I want to know what happened with Marnie. I couldn't help but plant that kiss on you when she showed up. I mean, I wanted to kiss you, but I loved getting that reaction. You know what I mean."

"Marnie," I said, pulling him to his feet and meeting his lips with mine. "Is just the tip of the iceberg. I have so many stories to tell you. Tons. We're going to shut down The Horse tonight."

"You're speaking my language, woman. Too bad the Celtics don't play until tomorrow night," he said, wrapping his arms around me. "Speaking of which, can we go sometime?" he asked almost sheepishly.

"You want to go to a basketball game with me, Mr. Holling?"

"Will I finally get to meet this elusive guy?"

I pulled him to the door. "Is that the only reason you want to go?"

Kyle closed my apartment door behind us. "He's really good, Devon."

"Don't I know it?"

THE END

ACKNOWLEDGMENTS

Thank you to Black Rose Writing and Reagan Rothe for publishing this book. I am so appreciative.

Many thanks to Stephanie Galvani and Jenn Haskin for all of your insight and editing assistance, as well as your friendship. You helped me to make *Considering Us* a much stronger story.

The following people offered me so much insight into the world of boarding schools, and I am so grateful: Liz Butler, Sarah Scoville, Laura Brandt, Liz K., Sarah Kennedy, Kelsey Banfield, Jocelyn Wise, Shannon Greenlese, Marty Fajerman, Sarah Schlechter, Karen Finocchio, and Alex Natalizio.

The Eleventh Chapter is the amazing group of writers who I have the privilege of knowing and working with every single day: Kerry Chaput, Sayword B. Eller, Jen Craven, Sharon M. Peterson, Caitlin Moss, Maggie Giles, Tanya E. Williams, Gloria Mattioni, and Colleen Temple. Thank you for asking me to join you. I am constantly in awe of your talents and love our work together!

Other writers who have been instrumental in supporting me over the past few years: Christina Consolino, C. D'Angelo, Leslie Rasmussen, Dara Levan, Meredith Schorr, Sara Goodman Confino, Sarahlyn Bruck, Kristin Contino, Lainey Cameron, Emily Belden, Lindsay Merbaum, and so many more...Thank you also to the WFWA, Every Damn Day Writers, and Bookish Road Trip for your camaraderie and collaboration! Special appreciation to Kathleen Eull and Suzy Approved Book Tours for helping to put me on the map back in 2021.

Thanks to everyone who has championed my writing and me through author events, stocking my book, interviewing me, or having me on your podcast. Special thanks to Belmont Books, Wellesley Books, Bank Square Books, Now You're Cooking,

Mockingbird Bookshop, Booklovers' Gourmet, Hummingbird Books, Hygge House Books, Illume Books, The Bee's Knees Mystic, The Sparrow Project, Fall for the Book, the Annapolis Book Festival, Nashoba Brook Bakery, Chip-In Farm, Made in Burlington, the Corinthian Yacht Club, J. McLaughlin in Wells and Concord, and everyone else who has been in my corner.

Seven women who live in my town have been my life raft over the past few years. Tara Goss, Sheila Mehta-Green, Amanda Lewis, Jane Holland, Monica Bou, Bhuvana Husain, and Liz Kaiser, I don't know where I'd be without you. And Tara, I think you named most of the characters in this book!

For all the friends that rallied to help me with book promotion for both *First Course* and *Considering Us*, thank you! From social media posts to ordering and reviewing books to, of course, Little Free Library placements, you have been amazing and wonderful.

Additionally, thank you to the Thursday Night Bates Ladies, all the parents sitting on the sidelines at all the sporting events with me (which is almost every single day), the women of the NHS Social Studies Department, and the lifelong friends from my years living in Virginia, Washington, Maine, Massachusetts, and Illinois.

My family has been a huge support on this adventure. Big thanks to my parents Bruce and Mary for their endless support and for talking me up all over southeastern Connecticut. My sister Rosemary and her crew of Jim, Mack, Abby, Greta, and Doris the Dog are always in my corner.

Grant and Avery have lived through the ups and downs of writing and publishing for several years now, and I am so grateful for their love and excitement over every little success. This book is dedicated to them! And Ryan, well, there aren't too many spouses who would drive through horrible Boston-area traffic to drop off a spool of award stickers that showed up late in the mail so I would have them in time for a book event. We have been together for a million years, and he still does this kind of thing for me all the time. I love our family.

Thank you to everyone who has read my books, brought them to their book club, interviewed me on a podcast or website or for a newspaper or magazine, or left a glowing review. You make my dreams come true.

ABOUT THE AUTHOR

Jenn Bouchard is the award-winning author of the novel First Course and several short stories. She is a graduate of Bates College and Tufts University. An avid cook, Jenn volunteers for good causes and is a devoted Red Sox fan. A high school social studies teacher of twenty-five years, she lives with her family in the Boston suburbs.

NOTE FROM JENN BOUCHARD

Word-of-mouth is crucial for any author to succeed. If you enjoyed *Considering Us*, please leave a review online—anywhere you are able. Even if it's just a sentence or two. It would make all the difference and would be very much appreciated.

Thanks!
Jenn Bouchard

We hope you enjoyed reading this title from:

BLACK ROSE
writing™

www.blackrosewriting.com

Subscribe to our mailing list – *The Rosevine* – and receive **FREE** books, daily deals, and stay current with news about upcoming releases and our hottest authors.
Scan the QR code below to sign up.

Already a subscriber? Please accept a sincere thank you for being a fan of Black Rose Writing authors.

View other Black Rose Writing titles at www.blackrosewriting.com/books and use promo code **PRINT** to receive a **20% discount** when purchasing.

Printed in the USA
CPSIA information can be obtained
at www.ICGtesting.com
LVHW041109151124
796562LV00001B/33